# MURDER ON THE BEACH
## A Destination Murders Short Story Collection

# Table of Contents

# A Tale of Two Sisters
## by Barb Goffman

MY BIG SISTER, EMMA, WAS NO BRIDEZILLA, but heading into her wedding today, she'd been wound up so tight she was like a jack-in-the-box ready to spring. Would the photographer be on time? (Yes.) Would a baby cry during the ceremony? (Not so far.) Would our beloved, klutzy cousin Janelle trip on her bridesmaid's dress as she walked down the aisle? (Yes, but she caught herself before she went splat, thank goodness.)

What's amazing is Emma actually didn't care about any of that. But our mother did. And even at age twenty-six, Emma's stomach still twisted into knots whenever Mom wasn't happy, which was basically anytime things didn't go exactly as Mom wanted.

So Emma gave up her desired intimate ceremony and dinner back home in Chicago with twenty of her and Braden's closest family and friends. Instead, here we were at a resort in Wisconsin, where Mom could impress people. Nearly two hundred friends, family, and folks Emma didn't even know (read: friends of our parents and Braden's) were staring while Rabbi Gelman, Emma, our parents, Braden, his parents and best-man brother, and I all crowded under the white chuppah. And my job as maid of honor had morphed. No longer Emma's sole attendant and cheerleader, I now wore an invisible cape over my soft crepe dress. Call me Robin the Magnificent, self-appointed fixer of everything that could go wrong so my mother wouldn't raise her right eyebrow—our family's bat signal for "look out, Mom's on the warpath!"—and my sister could enjoy her big day.

Thank you, Mom.

"And now it is time for the circling," Rabbi Gelman said, his kind sapphire-blue eyes contrasting starkly with his pale, wrinkled skin. I hoped he'd stick around tomorrow to enjoy the beach. He could use some color, as could I. Between my job as a marketing coordinator and helping with the wedding plans this past summer, I didn't get to the beach even once. I couldn't wait to dig my toes into the soft, golden sand while sipping a cold Bud Light.

As Emma lifted the hem of her fit-and-flare gown, Rabbi Gelman explained the custom. "Traditionally, the bride would circle her groom seven times to symbolize the creation of a new family circle—their new world—similar to how God took seven days to create the world. But Emma and Braden have chosen a modern approach. They'll each circle the other three times, and then they'll both complete a circle together."

Rabbi Gelman's description hadn't told the full story. Traditionally, circling was designed to create an invisible wall around the man, so he'd be protected in the future from "temptress women." Even the thought of this sexist tradition riled me up. Were men expected—or permitted—to have no self-control unless their wives gave them magical protection? Most of my married friends skipped this custom during their weddings. Emma claimed she wanted to do it, to create her own family circle, but I bet Mom pressured her into it. If anyone ever suggested I needed to circle *my* woman seven times to keep her from straying, I'd raise my own right eyebrow and inform them that I'd never marry anyone whose head might be turned so easily.

Finally, the horrid circling ended. Time to move on to the blessing over the wine. Much more my speed.

"Blessed are you, Lord, our God, king of the universe, who created the fruit of the vine." Rabbi Gelman said the blessing in his rumbly voice, first in Hebrew, then in English, before handing the cup to Braden and to Emma.

I took a moment to peek into the audience. My fiancée, Natalie, sat in the third row. Between her newly dyed black hair and the makeup she was wearing—purchased for this very occasion, as she'd owned none—I barely recognized her. She caught my eye and winked. It was the same flirty move that had attracted me three years ago during our senior year of college. Smiling, I twirled a strand of my swooshed-over wavy brown hair, just like I'd done the night we met.

"And now," Rabbi Gelman said, "it is time for the vows."

Vows aren't part of a traditional Jewish wedding ceremony, yet everyone I know has included them. Emma and Braden wrote their own vows, but they decided that their feelings for each other were too personal. So rather than share them now in front of a thousand of their nearest and dearest (I know I said it was two hundred guests, but looking out into the ballroom, I could swear the crowd had swelled), they planned to say them to one another a few minutes from now, when they'd be alone right after the ceremony. Once they walked back down the aisle, it would be time for the *yichud*—when the newly married couple spends a few peaceful minutes alone in a secluded room. Emma and Braden planned to drink champagne, eat strawberries, and share their personal vows then. For now, in front of all these people, generic ones would do.

"Do you, Braden, take Emma to be your lawfully wedded wife, to love, honor, and cherish all the days of your life?" Rabbi Gelman asked.

"I do." Braden's dimples appeared as he smiled, and I remembered the first time Emma told me about him three years ago. She raved about how smart and kind he was, but what had really attracted her were those dimples. "Hubba hubba," she'd said, fanning herself.

The best thing about Braden—besides his dimples—was that he had Emma's back. His calm countenance would serve him and Emma well, especially when he got to see Mom in her full overbearing glory. He thought he knew what she was like, but she'd actually been on relatively good behavior in his presence up until now. In a few minutes, he'd be one of us, and no number of warnings will have prepared him for an unleashed Stella Weiss.

"Do you, Emma, take Braden to be your lawfully wedded husband, to love, honor, and cherish all the days of your life?"

This was the moment she'd been looking forward to for so long. I hoped the videographer was capturing it because memories fade, yet Emma's joy deserved to be remembered, especially considering all the duds she dated before Braden came along. Her smile stretched into a grin, and when Braden dimpled back at her, she giggled, causing a wisp of her long brown hair to slide against her cheek. Her voice had a soft, lilting quality, and as she laughed the aquamarines and diamonds in her tiara caught the sunlight streaming through the window and glittered, as if they were blessing this union. "I do."

Braden took Emma's hand and slipped a gold band onto her finger, repeating the rabbi's words: "With this ring you are consecrated to me according to the laws of Moses and Israel."

Emma slid a gold band onto his finger, repeating the same words, and Mom sobbed loudly. What do you know—a baby had cried during the ceremony after all.

Rabbi Gelman then read aloud the ketubah, the Jewish marriage contract Emma and Braden signed before the ceremony. The ketubah outlines the protections the wife has in the marriage. Its focus is on the wife because in olden times, the husband held all the cards. Of course, times had changed, but since Braden supposedly held all the cards, Emma said she liked having her very own trump card. (Too bad for Emma, she had a little of Mom in her. I was lucky to be more like Dad.)

Finally, Rabbi Gelman explained the ritual of the man breaking a glass at the conclusion of the ceremony—another male-centered tradition. But as Emma said about circling, traditions can change. When Natalie and I get married, she'll want to smash the glass to smithereens, and nobody will be able to stop her.

"There are many interpretations of this ancient custom," Rabbi Gelman said. "Some people believe it represents the destruction of the Temple in Jerusalem. Others believe the shattered glass represents the fragility of love and the care the marriage needs to keep it strong. And," he said with a twinkle in his eye, "there is a contingent who believe that the glass serves as a reminder that this is the last time the man will get to put his foot down."

Everyone laughed, even my dad, who knew the truth of those words all too well.

"Emma and Braden," Rabbi Gelman continued, "believe when he smashes the glass, it will symbolize a break with the past. From then on, they will put their newly formed family above all others. Having watched Emma grow up, it doesn't surprise me that she and Braden would take this view, for Emma has always been a girl—and now a woman—who values her family above all."

The rabbi put a lightbulb into a cloth bag and set it on the floor. (Lightbulbs make a more satisfying popping sound than glasses do; they're easier to break too.) Braden stomped on it, spurring cheers of "mazel tov" from the audience as my sister had her first kiss as a married woman.

A sigh of relief escaped my lips. Finally, we could relax. Fingers crossed, it would all be smooth sailing from here.

* * *

While Emma and Braden enjoyed their quiet time together, and almost everyone else hustled into the ballroom next door for cocktail hour, it was picture time for the wedding party. It felt like we'd been at it for hours by the time Emma and Braden joined our fun. At least, that's what my rumbling stomach thought. Mom had kept me hopping all day, helping her make sure everything would go perfectly, so I hadn't eaten since breakfast.

Eventually we made our way out to the beach for some "candid shots." I couldn't imagine how they possibly could be candid when we knew they were being taken and our poses were suggested, but a photobombing golden retriever who missed peeing on me by inches proved me wrong.

Finally the photographer let everyone but the happy couple go. I brushed the sand off and hurried to the ballroom, thinking about the appetizers. Natalie was waiting for me by the door. For a woman who didn't like to wear dresses or heels, she was rocking the plum A-line sleeveless number that fell just above her knobby knees. It showed off her toned calves and pumped arms.

"I caught some of the photo shoot through the window," she said. "Cute pooch."

"Adorable."

She handed me a glass of merlot (I knew I loved her for a reason), and we started walking. I tried several times to score an appetizer—or three—from a passing server, but they were always gobbled up by the hungry hordes before I got close enough.

"Has everything been going okay?" I asked. Natalie had promised to be my eyes and ears during picture time.

"Just fine. As soon as the appetizers began circulating, Stella seemed calm."

"She must have gotten something to eat."

Natalie laughed as we neared one of the walls of windows overlooking the beach. Beyond the sand, Lake Michigan shimmered in the fading sunlight, with storm clouds gathering on the horizon.

"It's beautiful here," Natalie said. "I know this isn't the wedding Emma wanted, but she looked really happy during the ceremony."

"Yeah, she did. How long do you think it will take before Mom says, 'I told you so?'"

"You mean Stella hasn't said that already?"

I laughed and clinked my glass to hers. "Touché."

The loudspeaker buzzed, and the DJ's voice filled the room. "Ladies and gentlemen, please turn your attention to the main doors. Let's give a warm welcome for the very first time to Mr. and Mrs. Braden Roth."

As applause rang out, they strolled into the ballroom holding hands. Emma's tiara didn't glitter as much under the lights in this room, but her eyes sure did. Tony Bennett's "The Way You Look Tonight" began playing, and they made their way to the dance floor. Emma melted into Braden as they swayed. It wasn't the eye-catching number my mom had pushed for. (If I had a dollar for every time she said "nothing is classier than a waltz," I could move into this resort.) But when Braden claimed a few months ago to have two left feet, Mom had been forced to back off. I'd bet anything she'd be checking out how well those feet moved tonight.

"They are such an adorable couple," said a gray-haired woman standing a few feet away.

"And her wedding gown is to die for," another woman replied, adjusting the strap of the black quilted purse hanging on her shoulder. "Do you think it's satin?"

"Oh, it's satin," my aunt Hazel said, butting in. I hadn't noticed her standing nearby. She was wearing a sparkly silver dress that matched her hair, shoes, jewelry, and eyeshadow. She'd always been a fan of the monochromatic look, but this was taking things to extremes. "I'm the bride's aunt, so I've heard all about the dress, which is the latest style. In fact, I played an instrumental role in Emma's outfit today. That's my tiara she's wearing, with aquamarines surrounded by diamonds." Aunt Hazel raised her chin proudly. "In one fell swoop, I covered old, borrowed, and blue."

I rolled my eyes at Natalie. Bragging ran in Mom's family, though it had skipped my generation, thank goodness.

"Wow," Purse Lady said.

"It's a family heirloom," Aunt Hazel said. "It was one of the few items my grandmother took with her when she and her family escaped from Germany in 1939. She wore it at her wedding, as did her grandmother and mother before her. Eventually my mother and I both wore it too, as the oldest daughters."

"And now you've given it to your niece. How lovely."

From the way Aunt Hazel recoiled, you'd think Purse Lady had suggested she'd donated her only kidney. "Oh no. Only lent it to her. I'm saving it for my first granddaughter."

"I adore family traditions like that," Purse Lady's friend said.

While Aunt Hazel smiled, I suppressed a laugh. She and Uncle George had one child, my cousin Scott, who was standing across the room with his husband, Tristan, both in blue suits with white shirts and pale-pink bowties. Scott's suit was deep blue, which complemented his flawless pale skin. (He must have had work done. No one in their thirties looks that good without a little help.) Tristan's suit was a bold blue that befitted his personality as well as his spiky blond hair. Aunt Hazel knew darn well Scott and Tristan didn't want children, and since they're gay, there was no chance it would happen accidentally. But it was easier for Aunt Hazel to pretend she might get a granddaughter one day—repeatedly saying "people can change their minds"—than to admit to these strangers that if she had no direct female descendant to leave the tiara to, she planned to be buried in it. I thought Mom would have a stroke when Aunt Hazel told her that last year.

A couple of minutes later, after Purse Lady and her friend headed toward the bar, Aunt Hazel came over. She was nibbling a lamb chop she'd snagged from one of the servers milling around, providing food to everyone, it seemed, but me. My mouth watered just looking at it.

"Did you notice that knockoff Chanel handbag?" She nodded at Purse Lady. "I can't believe she brought it to a fancy affair."

*Heavens no.*

"How do you know it's fake?" Natalie asked.

"Oh, I can tell."

Of course she could. Aunt Hazel was a self-proclaimed expert about everything.

"Robin," Natalie whispered, "two o'clock."

I shifted my eyes in time to see Mom threading her way between the tables, headed straight for us. Her face was as red as the dye in her hair.

"Do you see what's going on out there?" she whispered furiously when she reached my side, motioning toward the dance floor.

I glanced that way, half expecting to find someone doing a striptease. But all I saw was Emma dancing with Dad while Braden danced with his mom. "What am I missing, Mom?"

"He twirled her."

"What?"

"Mr. Two Left Feet twirled his mother. Look! He just did it again."

*Lord save me.* The evening had barely begun, and we'd already pulled into Crazy Town. "What do you want me to do about it, Mom? Should I cut in and stomp on his foot?"

"No, of course not."

Finally, a little sanity—

"That would be too obvious," Mom continued. "Everyone knows you're a wonderful dancer."

*That's why I shouldn't do it?* I rolled my eyes. I'd probably be doing that a lot tonight. "Thanks," I said half-heartedly.

"You should thank me, since I'm the one who made you continue with dance lessons when you wanted to quit to play Little League."

"Little League would have made me happy."

"Little League was for boys."

"Could you be more sexist?"

"Robin." Natalie lightly squeezed my shoulder, and I immediately took a calming breath. Thirty seconds in Mom's presence and I'd reverted back to my thirteen-year-old self.

"I see you're getting along with your daughter again, Stella," Aunt Hazel said. "If only you weren't so controlling, you could enjoy this lovely evening."

*Oh good, another country heard from.*

"Controlling?" Mom's brown eyes narrowed, her brow furrowed, and her right eyebrow stretched so far toward her hairline, you'd think it was being pulled by a fishhook. The trifecta of anger. Uh oh. "At least I'm not selfish."

"Selfish?" Aunt Hazel said.

"You heard me."

Aunt Hazel planted her hands on her ample hips. "Just what have I been selfish about?"

"You know damn well."

Steam practically erupted from Aunt Hazel's pores. "That tiara is mine, and I'm under no obligation to give it your daughter!"

"No, you would rather wear it to the grave. A fifty-thousand dollar tiara!"

"It's my right!"

"That's crap and you know it. The tiara is supposed to go to the oldest daughter of the next generation, and that's Emma!"

"Mom," I whispered, "lots of people are listening."

She gawked at the staring faces around us—relatives, friends of the family, and a whole bunch of folks I didn't know—as if she'd forgotten where she was. Well, she had wanted to put on a show tonight. Thankfully, Emma hadn't seemed to notice. She was still dancing with Dad, a goofy smile on her face.

"This isn't over," Mom said to Aunt Hazel before storming off.

Aunt Hazel sighed loudly as she turned to me. "Who does she think she's fooling?"

"I really don't want to get into the middle of this tiara tussle, Aunt Hazel."

"Who's talking about the tiara? I was referring to that dye job your mother's got, as if anyone would believe a woman nearly sixty years old would have hair naturally that color."

*Wow.* "Could you try to make nice with Mom tonight? Please? For Emma."

Uncle George sidled up to Aunt Hazel, smoothing crumbs from his white mustache. He'd gotten to eat too. "Don't worry, honey," he said. "She'll be on her best behavior from here on out, right?"

Aunt Hazel shrugged. "I guess I can fake it. There's so much of that happening here anyway." She stared pointedly at the back of a woman standing nearby. "I asked her about her shoes earlier," she whispered. "She claimed they're Louboutin, but as soon as I saw her walking, I could see they're knockoffs. The soles aren't red."

"Let's bump her off now," I said.

Uncle George mouthed "sorry" over his shoulder as he pulled Aunt Hazel away. Natalie handed me a flute of champagne. "You look like you could use it."

"Bless you." It wasn't food, but it would do.

The song changed to John Legend's "All of Me," and Braden returned to Emma.

"Everyone's invited to the dance floor," the DJ announced.

Natalie offered her hand and led the way. This sweet song always made me feel good. As we rocked back and forth, Natalie said, "Do you think your uncle George will be able to keep your mom and aunt apart tonight?"

"I hope so, for Emma's sake."

Mom and Aunt Hazel loved each other, but there were always fireworks before those two made up. I just hoped they didn't rain down tonight on Emma—or me.

* * *

"All of Me" segued into some pop songs. Then "Hava Nag" began playing. This Israeli folk song was a staple at Jewish celebrations. Some people clapped along to the song, as a group gathered in the center of the floor for the hora, clasping hands and dancing in a circle.

Soon Braden's brothers pulled two chairs onto the dance floor, and with the help of some additional guests, Emma and Braden were hoisted up on the chairs. Up and down, up and down to the music, while the circle dancing continued around them, everyone celebrating the happy couple. Emma wasn't wearing her tiara anymore. Without it, her hair was flying. As she laughed, she let go of the sides of the chair to push her hair behind her ears. Heights sometimes made me queasy, and I had to fight not to yell, *Hang on*. It would be easy to fall off that chair.

After a minute or so, Emma and Braden were lowered to the ground. Emma ran to me and grabbed my hand. "Come on!" She pulled me to the center of the circle. "You're going up," she yelled over the music.

"Excuse me?"

"Remember my promise?"

*Dear Lord*. The chair dance also happened at bar and bat mitzvahs. I'd skipped my own hoisting at my bat mitzvah a decade ago because I'd faked an upset stomach. Emma had told me multiple times afterward how sorry she was I'd missed out and promised I could go up on a chair at her wedding. I'd always thought she was kidding.

"Oh no," I said. "Not necessary."

"Yeah, it is. It's happening."

And before I knew it, I was being lifted into the air. Up and down and up and down. It was a rollercoaster without seatbelts. I hung on to that chair like my life depended on it—which it likely did. *Oh yeah, this was a ton of fun.* I once got seasick on a family vacation, and Dad told me to focus on the horizon. It had worked then, so I forced myself to look out into the ballroom instead of at the people singing and dancing around me below, like I was a virgin sacrifice about to be thrown into a volcano.

It was a beautiful room, with gilt-edged plates sitting on cranberry tablecloths that matched the bridesmaids' dresses. Soft red and pink dahlias sat in tall glass centerpieces. Emma and Braden's small table for only the two of them—the "sweetheart table"—had a tall arrangement of roses, beneath which Emma had left the tiara. The wait staff was bringing out the communal baskets of warm rolls to put on each table. I love rolls, and I was starving, but the thought of them right now... Taking deep breaths, trying desperately to settle my stomach, I shifted my eyes and—no freaking way. Someone had just swiped the tiara and was walking casually toward the door, obviously trying not to attract attention.

I pointed repeatedly at the floor, yelling "down, down," but the music was loud and the guys below me must have been in the zone because when I neared the floor, before I could safely jump, back up I went. I was literally watching a crime in action and couldn't do anything about it. The thief was dressed for the wedding. Had to be a guest. Tall. Medium-build. Brown hair. There was nothing distinguishing about him from the back.

Nearing the floor again, I prepared to vault off the chair, when someone took a photo and the flash blinded me. *Son of a...* When I finished blinking, I was up in the air again and the thief was leaving the ballroom.

"Let me down," I screamed.

Someone must have heard me that time because the sadistic game of human yo-yo ended, even as the singing and dancing continued. I slid off the chair, ever grateful for solid ground, and Emma hurried over. "What's wrong? Didn't you have fun?"

I couldn't tell her the truth. It would ruin the wedding. I'd have to find the tiara before she noticed it was missing.

"You know me and heights. My stomach felt like I'd swallowed a fish tank."

She hugged me. "I'm sorry. I thought you'd enjoy it."

"I did. In the beginning." I gave her a reassuring smile, which she seemed to buy.

"Come dance?"

"I need to get some fresh air."

"Okay. Love you."

She hugged me before Braden pulled her into the circle, and I hurried off to the hall.

* * *

I burst through the doors. The area right outside the ballroom had a seating area perfect for introverts who needed a break—I might camp out there later—but the hallway was empty except for a middle-aged hotel employee clearing some glasses left on the table.

"Excuse me," I said. "Did you see a man leave the ballroom a couple of minutes ago?"

"No, ma'am. I'm sorry," she said.

*Shoot....* Wait a minute. Ma'am? I was nowhere near old enough to be ma'amed, especially by someone older than me. I took a breath. *Focus, Robin.*

"But I did hear the door to that stairwell close as I came around the corner," she said, pointing.

*Yes!* "Thank you."

I hurried off and opened the door. Halfway up the stairs, a couple was making out, with her back—and dress—pushed up against the iron railing. This was a hotel, for goodness sake. How hard would it be to get a room? "Don't mind me," I said as I started up.

They flew apart. Her lipstick was smeared, and his chin was quivering in fear. *Holy cow.* It was my married cousin Adam—and my klutzy cousin Janelle! Thank God they were from different sides of the family.

"Robin," he said, smoothing down his brown hair. "This isn't what it looks like."

I tilted my head in a who-are-you-kidding look. Unless she'd been choking and he'd been trying to extract the offending item with his tongue, it was exactly how it looked. Just three years ago, his wife walked around him seven times at their wedding. So much for magical protection.

"Okay, fine. It's how it looks," he said, throwing his hands out. My dad's side of the family was filled with people who gesticulated whenever they spoke. "But you can't judge until you've been inside a marriage."

*Whatever, dude.* "It's not my place to judge." Not out loud, anyway. "Did you see someone go up these stairs a couple of minutes ago?"

"Jason was heading up the stairs when we came in here," he said.

His older brother. I was going to kill him. "You know what room he's staying in?"

"He's in two fourteen," Janelle said.

Adam and I both stared at her. I didn't want to know why she knew that.

"Thanks." I started up the stairs again, then looked over my shoulder. "Go back to the party. The only person who should be consummating today is Emma!"

A minute later I banged on Jason's door. No response. "Open up. It's Robin. I know you're in there." Still no response. "Jason!" I pounded some more, the sound echoing down the hall.

The door opened. Jason stood there with his wavy hair messier than usual and his shirt untucked. "Sorry. I took a nap and overslept. I've been hurrying to get dressed. Did I miss the ceremony?"

Oh, he was good. I might have believed him if I didn't know better.

"Your brother already ratted you out."

"What?"

"He saw you going up the stairs...with the tiara!"

Yeah, I lied. But he asked for it.

He stomped his foot. "That kid has been a pain in my behind since the day he was born. You don't know what it was like growing up with him. Mr. Perfect."

*Yeah, he's not so perfect.*

I held out my hand. "The tiara. Now."

"Come on, Robin. I need the money. My business is in trouble."

"Not my problem."

"But your aunt's gonna be buried with it. I heard the argument, and your mom's right. Something so valuable should go to good use, not be used as worm food."

"A thief arguing ethics? Really?"

"I'll split the money with you." He clapped his hands together in supplication. "Please. It can be our secret."

"Give me the tiara right now or I'm going to tell my mother what you've done."

His eyes widened. "All right, all right!" He ran into the room and pulled it out of his suitcase. "You don't have to get nasty about it."

He grabbed his jacket, approached the door, and gave me the tiara. "So you'll keep this quiet?"

If Emma found out a thief—because that's what Jason was—had absconded with the tiara because she'd left it at her table, it would ruin her night and her memories of the wedding. Neither Mom nor Aunt Hazel would ever let her forget it, so I'd take this secret to my grave. But Jason didn't have to know that.

"There's going to be a limbo contest later," I said. "You're going to try real hard to win."

"Limbo? I hate limbo."

"Everybody hates limbo, except Emma and Braden. He thought it would be fun, and when Braden is happy, Emma is happy. You want Emma to be happy."

He sighed. "Fine. Limbo." He slammed the door behind us. "But if I hurt my back, I might need that tiara to pay for the doctor bills."

"Yeah, yeah. Keep walking."

* * *

I peeked inside the ballroom. People were still dancing. I hustled to Emma's table with the tiara behind my back, made sure no one was watching, and slipped it on the table. *Whew.*

The song ended. "Ladies and gentlemen," the DJ said, "please find your seats. Your salads are being served."

Natalie and I reached our table at the same time. "Where've you been?" she asked.

"You won't believe it."

"Let's give a warm round of applause for Braden's grandpa Fred," the DJ said.

"I'll fill you in later," I whispered.

Fred settled a royal-blue yarmulke on his head as he approached the microphone. His white hair was surprisingly thick for a man in his eighties. He said the prayers over the wine and challah. *Yes, thank you, God, for the sweet, eggy bread, and please bring some my way.*

Then Fred walked over to Emma and Braden, bent down, and kissed them each on the cheek. When Braden stood and hugged him, I blinked back tears, wishing my grandparents had lived to see this day. They would have loved it—and they would have been able to put Mom and Aunt Hazel in their places.

Braden's brother and best man, Michael, gave his toast next. Then finally it was my turn. This would my last official maid-of-honor duty of the night. I went to the microphone and gazed out into the ballroom. Servers were coming around, setting out mixed-greens salads and refilling wine glasses, which gleamed in the lights. Emma sat snuggled next to Braden, her head on his shoulder. Their sweetheart table was small, with only enough room for the plates and glasses. Emma had moved the tiara and floral centerpiece to a small empty table behind her, beside the wall.

"It's my joy to be here tonight to share in Emma and Braden's celebration. As Emma's little sister, we spent a lot of time as kids dreaming about what our lives would be like when we grew up. Would we live in a castle like Cinderella? Or save the world like Katniss Everdeen?"

A few guests were walking around, one heading to the bar, another to the door closest to the restroom. They couldn't have waited? I'd be done soon enough.

"You won't be surprised that Emma and I always assumed we'd do both things. But the third important question always was, would we live happily ever after with our very own Prince—or Princess—Charming standing by our sides." I beamed at Natalie. "Well, I'm still holding out for my own castle, but I'm delighted to say that for my big sister, the wait for Prince Charming is over. I knew it the first time she told me about Braden because she literally fanned her face and said, 'hubba hubba.'"

Emma covered her cheeks in embarrassment as laughter rang out.

"But seriously, I knew Braden was the perfect person for Emma because of the way she sparkled from the moment they met."

I kept talking, I know I did, but I don't know what I said from then on because I got distracted. My cousin Scott had slipped down the row right behind Emma, snatched the tiara with the ease of a big-city pickpocket, and slid it beneath his unbuttoned jacket as he sauntered toward the door.

*Are you freaking kidding me?*

* * *

I couldn't run after him or shout "stop, thief" because, once again, I couldn't ruin the wedding. But at least this time I knew who the thief was. I'd still have to find and reclaim the tiara pretty fast though, before Emma noticed it was missing.

"To Emma and Braden!" I raised my glass and heard a chorus of "to Emma and Braden" in return. Then I took a sip. I would have loved to chug it—boy, did I need it—but I needed to keep a clear head more.

"Ladies and gentleman," the DJ said. "Please enjoy your dinner. I'll be back with more music afterward."

I hustled to my table, slid into my chair, and leaned toward Natalie. "No one can know what I'm about to tell you," I whispered. "Keep your expression neutral."

She gave me side-eye. "Okay, Double O Seven."

All the bridesmaids and their plus-ones at the table were either chatting or eating. Still, I continued to whisper: "My cousin Scott just stole his mom's tiara."

Her eyes widened in a *no way* look.

"Is that neutral?" I sighed. "Anyway, this is on top of my cousin Jason stealing it during the hora. I got it back right before we sat down."

"Seriously? That's where you were? You have one effed-up family."

"Tell me about it. I need you to keep an eye on Emma. She doesn't know the tiara's gone. She left it sitting on the little table behind her, by the roses. If you see her start to search for it, or God forbid you see my mother realize it's gone, go spill the beans so they don't freak out. Tell Emma I'm on the case, and she doesn't have to worry." I stared at the ceiling. "Please let her not notice."

Natalie saluted me. "Go forth and kick butt."

* * *

I scurried to the table where Scott's husband, Tristan, was eating his salad—mixed greens with cranberries and cheddar cheese because: Wisconsin. "Hey," I said casually as I crouched beside him, breathing in his woody cologne. "You know where Scott is?"

"Forgot his cigarettes. He went to our room to get 'em. Why?"

"I'd like to ask him something—"

"What? Can I help?"

*Ummmm.* I couldn't tell if he knew what Scott had done.

"Would you look at her?" Aunt Hazel said from across the table. She'd nudged Uncle George as she stared behind me. "Like she's fooling anyone with those fake knockers."

I couldn't help myself. I looked. Aunt Hazel was right. No way those things were real. In my experience with boobs, and I had a fair amount, really skinny women like that chick don't have Dolly Parton breasts.

*Hmmm.* "I'm thinking about having some work done," I told Tristan. "I've started to sag, and I heard he knows a really good plastics guy." Heard. Guessed. Same difference.

"Sag? You're what? Twenty-six? Twenty-seven?"

"Twenty-four! And it can happen at my age when you're...well-endowed."

He stared at my chest. "You look fine to me."

"What do you know? Have you even seen any up close? I'm saggy I tell you!" I might have said it a little loud. Aunt Hazel glanced my way, as did several other people. Great. In an hour everyone would know. And it wasn't even true! "Anyway, I'd like to talk to Scott without prying ears."

He shrugged. "If he's not on the deck, you can check our room. Three sixteen."

"Thanks."

Scott might have gone out on the deck already to smoke, having stashed the tiara. I stepped outside and shivered. Boy, the wind had picked up, which explained why no one was out there.

"Shhhh!"

Or was I wrong? My heels clicked against the wooden planks as I approached the stairs down to the beach. I saw someone below scurry into the darkness. If it was Scott, who was he talking to? Was *he* cheating on his spouse too?

"I saw what you did," I called as I started down the stairs. "You should come out." No response. "If you make me get sand in my shoes, you're going to regret it." I actually regretted coming out there at all because sand was blowing right at me, landing in my hair and on my face and down my dress. But I'd come this far. "Last chance. Come out or I'm going to tell my mother."

"No, please, no!"

The threat of Stella Weiss worked again. If only I could bottle the fear Mom inspired.

My twin teenage cousins, Chloe and Olivia, jumped out into the light, barefoot and holding a half-empty bottle of vodka they must have swiped from the bar. This was not the theft I was interested in.

"Please don't rat us out," Chloe said. "It's just so boring in there."

*I wish.* "Have you seen Scott out here?"

They shook their heads, their long brown hair swishing in the wind. Maybe he was still in his room. I turned to go inside as rain began to fall.

"Wait," Olivia yelled. "Are you going to tell?"

I was supposed to do the right thing. Teach them a lesson. Keep them safe. Yadda yadda yadda. But it wasn't that long ago that I was underage, and I liked being the cool cousin. "I have three conditions."

"What?" Chloe asked.

"First, you promise to never drink and drive or get in the car with someone who's been drinking."

"Okay," she said.

"Second, if Natalie or I ask for your help later tonight, you give it, no questions asked."

"Will do."

"And third, when the limbo game starts, you both join in and act like you're having fun."

"Limbo?" Olivia said. "That's lame."

I raised my right eyebrow.

"We're in," Chloe said.

"Fine," Olivia said. "What are you going to need help with anyway?"

"That sounds like a question to me," I said.

"Sorry."

Right then the heavens really opened up. I dashed up the steps, hearing movement on the deck. Scott? But when I reached the top, I didn't see him. Eager to get out of the rain, which had begun blowing sideways, I opened the door and heard running behind me.

"Robin, look out!"'

I turned. The golden retriever that nearly peed on me this afternoon was sprinting straight at me from the other end of the deck. He must smell the food inside. Mom had sprung for the beef tenderloin to impress the relatives. A dog running through the reception would definitely not impress them.

With barely a second to spare, I bent into a catcher's stance to block him from going inside. *Bam!* The dog knocked me flat on my butt, then scrambled over me to dart into the ballroom. Maybe if Mom had let me play Little League this wouldn't have happened.

"Stop that dog," I yelled.

Olivia and Chloe jumped over me—they should run hurdles—and ran inside. I followed. We all stood there dripping wet, looking around. Some guy at the closest table pointed his fork and said, "He went that way."

"Come on." I hurried as quickly as I could without calling attention to myself, as if three drenched women weren't going to turn some heads. Thank God Mom and Emma weren't sitting nearby.

"There he is." Chloe pointed.

The soaked pup was trotting past some tables, his nose to the ground. He seemed on a mission. But to where?

And then I realized his destination. *Oh no.* There was an empty chair at a table full of people eating their dinners, and right in the middle of the isolated place setting was a plate with baby roasted potatoes, mixed vegetables, and one delicious-looking steak.

I double-timed it. Or tried to. But these heels were made for walking, not running, and I reached the table just in time to see the dog leap onto the chair, sink his teeth into the steak, and bolt toward the hallway.

"Is that your dog?" The woman sitting beside the empty chair looked indignant.

*Yes, I always bring my dog to fancy affairs. That wouldn't bother my mother at all.*

"No, he probably belongs to someone staying at the state park a couple of miles from here." Some careless person whom I'd happily kill. "He ran inside when I opened the door."

"That's great. Now my husband has no dinner."

"No dinner?" A large man—in height and width—loomed over me, and he sounded sad. Another problem to deal with.

"Chloe, there should be a steak waiting for me at table four. Go get my plate, please, and bring it to this man. And for all that is holy, do not let my mother see you."

"Don't worry." From the fear in her eyes, Chloe understood the importance of stealth on this mission.

"I can't take your dinner," the man said.

"You're welcome to it," I said. "I couldn't eat tonight anyway. Dieting." Or, rather, it seemed I *wouldn't* eat tonight. Not a single morsel.

"Thanks. I'll be sure to tell Emma what you did for me."

*Oh no no no.* I forced a smile. "Please don't do that. It would upset her to hear a dog ran through the reception and stole your food. Could this be our little secret?"

"Sure. I guess."

"Great." I started toward the hall, then turned back. "How do you know who I am? Do I know you?"

"Nah. I work with Emma. She has a photo of the two of you on her desk."

*How sweet.* Emma was worth every moment of this horrible evening.

Chloe returned with the steak. It smelled so good I nearly drooled. "Come on, girls."

In the hallway I said, "You're both in charge of making sure that dog doesn't get back into the ballroom tonight."

"Is this the help you were talking about before?" Olivia asked.

I gaped at her. Did she really think I'd expected a dog to run off the beach, into the ballroom, steal a steak, and make a run for it? She gazed back at me expectantly. It seemed she did.

"Yep. That's what I was talking about."

"There he is," Chloe said.

The dog stood several yards away. He stared at us. We stared at him. I padded toward him slowly, the girls following. He came toward us, also slowly. It was like a showdown at the O.K. Corral, but I had backup.

"He's wearing a collar," I said. "Whichever one of us has the opportunity, grab that collar and hold on tight."

"I don't see the steak," Olivia said. "He must have eaten it already. He might be easier to catch if he's full."

"Yeah, but he was heading back to the ballroom," Chloe said. "Maybe he wants seconds."

"Not on my watch," I said.

We inched closer and closer. "On three," I said. "One. Two. Thr—"

And that's when the dog started shaking. A veritable waterfall of rainwater—and maybe Lake Michigan too—flew off of him, right onto me. It was a clever ploy on his part because we were all so stunned, we stood there as a puddle grew beneath me, giving him time to dash past us toward the ballroom.

"Get that dog," I yelled.

Chloe and Olivia took off while I shook myself. Turns out that drying method doesn't work with people. If I ever learned who owned that dog, I would kill them.

I squeezed some water from my hair and pumped myself up for round three of Catch That Dog when the elevator dinged. I twirled around, and out walked my other prey.

Scott.

* * *

I hoped Chloe and Olivia could deal with the golden themselves because I wasn't going to let Scott get away again.

I approached him with a furrowed brow and narrowed eyes. I even tried to do a full-on raised right eyebrow. I must have pulled it off because he cringed.

"Why are you all wet?" he said.

*Darn.* Maybe that's why he cringed. But I would not be deterred from my mission. "Where've you been, Scott?"

He paused. That was his tell. He always paused before he lied. "Had to make a phone call."

"Really? I thought you were going out on the deck for a smoke. That's where Tristan thought you went."

"I'm heading there right now." He tried to pass me. I clutched his shoulder.

"Not so fast." When he turned, avoiding my gaze, I moved in for the kill. I invaded his personal space, nose to nose. At least the heels Mom had pushed me to wear today had a good use after all. "Where's. The. Tiara?"

He swallowed hard. "I don't know what you're talking about."

He was lucky I didn't kill him on the spot. "I'm talking about the family heirloom that belongs to *your* mother, was loaned to *my* sister, and which *you* swiped while I was giving my toast."

Scott glanced around. Seeing we were alone, he said, "Why do you care? Emma got to wear it during the ceremony and in the photos, like she wanted. Then she took it off, so clearly, she's done with it. Besides, it belongs to my mother."

"And she'd never let Emma hear the end of it if the tiara was stolen while Emma was responsible for it."

He shrugged. "Sorry, but the tiara should be mine."

"How do you figure?'

"I'm the oldest child of our generation."

"It's supposed to go to oldest daughter." I glanced down at his pants. "Has there been a change I'm unaware of?"

He huffed out a breath. "No. But isn't that sexist? Just because I'm a guy I'm not allowed to inherit the tiara?"

I felt a headache coming on. "Who would you leave it to? You and Tristan don't want kids."

"So?"

"So...I don't get it. You want it simply to have it?"

"Better than my mom being buried in it one day. And...maybe I want to wear it myself. Maybe Tristan and I want to renew our vows in a few months on our tenth anniversary and I want to wear it. Did you ever think of that?"

My mouth hung open. "Actually...no. That hadn't occurred to me for a second." Scott had never struck me as particularly femme. "Well...that's nice. That's really nice, Scott, and I'm glad you shared it with me. But wouldn't your mom notice when you walked down the aisle with the missing tiara on your head?"

"It's going to be a very small event. No moms allowed. Nothing like this extravaganza."

"That's what Emma wanted." Well, maybe I wanted the no-Mom part.

"At least she got to wear the tiara."

I sighed. For all my anger over sexism in today's ceremony, I'd never realized how sexist our family's tiara tradition was. "Look, I'm sorry about all this. You have a really good point about the sexism. But you're still going to have to give the tiara back."

He crossed his arms over his chest. "No."

I widened my eyes. "You can steal it from your mother's house some other time. I'll even help you if you want."

"No."

Growling, I poked his chest. "We're going to your room right now and you're going to give me the tiara or I am going to tell my mother what you did."

He visibly gulped.

"And then I'm going to tell your mother."

He jumped back and punched the elevator button repeatedly. "Okay, okay. You don't have to play dirty."

As the elevator arrived, he said, "Will you really help me steal the tiara?"

"On one condition."

"What?"

"You have to participate in limbo later tonight."

"Limbo? Really?"

I raised my right eyebrow at him. I was getting pretty good at that.

"Ugh. Fine. You win. Limbo."

* * *

When I got back to the ballroom, the music and dancing had resumed. Emma wasn't at her table, so I snuck over and slid the tiara back under the flower arrangement.

Across the room, Natalie sat alone at our table. I hurried over.

"I saved you a slice of cake."

If we hadn't been in public, I would have picked it up with my fingers and swallowed it whole. As it was, I used a fork and ate reasonably sized bites. One after the other, with barely time to breathe in between. This ginger spice cake with vanilla frosting was so tasty it almost made up for missing out on the tenderloin. And the salad. And the appetizers. And lunch.

"Emma never noticed the tiara was missing," Natalie said.

"Oh, good." Emma was out on the dance floor, shaking her booty.

"Yep. Of course, she might have been distracted by a big dog running through the room about ten minutes ago."

A piece of cake fell out of my mouth, down my cleavage. "Oh no!"

"Oh yeah."

"Oh God. What happened?"

"I was sitting here, eating my cake, keeping my eye on Emma as she ate her cake, so I didn't notice the dog until I heard the commotion."

"Commotion?"

"Lots of people reacted to that dog as he trotted to the dance floor. Gasping and pointing, like they've never seen a big wet dog before at a fancy affair thrown by Stella Weiss."

Yep, I was definitely getting a headache.

"Did she see the dog?"

"Oh yeah."

"So what happened?"

"Your cousins Chloe and Olivia started chasing the dog. You know what happens when you chase a dog, don't you?"

"It thinks it's a game and runs faster."

"There you go. It's like you were here. It ran around the tables, under the tables, shoving its nose in places it shouldn't have. Then..." Natalie laughed. "Then it ran onto the dance floor. Your mom threw down her napkin and marched red-faced over to it. Her eyes were narrowed. Her brow was furrowed."

"Her right eyebrow was raised to the ceiling," we both said at once.

"And?" I said.

"And she scared the poor thing so bad, it took a dump, right there on the floor. See that white napkin? It's covering the spot."

I felt faint. "Oh God. Oh God, poor Emma."

"That's what I thought too, until she started to laugh. And when she laughed, everyone else did too. Everyone but your mom, of course."

"Of course. Emma laughed?"

"She sure did."

"And my mom?"

"Last I saw, she was demanding one of the servers find the manager of the hotel, while your twin cousins cleaned up the poop, begging me to tell you they tried their best. You want to tell me what that's all about?"

"It's a long story."

"I have all night. Don't forget to include the part about how you got all wet, with your makeup smeared and sandy paw prints on your stomach."

I looked down. There they were.

"Yep." Natalie broke into a grin. "This may be the best wedding I've ever been to."

Emma approached us, her mouth open wide. "Robin, what happened?"

I shrugged. "I went outside for some fresh air, and it started pouring before I could get back in."

She glanced at my stomach. "That's all?"

*Stupid dog.* "That's all." No need to tell her how hard I'd tried to make this evening a good one for her. "You having fun?"

A blissful smile blossomed on her face. "I am."

"You should put your tiara back on. Enjoy it while you can." Then I could stop worrying about it.

"No. It pinched." Neil Diamond's "Sweet Caroline" started playing. "Oh, I love this song. You guys should come dance," she said as she scampered back to Braden.

My cake was all gone, except that piece in my bra, which I guess I was saving for later. "You want to?" I asked Natalie.

"Let's do it." Her mouth fell open. "Robin..."

"What?"

She turned to me, her face confused. "I hate to tell you this, but...your dad just stole Emma's tiara."

* * *

As I watched Dad scurry toward the back of the ballroom with a crescent moon-shaped bulge under his tuxedo jacket, I knew Natalie was right. If Dad had picked up the tiara to look at it or move it to a safer spot—which it clearly needed—he wouldn't have hidden it.

"I can't even." Words failed me. The goody bags Emma and Braden had made for everyone had Tylenol in them. I needed every last pill. "I have to talk to my dad."

Natalie laughed in disbelief. "Yeah, you do." She waved me off.

I hurried after him. I couldn't begin to figure out what he was thinking. Did he hope to sell the tiara to help pay for the wedding? That would be completely out of character for him. I'd never known him to do anything dishonest.

I was so focused on Dad that I didn't notice I was on a collision course with some guy until I smacked into him and his glass of beer splashed my face and dress. I loved beer, but not like this.

"I'm so sorry." He handed me his cocktail napkin.

I tried to blot my face and neck with the small triple-ply napkin engraved with "Emma and Braden" in gold script. As with so much this weekend, it was clearly designed for show. Not up to the task at all. "Don't worry about it. This development is right on trend for tonight."

"What?"

"Nothing. I'm sorry about your drink."

"No worries. I'll get another. Open bar."

Was that why Dad stole the tiara? To cover the bar tab?

When I reached the hallway, Dad was down at the far end, stepping into the restroom. The ladies' restroom.

He'd passed a closer set of restrooms, which everyone at the reception had been using. Did he go down there for privacy? Why the ladies' room? I couldn't figure it out.

I sped there and pushed the door open warily. Dad was leaning against a dove-gray wall, his bald spot shining in the ceiling light, while my mom sat at a slate-gray vanity table *adjusting the tiara on her head.*

"What the heck?" I said.

Mom glared at Dad over her shoulder. "You let her follow you here."

Throwing his hands in the air, Dad said, "Sorry I skipped the class on sneakiness at burglary school. I knew I shouldn't have let you talk me into this."

Dad kissed the top of my head, dabbed water off his face, then walked out. When the door clicked shut, I sauntered toward Mom. "Let me see if I've figured this out. You had Dad steal the tiara so you could keep it from Aunt Hazel?"

She gave me a *duh* look. "You think I'm going to let her be buried in it? My grandmother smuggled this tiara out of Germany. It might technically be Hazel's now, but it belongs to the oldest daughter of each generation, those before us and those to come. It belongs to Emma!"

"Does she know about this?"

"Of course not. I'm going to leave it to her first daughter in my will. Won't that be a nice surprise?" She turned back to the mirror and patted her hair. "This is the only time I've ever worn it. It's pretty, don't you think? Though not as shiny as I'd have thought."

"Gorgeous." I rolled my eyes at her priorities. "Mom, have you considered how Emma's going to take it when she realizes the tiara is missing? It's her responsibility. This will ruin the wedding for her. And you know Aunt Hazel will never let her hear the end of it."

"You leave Hazel to me."

"So you don't care Emma's going to feel terrible about this? For years to come."

"Stop being so dramatic. She'll get over it."

I chuckled in disbelief. I'd jokingly (sort of) thought about killing several people tonight because they'd been greedy, selfish, or irresponsible. None of them had considered how their actions might upset Emma. That's why Mom's theft was on a whole other level. She knew this would hurt Emma, and she didn't care.

*Maybe I could kill her.*

"You know, Mom, you're right. Aunt Hazel's incredibly selfish, wanting to take the tiara with her. But what you're doing is worse, letting Emma twist in the wind. I won't let you do it."

Mom stood and turned toward me, fists on her hips. "Excuse me?"

"You heard me. Hand over the tiara."

Her eyes narrowed, her brow furrowed, and she raised her right eyebrow. I admit my resolve wavered a bit.

"I have spent the better part of a year doing everything I could to make this a perfect night for my first-born child," she said in a haughty tone. "And here you stand looking like something the cat dragged in, with your hair wet and scraggly, your makeup a mess, paw prints on your beautiful dress, sand stuck to your shoes, and on top of all that, you smell like a brewery mixed with wet dog. Yet you're telling me *I'm* going to be responsible for ruining this wedding?"

Oh, that was a low blow. "Give me the tiara, Mom."

"No. I'm saving it for the daughter Emma will have one day, and that's final."

With my anger rising, I stretched up as tall as I could, trying to look my most imposing. "Give me the tiara."

"Don't try to intimidate me."

"Last chance. Hand it over."

She laughed. "Or what?"

I narrowed my eyes, furrowed my brow, and raised my right eyebrow.

Surprise registered on Mom's face. "That is not a good look on you."

My anger boiled over. I thrust my arm forward and yanked the tiara right off her head! Got some of her dyed hair with it, including the roots.

Then I ran for it.

* * *

I returned to the ballroom having made a decision. "Emma," I said, approaching her on the dance floor, holding out the tiara. "Could I wear this for the rest of the night? I need something to keep my hair off my face." And a way to ensure the tiara didn't get nipped again.

"Sure."

"Ladies and gentlemen," the DJ said. "Come on out to the dance floor. It's time to limbo!"

Emma punched her fist in the air. "Woo-hoo!"

Natalie and I got in line. I settled the tiara on my head, heard my name, and turned just in time for the photographer to take a photo of me in all my bedraggled glory—as if this night wouldn't be burned in my brain already.

The music started and the game began. I checked to make sure Chloe, Olivia, Scott, and Jason were all in line. They were. That raised right eyebrow was powerful stuff.

After several rounds, my cousin Janelle and I were the only ones left. I kept waiting for her to slip and fall, like on any normal day, but she was proving to be surprisingly limber. How was she still single (wedding hookups aside)? Finally Janelle nudged the stick as she tried to shimmy under it.

"All right," the DJ announced. "We have one contestant left. If you make it under this time, you win!"

After the night I'd had, it was insane how much I wanted to win.

"Come on, Robin," Natalie yelled as I bent backward.

One little jump forward. Another little jump forward. Leaning back. Leaning back. I was going to make it. I—

Something slammed into my leg. My balance shifted, and down I went, flat on the floor. People started laughing as I wondered who'd pulled a Tonya Harding on me.

"We have a winner!" the DJ said. "A last-minute entry. I don't know his name, but he's blond."

I sat up to see who the cheater was.

Of course.

The dog won the limbo contest.

* * *

The next morning, Natalie and I made our way down to the beach. I kept my eye out for that dog as we traipsed along the golden sand, but I didn't see him. With the wedding over and a good night's sleep—and a solid meal—in me, I felt kinder toward him. I hoped the hotel had found his family.

It was a beautiful warm day for September. Nice enough to enjoy the sun, even though the clear blue water would be too cold for swimming.

A lot of people from the wedding were here, including the twins, who had no hangover, thank goodness; Rabbi Gelman, who was getting some needed color; and Adam and his wife, who remained oblivious to his cheating ways. I felt bad about that, but I couldn't solve every problem, at least not at this wedding.

Eventually we grabbed some canvas beach chairs and sat in a quiet spot. Natalie read while I scrunched my toes in the sand and stared out at Lake Michigan. You'd never know it wasn't an ocean. The state of Michigan was out there somewhere on the other side—more than a hundred miles away. Staring at the vastness of the lake let me shake off the last of my stress from the prior night.

After about an hour a shadow fell over me.

"This spot taken?" My dad wedged a chair into the sand beside me and settled into it. "A little birdie told me about everything you went through last night."

"Cheep cheep cheep," Natalie said.

I rolled my eyes. She and Dad are early risers and had eaten breakfast together this morning.

"You're a good sister," Dad said. "Emma's lucky to have you. Don't worry about your mother. She'll get past this. You were right to stand up to her last night. I should've done it myself. She's just had such a fiery relationship with Hazel all her life, with Hazel getting what your mom calls 'special treatment' simply because she's older, including control of the tiara. She'd worked herself into a frenzy thinking it'd be buried one day. I'd wanted to calm her down. Unlike you, I hadn't focused on the consequences."

"If I can add my two cents, from an outsider's perspective?" Natalie asked, and I nodded. "I'm sorry to say this, but you and your mom are a lot alike."

"Excuse me?" As my right eyebrow rose, I recalled Mom saying that exact thing last night in the same outraged tone. I cringed.

Natalie grasped my hand. "You're both fierce. Determined to do what you believe is right. You want to protect Emma. Your mom thinks Emma's too shy for her own good. She doesn't want her to miss out on things she believes Emma really wants deep down, so she pushes to get her way. Maybe Stella's not unfeeling. Maybe she simply sees things differently."

I felt the color draining from my face as the truth of Natalie's words struck me. I was just like Mom.

"Tylenol," I croaked. "I need more Tylenol."

Dad laughed. "If I haven't said it before, Natalie, you are a welcome addition to our family. I'm looking forward to your wedding."

I whimpered. "No more weddings."

Natalie squeezed my hand. "Maybe we'll elope."

"This is why I love you."

My phone buzzed. I read the text.

"Braden's heading to the restaurant for brunch. You and Nat should join us. But meet me in my room first alone? I'd like a few minutes of sister time before we leave on our honeymoon."

* * *

Emma and I were sitting on the striped sofa in her suite. To the soundtrack of waves whooshing toward the beach outside, I'd just told her everything that happened last night. She'd known something was up.

"You did all that for me? To save the tiara?"

"Yep."

She reached into a canvas bag on the carpet. "This tiara?"

"I thought you returned it to Aunt Hazel. Didn't she and Uncle George already go home?"

Emma smirked. "She went home with *a* tiara."

I gawped at her, then at the tiara. It was much shinier now than it had been last night—except during the ceremony, when its gems had really glittered.

"I love everything you did for me," Emma said. "But I wouldn't have minded if that tiara had gone missing because this one—the real one—was tucked safely away in the locked *yichud* room."

I needed a carton of Tylenol. "Explain."

"When I wrote my vows, one of them was that I would put my new family ahead of everyone else. Mom. Aunt Hazel. It's what the circling was about during the ceremony. I want the daughter I'll have one day to wear this tiara. It's her birthright. So I had a duplicate created, and after I made my vows to Braden in the *yichud* room, I hid this tiara and put the fake one on."

"*That's* why you weren't worried it might get stolen when you took it off during the party."

"It really did pinch." She grinned. "You know the best part of all? Turns out Aunt Hazel *can't* tell when everything is fake."

*Wow.* "No offense, but when I think of what I went through last night for you, I'm a little angry you kept me in the dark."

Emma laughed. "No offense to you, but while I may be a little timid—or at least the old me was—you can be a bit judgmental. I didn't know how you'd feel about this. I didn't know if I could trust you."

"You didn't know if *you* could trust *me*?" I narrowed my eyes, furrowed my brow, and raised my right eyebrow.

"Oh, Robin. That is not a good look on you."

*Lord help me. I may kill her.*

* * *

**Barb Goffman** has won the Agatha, Macavity, Silver Falchion, and 2020 Ellery Queen's Mystery Magazine Readers Award. She's been nominated for major crime-writing awards thirty-two times, including fourteen Agatha Award nominations (a category record), and multiple nominations for the Anthony, Macavity, and Derringer awards. In addition to *EQMM*, her stories have appeared in *Alfred Hitchcock's Mystery Magazine*, *Black Cat Mystery Magazine*, and many anthologies. Later in 2021, you can read new stories from Barb in *BCMM*, *Malice Domestic Presents: Mystery Most Diabolical*, and *Monkey Business: Crime Fiction Inspired by the Films of the Marx Brothers*. Barb blogs every third Tuesday at www.SleuthSayers.org, often about writing. She lives with her dog in Winchester, Virginia, where she works as a freelance editor, focusing on cozy and traditional mysteries. She also has her own invisible cape (in case you were wondering). You can find more, including a complete list of her published stories, on her website: www.BarbGoffman.com.

# Footprints in the Sand
# by Shari Randall

I HAVE THREE RULES IN MY LIFE:

1) Always pet a friendly dog.

2) Never chew gum in the ballet studio.

3) Never rise before the sun.

So why was I awake before dawn? Me?

There was no glimmer of light around my bedroom window shade, just a lighter shade of gray. I tossed onto my side, relishing the feel of my silky sea green sheets, willing myself to go back to sleep. I turned the other way, bunched my pillow and closed my eyes. Nope, not sleepy. Well, there was nothing for it. I stretched and decided to channel my relentlessly cheerful Aunt Gully and look on the bright side. I had time for a swim. Business had been so brisk at her Lazy Mermaid lobster shack I hadn't had any beach time in weeks. Before I had a chance to talk myself out of it, I slipped into a swimsuit, grabbed my phone and a towel, and jogged down to the beach.

Aunt Gully's cottage was a short walk from our neighborhood's quarter mile of sand, Kidde Beach. Like most New England beaches, it was rocky and pocket-sized, but there was a gentle slope of sugary sand with a great view of Long Island Sound and little Harvey's Light. The name was pronounced "kiddy" and was where many Mystic Bay kids learned to swim. It was a very bare bones beach, unspoiled, the only concessions an outdoor shower and a trash can by a small parking area.

As I arrived, pink dawn light stretched across the horizon and spilled into the water where a few fishing boats bobbed in the distance. The light breeze was already warm and not another soul walked the beach. Perfect.

I tossed my towel onto the sand and was surprised to see a line of footprints—footprints so large I put my foot next to one and laughed. These were made by some impressively large feet. My size eight foot isn't exactly tiny, and it was about half the size of the print in the sand.

The line of footprints led directly into the ocean. I left my phone on my towel and followed them, noting that the shape of the prints changed the closer they got to the water—the weight shifted to the ball of the foot. Someone had run full speed into the water.

I cast a glance down the beach. There was no beach chair, no towel, no umbrella, just empty sand and a strip of dark green seaweed that marked the high tide line.

I scanned the ocean for the footprints' owner, squinting against the sunlight that now glittered on the gentle waves. The ocean was calm, and I saw no one swimming, no head or arm breaking the surface, nothing except those far off fishing boats. I did a running dive into the cool water and swam the length of the beach, then flipped onto my back and let the tranquil swells carry me. I wondered if the guy—it had to be a man with footprints that large—was training for the weekend's Mystic Bay Triathlon. The triathlon was a mile swim, ten-mile run, and twenty-mile bike ride. I splashed up the sand and walked the length of the beach, enjoying the feel of the water lapping over my toes. I returned to where I'd started, but no supersize footprints leaving the water crossed mine.

Familiar voices pulled me from my examination of the prints.

"Allie, how's the water?"

Aunt Gully and her chum Aggie Weatherburn, owner of Fairweather Antiques, crossed the sand toward me. The lifelong friends were an odd couple; Aunt Gully short and curvy, Aggie tall and angular. While Aunt Gully was outgoing and talkative, Aggie was reserved and given to New England reticence. Both wore plastic swim caps; Aggie's navy blue to match her no nonsense one piece, Aunt Gully's a bright pink dotted with plastic flowers that matched her tropical print swim dress.

"Look at this footprint." I lined up my foot next to it.

"Who knew Bigfoot could swim?" Aunt Gully laughed.

"It's odd." I pointed. "The prints go out, but there are none returning. And I don't see anyone out there."

Aggie windmilled her arms and lifted her knees in a warmup march, stepped gingerly into the water, and sank in with a sigh. "Hard for a swimmer to get in trouble here. The water's always calm."

Aunt Gully walked alongside me, looking at the footprints. "Looks like he got a running start into the water," she said. "Like at the polar plunge you crazy people do in January."

I shivered at the memory of diving into the frigid waves on New Year's Day. "Good point. If someone were running into the water, it means they're a confident swimmer."

"One of those triathaloners," Aggie called. "By the way, my nephew's coming this weekend to do the triathlon."

Aggie had an inexhaustible supply of nephews she was always trying to set me up with. I tried to think of a response that wasn't "thanks for the warning."

I made a noncommittal sound as I picked up my things, shook the sand off my towel, and tucked it around me. A glint at the waterline caught my eye and I stepped into the shallow water to see what it was. I plunged my hand in and swooped up a smooth, metal object.

"Sea glass?" Aunt Gully asked.

I swished the sand-encrusted object in the water to rinse it off and turned it in my palm, my surprise turning to wonder. It was a ring with a gold setting holding a huge diamond encircled by a dozen smaller diamonds. It was the biggest gem I'd ever seen. I held out the ring and breathed, "Look at this!"

Aunt Gully whistled. "What a rock!"

Aggie side-stroked over to us and plucked the ring from my fingers. "I see a lot of vintage jewelry at the shop." She hefted the ring, then squinted at it. "That *is* a rock. Halo setting. Nice."

"It's so big it looks fake," I said.

Aggie handed me the ring. "I need my glasses and my jeweler's loupe to be sure, but it's not bad."

Aggie's New England understatement made me raise my eyebrows. "Not bad? It's gorgeous." I slid it onto my ring finger, then took it off and read the inscription. "Fifty beautiful years. JS to MS."

"You don't think Bigfoot lost it?" Aggie said.

"That ring barely fits me. I can't imagine it would fit Bigfoot," I said.

"I'll post on Neighbornet," Aggie said, naming the neighborhood website. "Found. One heck of a ring."

"I'll ask around, too," Aunt Gully said. "Since you're heading back," she lowered her voice, "hide it in the sugar bowl for now."

We looked at the ring glittering in my palm and sighed.

"If only I were less honest," Aunt Gully said.

We laughed.

"Let's think," I said. "Someone married for fifty years—"

"They'd be probably in their seventies or so." Aunt Gully tapped her chin.

I wrapped my towel more tightly around me. "Who has the initials MS, who's the right age, and swims at this beach?"

"Marian Santiago?" Aggie said.

"Moved to Fort Myers two years ago." Aunt Gully was already moving slowly through the water, head down, scanning the sandy bottom. Aggie joined her. I knew they'd mentally thumb through years of friends, relatives, friends of friends, business associates, old school chums, customers, and acquaintances as they looked for more jewelry.

My thoughts returned to the footprints as I turned to go. The incoming tide had been busy erasing them. I put my foot next to the last remaining print, snapped a photo, then wrapped my hand more firmly around the ring and headed home.

* * *

I did put the ring in the pink Depression glass sugar bowl on the kitchen table. I felt silly, but if anything happened to me, at least Aunt Gully and Aggie knew where it was. I dashed through a shower and dressed in my work uniform, a pink T-shirt with strategically placed red seashells and khaki shorts, thinking about the ring and trying to imagine the woman who owned it.

Our neighborhood was home to a few blocks of rustic cottages that had originally been built by fisherman and lobstermen working the fleets out of Noank and Mystic in the early 1900s. Aunt Gully's snug Cape Cod style home, Gull's Nest, was typical—shingled with cedar that had grayed in years of exposure to the elements, with a broad front porch to catch the breeze. Every home had a share in Kidde Beach, and I'd grown up swimming there.

Who in our neighborhood would own an elegant ring like this? I took the ring out of the bowl and brushed sugar crystals from the sparkling gems. The diamond was huge, meant to be noticed. Glamorous. I felt that JS was celebrating more than fifty years of marriage. He'd made it, perhaps in business, and wanted this splashy symbol of success for his spouse. This was more in keeping with Fox Point, a neighboring village that had always been a vacation escape for well-to-do summer people or folks renting a vacation home. The summer people probably wouldn't be on Neighbornet.

I snapped a pic and sent it to my friend Bronwyn, a police trainee, then put the ring back in the sugar bowl and replaced the lid. Outside, the door to the shower creaked and the sound of running water and Aunt Gully singing "Under the Sea" from *The Little Mermaid* streamed through the open kitchen window.

Bronwyn called me immediately. "Are you engaged? Have you been keeping secrets from your best friends?"

I laughed. "No!"

"Thank goodness," Bronwyn said. "I thought you'd said your last date struck out."

I cringed. "Very funny." Aggie's latest nephew, Brad the baseball fanatic, had buttonholed me for three hours of baseball statistics. "Hope I'm not interrupting any exciting arrests."

"I wish," Bronwyn said.

"I wanted to ask if anyone had reported a missing ring." I explained how I'd found it.

"I'll check in and ask."

"Thanks."

Aunt Gully burst in, wrapped in a leopard-print towel. "I thought of an MS!" she crowed. "Mary Sabino, been married quite a while, right age." Aunt Gully bustled into her bedroom to dress. "Eight kids. I can't see her with a fancy ring like that, but you never know. Maybe her husband's plumbing business is doing better than I thought."

"We can swing by on the way to the shack," I said. That was one good thing about insomnia. It got you up early so you could get a lot done.

A few minutes later, Aunt Gully took the ring out of the bowl and held it up to the light streaming over the yellow gingham café curtains. She returned it to the bowl with a sigh. "When she gets a chance, Aggie's going to stop by with her loupe and take a look at this baby, see if it's real. By the way," she added with exaggerated nonchalance as she busied herself scrubbing the already pristine porcelain sink. "We're invited to her house for a picnic Saturday."

My guard went up.

Aunt Gully gave the sink an extra scrub. "One of her nephews is coming for a visit."

I groaned. "Not Brad the baseball nut."

"No, no, another one."

Aggie lived right next door so it was difficult and delicate to evade her matchmaking. "I'll check my social calendar," I said as we headed out to her van. *And try to come up with a believable excuse.*

Aunt Gully and I swung by Mary Sabino's house on the way into Mystic Bay. A sprawling split level, it took the nautical décor of the area to the extreme. Lobster buoys hung from every available inch on the weathered wood exterior. All the curtains were closed and a newspaper sat on the front mat.

I parked next to a mailbox attached to a five foot tall scale model of the New London Harbor Light.

A neighbor peeped over the fence and waved. "Gully, is that you?"

"Laurie!" Aunt Gully returned the wave and asked about Mary and the ring.

"Mary's gone to Canada for her grandson's baptism. A fancy ring?" Laurie shook her head. "I know for a fact they put another mortgage on their house to pay for one of their grandkid's college fees. Besides, they had an anniversary party in the spring. Forty-five years."

I thanked Laurie and turned the van toward the shack. "Who else could MS be?" I mused.

"You've got that detective fever again," Aunt Gully teased as we turned onto Pearl Street. "I can tell. Me too. It is nice that it isn't a murder, although..." her tone was wistful, "it has been so quiet this summer."

I shook my head. Last summer had been a whirlwind for me. After the accident that broke my ankle and put my dance career on hold, I'd moved back to Mystic Bay while I healed. There'd been several murders in our sleepy village, and I'd somehow become entangled in all of them—entangled to the point that *The Mystic Mariner* dubbed me the Dancing Detective. What I didn't enjoy were all the jokes comparing me to a character in a TV show where a murder happened every time the sleuth showed up. It was killing what little social life I had.

The last few months had been murder free and I hoped, for Mystic Bay's sake, it stayed that way. I might've been alone. Aggie had bought a police scanner and, judging from the excitement gleaming in Aunt Gully's big brown eyes, I wondered if Gull's Nest would soon have its own scanner, too. Maybe I was a bad influence.

I parked Aunt Gully's van by the kitchen door of the Lazy Mermaid. We'd left up the patriotic bunting from the Fourth of July, and Aunt Gully had added a banner to the porch that proclaimed WELCOME TRIATHLONERS! The life-size wooden mermaid statue by the front door sported a "Mystic Bay Tri" T-shirt and baseball cap.

Two ten-year-old boys, tanned and wiry in oversized T-shirts and board shorts, were busy working on the porch. Bit Markey watered the geraniums in the half barrels while his friend Jack swept sand and debris from the mat by the door. Aunt Gully had hired them to "police the grounds" and gave them a small salary along with what seemed to be their weight in lobster rolls in return.

The boys were deep in conversation as Aunt Gully and I greeted them. She hurried inside, but I pulled up short when I heard what they were discussing. "Loch Ness Monster?" I said.

Bit and Jack exchanged a look, then shrugged, deciding I could be trusted with a confidence.

"We saw something big and dark in the water this morning, and maybe it was a sea monster," Bit said.

Jack spoke with confidence. "All I'm saying is, if there's one Loch Ness Monster, there could be another."

"When was this?" I asked. "Where were you?"

"An hour before dawn," Bit said.

"Four-twenty, to be exact." Jack spoke with assurance.

I hid a smile. "You were out early."

The boys' words tumbled.

"We were fishing. And we saw—"

"This thing, this dark thing splashing in the water off Kidde Beach."

"I thought it could've been a harbor seal."

Jack shook his head. "Not at this time of the year. They head north when the water gets warm."

Bit put his hands on his hips. "If it wasn't the Loch Ness Monster, what was it?"

I held up a hand. "Wait a sec. What were you guys doing out on the bay in the dark?"

The boys looked around, then shared a guilty look.

Bit said, "Allie won't tell."

"Won't tell what?" I folded my arms. "You didn't, ah, borrow a boat—"

"No, it was Jack's dad's Boston Whaler. He was cool with it." Bit nodded so vigorously I was certain Jack's father had no idea the boys had taken it.

"I'm helping Bit do the stargazer and fishing badges for Ocean Scouts," Jack said. "We went out around two and got home around five."

I recalled the footprints on the beach. The timing would be right. "Where did this sea monster go?"

"Toward Fox Point. We had to get back, so we didn't follow it."

I mulled over what the boys had said as I went inside, put on an apron, and shared news of the ring with our cook, Hector Viera, and his wife, Hilda, as we did the morning's prep work. Despite the pink Lazy Mermaid apron with strategically placed shells, Hilda always looked elegant, her dark hair styled in a smooth chignon, her lipstick a classic red. Hector was bald, well over six feet tall, and had the rakish air of a good-natured pirate.

Hector wagged his eyebrows. "Another mystery for you, Allie."

Soon Aunt Gully opened the door to our first customers, and it was all hands on deck as they streamed in.

"Aggie texted me," Aunt Gully said. "She had a burst pipe at her shop so she's been dealing with that all morning and hasn't gotten over to check the ring yet. But she did post about finding the ring on Neighbornet. She asked all the people who said it's theirs to describe it." Aunt Gully shook her head. "A lot of people are missing rings."

"They're fishing for a free ring," Hilda scoffed as she set mugs of coffee in front of two guys in triathlon T-shirts.

Hector emerged from the kitchen and wrapped his arms around his petite wife. "Would you like a big diamond ring, *mi amor*?" He had to bend his six foot frame to rest his cheek against hers.

"Not me," Hilda said. "Pearls are this girl's best friend." She turned to show off the pearl studs in her ears.

"My pearl." He kissed her cheek and returned to the kitchen.

"I'm a lucky woman." Hilda smiled. "Hector has always bought me gifts I liked. Not what he *thought* I liked."

"Good point," Aunt Gully said. "I have a friend whose husband keeps buying her jewelry, but she'd rather have a Harley."

Customers crowded the counter and as I served them, the sparkling ring wasn't far from my mind. At break time, I hung up my apron.

"I have an idea, Aunt Gully," I said. "The ring's so distinctive. I'm going to run up to the jewelers to show them the photo and see if they remember selling it."

Hector waggled a finger. "Finders keepers."

I smiled. "The ring's not quite my style."

Aunt Gully got a faraway look in her eye. "It could be mine."

* * *

There was one jeweler in our small village, Muse of Mystic. I straightened my spine as I entered the hushed showroom of the elegant shop across from the town green. The whole place was a jewel box itself, replete with blue velvet, sparkling crystal, thick oriental carpets, and the hush of serious money.

"May I help you?" A woman about my age wearing a sophisticated teal silk wrap dress greeted me. She smiled, but it was carefully calibrated and didn't reach her icy blue eyes. She'd already assessed, correctly, my potential as a customer.

I straightened my shoulders to full ballerina mode to exude confidence. "I was hoping you could help me."

A gray haired man in a dark suit emerged from the back of the store, carrying an armful of blue velvet fabric. When he saw me, he stopped short and his eyes widened behind his tortoiseshell glasses.

"Why, it's Allegra Larkin!" He used my full name, which I only used professionally. "Jill, don't you know who this is? Miss Larkin, I'm delighted to meet you. I'm a big fan of your dancing. I'm Jason d'Amboise. Jillian's my niece." He set down the velvet and extended his hand. "How can we assist?"

I shook his hand. "Nice to meet you." I showed them the photo I'd taken earlier. "Do you recognize this ring? I found it on the beach this morning. I was wondering if maybe your shop sold it and you knew who it belonged to."

Jason peered over his glasses. "That beauty belongs to Millicent Sutcliffe up on Fox Point!"

*Millicent Sutcliffe. MS.*

Jillian shot him a withering look then turned hard eyes on me. "You found this on the beach? What beach?" Her tone was so skeptical I got the message: *she thinks I stole it.*

"Kidde Beach." I took a deep breath to calm myself. "I'm trying to reunite the ring with the owner. I imagine she's desperate to get it back."

"I remember selling that ring to Mr. Sutcliffe, I think, fifteen years ago," Jason said. "We haven't seen the family since we did an insurance appraisal for them in April. That's when Mrs. Sutcliffe had a terrible fall—she was lucky to survive it with only a broken hip—so we dealt with the grandsons. I guess she's back to swimming now. Well, that's great news."

Jillian folded her arms. "Of course, we'd have to check if it's the same ring."

Jason scoffed. "That was a custom-designed piece. Mr. Sutcliffe wanted something no one else had."

Jillian's expression softened. "Why don't you have a seat and I'll check our records. Just a moment, please. Uncle Jason, why don't you get Miss Larkin something to drink?"

Jason grinned. "My pleasure. Coffee? Tea?"

I shook my head, still annoyed by Jillian's accusatory tone. "I'm fine, thank you." I settled onto a side chair.

Two people came in and Jason excused himself to help them. From his exclamations, it was a newly engaged couple looking for wedding bands. Their chatter faded into background noise as minutes passed. Jillian was taking her sweet time and my mind wandered. Mrs. Sutcliffe had broken her hip. She lived on Fox Point. Even if she'd recovered well enough to swim, Fox Point had a beautiful sandy beach and, if the ring was any indication, their house might even have its own private stretch of sand. Odd that she'd swim on Kidde Beach.

I stood and walked among the cases, admiring the sparkling gems. Finally, Jillian emerged from the back room.

"If you don't mind waiting there," she said, pointing to a chair by a case of pearl necklaces.

"Waiting?" I said. "You said you were checking your records. Did you find anything?"

She lowered her voice. "I hope you won't make a scene. I called Mrs. Sutcliffe and spoke to her grandson." Outside the picture window, a police cruiser pulled to the curb. "There was a break-in at their home last night and her jewelry was stolen. Including that ring." She lifted her chin. "I've called the police."

* * *

Having one of your best friends called to arrest you is an interesting experience.

I had to give Bronwyn credit. When she entered the shop and saw me with Jillian, she blinked only once.

"But, I was trying to find the owner and return it," I stammered. Jillian didn't respond, just pressed her lips more tightly together.

"Stay here," Bronwyn said, then asked Jillian to accompany her into the office. A few minutes later, Bronwyn returned and nodded toward the door. I jumped to my feet.

"I'll take it from here," Bronwyn said to Jillian. She stepped close to me and muttered, "This is awkward."

Jason and the engaged couple gaped from across the store as Bronwyn escorted me outside. The bride-to-be raised her cellphone to snap a photo as the door closed behind me.

"I can't believe it!" I burst out, indignation and embarrassment heating my face. "Jillian thinks I'm a thief?"

"Get in." Bronwyn opened the passenger door of the cruiser and I complied. She made a phone call as I slid down in my seat and covered my face, praying no one walking by recognized me. At least she let me ride in the front.

Bronwyn finished her call, got in the cruiser, and turned to me, her lips curved in a smile.

"Are you enjoying this?" I asked.

She resumed her professional expression, but not before I saw the laughter in her gray eyes. "You're not under arrest. I just spoke to Chief Brooks. He's headed up to Fox Point to investigate the burglary. He wants me to pick up the ring and take you to the Sutcliffe house."

As we drove to Gull's Nest, I filled in Bronwyn on everything that had happened since the discovery of the ring.

Bronwyn parked the cruiser in the driveway and we hurried in the kitchen door. "You know, you can't blame Jillian. She saw you with a photo of a ring she knew belonged to someone else. Didn't they tell you it's one of a kind? Then she calls the owner and they tell her there was a burglary..." She slid on a latex glove.

I held out the sugar bowl and lifted the lid. "Sorry, but it already has my prints, Aggie's, and Aunt Gully's."

Bronwyn's eyebrows rose. "That *is* a ring."

I set the bowl back on the table and brushed sugar off my fingers. "We can't hand it back like that. It needs a box."

Bronwyn shook her head, "I'll put it in an evidence envelope. Best not to broadcast what we're carrying around."

We drove the short distance across a narrow stone causeway into upscale Fox Point. Bronwyn pulled up to a sprawling three-story home perched on a rocky point overlooking the bay. The home didn't have a private beach, but it did have a spectacular view. In New England fashion, a small sign proclaimed the home's incongruously humble name: Sandy Feet. Two police vehicles were there, one of them the Chief's SUV, blocking in two gleaming sportscars and a rust-spotted blue Volvo station wagon with a UCONN sticker on the back window.

A silver haired woman in navy blue pants and a Fox Point Country Club polo shirt stood by the door, bent almost double, her hands clutching the bar of a walker. A tall young woman, her honey blond hair in a long braid, stood protectively at the older woman's side, while an even taller guy clad in running shorts and a sweaty triathlon T-shirt emerged from the back yard.

The older lady straightened and beamed as we approached. "Allegra Larkin! I'm Millicent Sutcliffe." Though she looked frail, her voice was strong and musical. "Olivia took me to see you dance in *The Nutcracker*. Oh, it was marvelous! Your dancing was exquisite! And I remember your costume was such a lovely shade of green, it set off your red hair so beautifully."

"Thank you, Mrs. Sutcliffe."

"This is Olivia, my granddaughter, and Marc, my grandson," Mrs. Sutcliffe continued. "My other grandson, Dustin, is on a bike ride, training for the triathlon."

"Nice to meet you," I said. "This is Police Trainee Bronwyn Denby."

Bronwyn nodded, then said, "I'm going to check in with the chief. Excuse me."

"My grandsons arrived yesterday morning. Marc's also doing the triathlon," Mrs. Sutcliffe said. "Olivia's been staying with me while I rehab, till she goes back to college." Mrs. Sutcliffe patted her granddaughter's arm. "She plays basketball at UCONN."

Olivia blushed. "Watch out, Gran's my number one fan. She'll talk your ear off about basketball."

Mrs. Sutcliffe's smile faded as we crossed the threshold into the house, passing a security keypad on the wall. "I could swear I locked the doors last night, I could swear I keyed in the code." Her voice faltered as her hands tightened on the bar of the walker, and my heart twisted for her.

"Sometimes you forget, Gran," Marc said, pushing back his sun-streaked blond hair, his expression soft and affectionate. "Want to sit in the sunporch?" Marc's bare feet slapped on the pristine blue tile floor as he led the way through a two-story foyer. He had bandages on his heels and a recently healed scar on his heavily muscled calves.

Olivia hovered over her grandmother as she made slow progress down the hallway, past a staircase that led to the gallery on the second floor. I wondered if this was where Mrs. Sutcliffe had fallen.

She read my mind. "I had a terrible fall in April. I was so lucky that all my grandkids had come to visit me that weekend. I'm so clumsy. I managed to trip on my way downstairs to get a glass of warm milk."

Olivia squeezed her grandmother's shoulder, worry evident in her furrowed brow.

Mrs. Sutcliffe gave her a smile. "Olivia just happened to get up shortly after that, and she found me. I don't know what would've happened if she hadn't called the ambulance right away. She insisted that I install this elevator."

As we passed the narrow metal door of the elevator, I glanced into a small room off the hallway, an office stuffed with cardboard boxes and teetering stacks of papers.

We went through a great room furnished with a massive television, low, angular furniture, and an incongruously homey and worn recliner covered with a crocheted afghan. Mrs. Sutcliffe stopped in front of a fireplace topped with a family portrait in which everyone wore matching white pants and blue shirts, posed against a backdrop of ocean and sky. In it, a younger Mrs. Sutcliffe stood tall next to a bald man with a prominent nose, who didn't look at the camera; instead, his adoring gaze was turned to her. Next to them was a younger version of the bald man and a woman with Olivia's honey blond hair. Flanking the four of them were younger versions of Olivia and Marc and another young man, who must have been Marc's brother, Dustin.

"I'm the only shrimp in the family," Mrs. Sutcliff laughed. "My husband, Jim; our son, Paul; and his second wife, Ella, Olivia's mom. Sadly, the boys' mom, Robin, died in a boating accident."

*Jim Sutcliffe. JS,* I thought.

We stepped into the sunporch, a room enclosed on three sides by glass walls. French doors overlooked a brick patio open to a spectacular view of the Sound. Just to the north, Kidde Beach was visible. Marc sprawled on a chair at a glass-topped wicker table, scrolling his phone. We took seats, Olivia hovering as Mrs. Sutcliffe settled on her chair.

"Lemonade?" Mrs. Sutcliffe said.

"No, thank you."

"Liv, get me some?" Marc gave his stepsister a crooked smile. She rolled her eyes but went into the kitchen and returned with a glass for him.

Hard-soled shoes clicked across the tiled floor, then Chief Brooks and Bronwyn joined us. My path had crossed with the chief's several times in the course of my amateur investigations, and let's just say he hadn't always welcomed my contributions. Bronwyn must have prepared him, because although he wiped perspiration from his rapidly receding hairline, he nodded at me in a friendly way. "Looks like Miss Larkin found one of your rings on the beach," he said.

Bronwyn handed Mrs. Sutcliffe the evidence bag. She opened it and her pale blue eyes welled with tears. "Oh thank you, thank you for returning it." Her expression softened as she looked at the gleaming ring. "I can't wear it now, because of my arthritis, but I'm glad it's back. I'm giving it to Olivia when she turns twenty-one next month."

Olivia's eyes welled, too. "Gran told us last night over dinner. She's going to sell all her other jewelry and donate the money to St. Peter's soup kitchen." She threw her arms around her grandmother.

"Don't worry, Gran, the police will get the rest of your jewelry back." Marc reached over to squeeze his grandmother's hand. "And even if they don't, it was all insured anyway."

Mrs. Sutcliffe raised her hand where a thin band of gold gleamed on her ring finger. "I'm not worried, Marc. Honestly, my wedding band's the only ring that matters to me. Olivia doesn't want my other jewelry, so I'm glad the money from selling it'll go to a good cause."

The heavy footsteps of the CSI team thudded overhead. I was sure Mrs. Sutcliffe had already given a statement, but I launched in before the chief could tell me to go away. "When did you realize the ring and your other jewelry was missing?"

"Olivia and I were making grilled cheese sandwiches for lunch"—Mrs. Sutcliffe pressed a hand to her forehead—"when Jillian called from the jewelry store and said you found my ring."

"Did you take the call?"

She shook her head. "Marc did. Dustin was on his bike ride. I heard Marc's voice out here in the sunporch and then he ran upstairs into my dressing room. Olivia and I went up in the elevator. Marc showed me my jewelry box, the one with my special occasion jewelry. It was empty. Marc said someone must've broken in."

Marc pointed at the French doors that led to a patio. "I noticed those doors were unlocked this morning. The thief must've gotten in that way."

Mrs. Sutcliffe frowned. "And I slept in the recliner by the TV last night. I get insomnia and sleep there some nights. I can't believe I didn't hear the thief go right past me upstairs into my bedroom."

A guy who was a carbon copy of the one sitting at the table opened the door from the patio and entered. "Take off those shoes, young man," Mrs. Sutcliffe said with mock seriousness. "You track sand all over the house."

Humor flashed in his blue eyes. "Yes, Gran."

"That's Dustin, Marc's twin. He's quite an athlete," Mrs. Sutcliffe smiled. "He's been training for triathlons since he graduated from college."

Dustin took off his shoes and dropped them on a mat that was already full of high tech running and bike shoes.

Marc nodded his head toward me. "Gran got her ring back from Allegra, here."

"That's great news." Dustin gave his grandmother a kiss on the cheek and smiled at me. "Thank you, Ms. Larkin."

"Ma'am," Chief Brooks said, "we'll have the report done later today. You'll just have to work with your insurance company."

Marc said, "I've gotten the papers together, Gran."

"Thank you, dear."

The chief cleared his throat and I took that as my cue to leave.

"I'll give Allie a ride back," Bronwyn said. A look of relief crossed the chief's face and I tried not to laugh.

Olivia stood. "I'll see you out."

As we walked to the door, I asked, "By the way, what jeweler did your grandmother use for the insurance appraisal?" I knew the answer but wanted to confirm.

Olivia said, "Muse in Mystic. Marc's girlfriend Jillian works there."

* * *

Back in the cruiser, I turned to Bronwyn. "Doesn't it all seem off to you? The thief passed right by a woman with insomnia and she didn't wake up? You could hear everyone's footsteps on that tile floor. And the thief struck on the night she conveniently forgot to arm the security system?"

Bronwyn ran her hand through her pixie cut brown hair as we drove out of Fox Point. It was a gesture she made when she was stressed or thinking hard.

"Marc made a point of saying she was forgetful, but she seemed pretty sharp to me. Although," I hesitated, "she didn't notice the jewelry was taken when she got dressed."

"It was her special occasion stuff," Bronwyn said. "She has two jewelry boxes and both were closed when she dressed this morning. She told the chief nothing upstairs was disturbed at all."

I folded my arms. "So the thief knew where to look."

Bronwyn threw me a shrewd look. "Yep."

My cellphone buzzed at the same time the police radio squawked. "Break-in. 22 Mermaid Lane."

"22 Mermaid Lane?" Shock lanced through me. "That's my dad's house!"

"Isn't your dad sailing with Esmeralda in the Caribbean?" Bronwyn spun the wheel.

I was too stunned to do more than nod.

Bronwyn keyed the mike. "On my way." She threw me a glance. "Don't freak. I'll check it out. With all the people in town training for the triathlon, we're getting a lot of trespassing calls. Some of the runners get lost and cut through yards." Her voice was steady, but she ran a hand through her hair again.

We pulled up to the house I'd grown up in, a brown cedar shingled Dutch colonial with a small burnt-wood sign that dad had carved when I was a little girl. It read: Mermaid Motel. I'd moved in with Aunt Gully a few years back, giving Dad his space when he finally started dating twenty-eight years after my mom passed away. He'd met his girlfriend, Esmeralda, when she'd hired him to pilot her yacht into Mystic Bay.

A woman with glossy brown hair styled in a sleek bob waved from the cottage next door, her black and white beagle mix barking as I jumped from the car before Bronwyn could kill the engine. "Allie!"

"Ms. Goffman?"

"Jingle started barking about an hour ago when I was streaming my soaps, and when I looked out I didn't see anyone, but now I realize your dad's back door's been banging in the breeze, and what with your dad and Esmeralda gone, I thought it could be a burglary." She paused for a deep breath. "I'm sorry I didn't check sooner."

"I appreciate it. We'll check it out." Bronwyn and I ran through the yard and up the back steps. The screws that held the screen door's top hasp anchored to the wall had been pulled out and the door hung crookedly.

"Someone yanked the door so hard they pulled it off the hinges." The inner door was ajar and scratches marred the wood beside the knob. My body heated with anger and adrenaline. "They kicked in the door!"

"Stay here," Bronwyn muttered as she entered.

I snorted but gave Bronwyn a few seconds' head start into the house. I knew this house so well. I listened to the familiar sounds of gulls squawking and windchimes ringing on the front porch. I didn't sense any unusual presence, but still my heart rate ticked up. I stepped inside and heard the tap of Bronwyn's police issued shoes as she ran upstairs.

I froze. The kitchen cabinets and drawers hung open, Esmeralda's cookbooks were strewn over the floor, and her herb plants had been knocked from the windowsill. My heart hammered in my throat as I ran upstairs. The bedroom bureaus had also been ransacked, with clothes pulled from the drawers and Esmeralda's trinket boxes upended. She kept her good jewelry in a safe deposit box and, judging from the size of the pile of Esmeralda's everyday jewelry, the thief hadn't been tempted by any of the rainbow-hued bangles and beads Esmeralda favored.

Bronwyn panted behind me as I picked up socks and T-shirts. "Wait. Let me make sure the house is clear."

I heard her run through the rest of the house, opening and closing closet doors. Shock gave way to anger, then gratitude that both Dad and Esmeralda were safe on the yacht. There was little here for a thief to take beyond Esmeralda's costume jewelry and clothes, and Dad's flannel shirts and fishing tackle, and nothing appeared to be missing.

Bronwyn pulled me downstairs and we went into the kitchen. "Does your dad have a doorbell camera?"

I shook my head as I gathered cookbooks from the floor. "The only reason people around here get cameras is to watch for foxes or birds. Besides, Ms. Goffman's the neighborhood watch."

"Too bad this break-in happened during her soaps." Bronwyn took photos as I righted the plants and swept up spilled soil, my mind whirling as I rattled off everything that had bothered me about the visit to Sandy Feet.

"Didn't Sandy Feet have security cameras?" I asked.

"Captain Brooks checked first thing," Bronwyn said. "The camera in the back of the house had some debris on the lens so the video was obscured."

"Convenient." I walked through the living room to the front window that overlooked the ocean. "Most houses in Fox Point have security cameras, right?"

Bronwyn joined me. "Practically every single one. Tell me what you're thinking."

Mentally I retraced the route from Mrs. Sutcliffe's magnificent oceanfront home to Kidde Beach. "Kidde Beach is the first beach you come to when you leave Fox Point." I remembered Bit and Jack's Loch Ness Monster. "Remember the footprints I saw on the beach?"

Her forehead wrinkled. "You think the thief swam away with the jewelry? That's nuts. You'd take a chance on losing some..."

I raised my eyebrows. After a moment, her eyebrows popped, too. "Unless..."

"You want to lose it," I said. My phone buzzed. "Hi, Aunt Gully."

"You didn't answer the texts I sent," she said. "You're not upset about Aggie's picnic, are you? This nephew's not bad."

"No, that's not it."

Aunt Gully gasped when I told her about the break-in.

"Don't worry. I don't think anything was taken."

"I'll come over later to help set things right," she said. "I texted to tell you that Aggie called. She did come over this morning and checked out the ring with her loupe, but with the plumbing emergency she didn't have a chance to call me until now. You're not going to believe this."

As I listened, I felt pieces fall together. "Actually, Aunt Gully, I do believe it. I'll talk to you later."

Bronwyn said. "What is it? I know that look on your face. You've figured something out."

I slid the phone back into my pocket. "Aggie examined the ring. The diamond is fake."

* * *

Ms. Goffman was waiting for us, sweeping her tidy front walk where not a bit of sand was to be found. Jingle loped over for a pat and I obliged him.

"Ms. Goffman, remind me. When did Jingle start barking?" I asked.

She squinted. "Little more than an hour ago? Hour and a half?"

We thanked her and got in the car. "Bronwyn, where were we a little more than an hour ago?"

She slid on sunglasses and pulled from the curb. "I was picking you up at Muse."

"More specifically, an employee at Muse was making a phone call." I searched on my phone. "If you look up my address, there isn't a listing because—"

Bronwyn jumped in. "You live with Aunt Gully. Whose last name's Fontana."

"Yep," I said. "The only listing for a Larkin is Dad's."

"All this for a fake ring?" Bronwyn shook her head.

I nodded. "I have to talk to the chief."

* * *

Aunt Gully's news put everything in focus. As Bronwyn drove, I walked through the reasons for my theory.

Mrs. Sutcliffe's announcement of her decision to donate her jewelry.

Mrs. Sutcliffe's insomnia.

Large footprints running into the water, none returning.

Bit and Jack's Loch Ness Monster splashing off Kidde Beach.

As the cruiser sped past Kidde Beach, Bronwyn said, "So they had to get that ring back before anyone could discover it was a fake and that it was part of an insurance scam."

"And hide the fact that Marc sold the original pieces and replaced them with copies," I said. "The thief didn't want the jewelry. The thief was swimming the jewelry out to drop it onto the bottom of the ocean because Millicent Sutcliffe announced she planned to give the ring to Olivia for her birthday and sell the other pieces to give to charity. At that point someone would discover that Mrs. Sutcliffe's gems were replaced with fakes."

"So Jillian and Marc are in on it," Bronwyn said. "Do you think Dustin's involved?"

I turned to her. "Did you notice that Dustin knew my last name, even though no one had mentioned it?"

"Maybe he's a ballet fan," Bronwyn said.

I snorted. "Kidder."

Bronwyn said, "I'm serious. Okay, so how did he know?"

"When the accomplice called from the jewelry store," I said. "Jillian."

"But Marc took the call from Jillian."

I nodded. "And Marc told Dustin that Allegra Larkin had the ring. That's how Jillian's uncle introduced me. Dustin took off on his bike to the only house in Mystic Bay owned by a Larkin and broke in, setting off poor Jingle. Dustin didn't find anything, so he biked home where we were all cozily chatting on the sunporch. He took off his shoes—very large shoes, by the way—and put them in the pile by the door."

"But everything's circumstantial," Bronwyn said. "There has to be some physical evidence that links the brothers to the theft."

I remembered the footprints in the sand. "The footprints in the sand? I took a photo."

She shrugged. "It's not against the law to go for a swim. I wonder which one actually did the theft?"

I remembered the blisters on Marc's heels. I grabbed Bronwyn's arm. "Bronwyn, go to Kidde Beach."

She spun the cruiser into a U-turn.

Surely Marc hadn't run barefoot from Fox Point to Kidde Beach. "I didn't see any shoes left behind on Kidde Beach this morning when I found the ring. Shoes would've been too heavy to swim in. He'd have to leave them somewhere near the beach. When I saw Marc at Sandy Feet, he had blisters on his heels. He must've used a new pair of running shoes this morning and they gave him blisters."

Bronwyn parked the cruiser by the path to Kidde Beach and we ran to the dented metal trash can by the outdoor shower. I lifted the lid. Among the discarded pizza boxes, ice cream wrappers, and bottles was a pair of very large running shoes.

* * *

Later that day after her shift, Bronwyn joined me at Kidde Beach. We spread beach towels on the warm sand and I covered myself with sunscreen, an oversized T-shirt, and a broad brimmed hat—the lot of a redhead at the beach. I sipped some of Aunt Gully's homemade lemonade and watched a flotilla of rowboats, kayaks, and dinghies converge at the base of Fox Point. Aggie's post on Neighbornet and news of the missing jewelry had set off a treasure hunt. Judging from all the boats, people didn't care that the jewelry was fake. I shaded my eyes and watched as Bit and Jack's Boston Whaler pulled up to the crowd of boats and dropped anchor.

"Chief Brooks told me to thank you," Bronwyn said. "He thought the whole theft at Sandy Feet was a little too tidy—the security camera conveniently obscured, the thief passing right by Mrs. Sutcliffe on a tile floor, then knowing precisely where to get the jewels, and so on. He said that you finding the ring rattled Marc and Dustin into making their big mistake."

I nodded. "The break-in at Dad's house."

"When the chief returned to Sandy Feet to question them, Marc and Dustin didn't lose any time trying to implicate each other." Bronwyn sipped from her water bottle and I noticed a scratch on her wrist.

"What happened?"

Bronwyn adjusted her sunglasses. "Jillian wasn't exactly cooperative when I arrested her."

I shook my head.

"It's the job." Bronwyn shrugged. "So Jillian was in a relationship with Marc. Marc knew that his grandmother wanted to sell her jewelry and give the proceeds to the soup kitchen. He took his grandmother's jewelry to Jillian for an insurance appraisal and while it was in her possession, she had the jewelry copied. She returned the fakes and the two of them sold the real pieces for a tidy sum."

I recalled the brothers' sports cars. "But Dustin found out and wanted in on the action. Then Mrs. Sutcliffe announced last night that she was giving Olivia her ring as a birthday present. They couldn't take a chance of Olivia finding out the ring was fake."

"Exactly," Bronwyn said.

"Plus," I continued, "if the fake jewels were stolen, they could put in the insurance claim. That way they'd get the insurance money and hide their theft. Win win." I sat up and rested my chin on my knees. "Something else bothers me. Mrs. Sutcliffe's fall. I wonder if that fall wasn't accidental."

Bronwyn frowned. "It's a good thing those guys won't be spending too much time with their grandmother in the future."

Bit and Jack dived off the Whaler. I hoped they'd find something on the ocean floor.

Bronwyn applied sunscreen to her legs. "Anyway, finding Marc's footprints and shoes foiled their plan."

I sipped my drink. "Actually, you know who really did? Aggie Weatherburn. She's the one who confirmed the ring was fake."

"Gotta give her credit." Bronwyn looked down the beach and jutted her chin. "Speak of the devil."

I turned and saw Aggie and Aunt Gully walking down the sand, flanking a tall guy who was so good looking I almost dropped my drink.

"Whoa," Bronwyn whispered. "I hope that's a nephew."

Aunt Gully lowered her sunglasses, caught my eye, and winked.

"I think I'm going to a picnic on Saturday," I said.

* * *

**Shari Randall** is the Agatha Award-winning author of the Lobster Shack Mystery series. She loves books, dancing, mermaids, and all things New England. You can learn more about Shari and her books and short stories at: @ShariRandallAuthor on Facebook, as well as at her website, www.ShariRandallAuthor.com.

# Bay of Reckoning
## by Shawn Reilly Simmons

*Briny Bay, Maryland, July 1999*

THE GIRLS GOT YOUNGER EVERY YEAR. At least it seemed that way to Sabrina Westfall. She wouldn't have been surprised if this year's flock of beauty pageant contestants toddled in done up in pigtails and wearing onesies. Of course she was the one getting older, another year gone by on the calendar each July when Briny Bay's Miss Crab Pageant and the Summer Crab Festival rolled around.

Sabrina had worn the crown herself thirty years earlier, and never forgot the feeling of elation when her name was called. For the last twenty years, she had helmed the pageant, months of work that always ended in that same moment she craved: the crown, the cheers, the satisfaction of an event well planned.

Sabrina paced slowly in front of the stage, eyeing this year's crop of local beauties, gazing up at them from knee height. She tapped a rolled-up copy of the pageant script lightly on her palm. "Good posture builds confidence, ladies. Nothing is more important in life than how you carry yourself."

A soft titter floated through the air from someone Sabrina had already passed. She stopped, pivoted her high heels, and tilted her head, her updo defying the motion and the humidity in the air. The first girl in line was rubbing her nose, pretending to suppress a sneeze.

"Something funny, Connie?" Sabrina said, slowly clicking her heels back down the line.

The girl's cheeks reddened and she straightened her spine, her long legs wobbling on platform heels. Underarm sweat darkened her bathing suit, a modest one-piece that was blue and white with tiny cartoon crabs. "Sorry, Mrs. Westfall."

"Oh dear, call me Sabrina. I'll be your mother-in-law soon."

"Sabrina," Connie said awkwardly, as if she'd never said the name before. "It's just that—"

"What?"

"Isn't this kind of silly? I mean, it's not like we're in the Miss America pageant."

"All I ask is that my girls be their best and take themselves seriously," Sabrina said, her eyes on the young girl's sweaty cheek. "If you can't do that, you may leave now. Your mother would be disappointed though, I imagine. I'd think she'd want you to advance further in the pageant than she was able to. She was in sixth place behind me, if I remember correctly?" Sabrina's lip twitched but she resisted the smile just below the surface. She remembered exactly the rank and where everyone had fallen in line behind her.

Connie's legs quivered even more and Sabrina thought she might fall forward onto the sand-dusted floorboards. Better to find out during rehearsal which of them couldn't take the heat. The Miss Crab contest was the biggest draw of the festival weekend, next to the Briny Bay Spice Competition, and Sabrina worked all year to make sure it was as close to perfection as it could possibly be.

Sabrina continued her inspection. "You're not just representing yourselves or your families," she said. "You're representing me, and I hope to be proud of each and every one of you."

"Mrs. Westfall!" A small man with a sweaty bald head rushed toward the stage, the damp air wilting his shirt collar. "Something has happened."

"Jerry," Sabrina said, "what can possibly be so urgent you must interrupt me? We only have one rehearsal left before the festival begins."

"I'm sorry," Jerry said. "But it really is an emergency. Someone..." Jerry trailed off, crushing the rim of his floppy sun hat in his hands.

"Someone what? Let's assume for the moment I'm not a mind reader," Sabrina said.

"A body has been pulled from the Bay. It was attached to a Westfall crab pot," he said, lowering his voice. He glanced at Connie on the stage, then looked away quickly, as if holding his gaze on her would burn his corneas.

"Why does everything have to happen during the Crab Festival?" Sabrina muttered under her breath.

"Sorry," Jerry said. "Mr. Westfall has called the police."

"If my husband is handling things, why disturb my rehearsal? There have been accidents out on the Bay before, poachers...wait, was it someone from the Westfall fishing crew? It's not Darius, is it?" Sabrina's son was spending the summer on the largest trawler in an effort to learn every aspect of the family business.

"No, it's not Darius. That's the thing," Jerry said, scurrying behind the much taller Sabrina. "I'm afraid it's Albert Eastman." He whispered the last two words, but not softly enough.

Connie Eastman cried out, then fell to her knees.

The roll of papers Sabrina clutched fell to the floor. "Albert?" she gasped, turning to Jerry. Connie pressed manicured fingertips to her mouth.

Sabrina pressed a palm to her forehead and closed her eyes for a second, feeling the heat of the morning for the first time. "Where is my husband?"

* * *

"Rufus?" Sabrina said, stepping outside the tent. She hurried toward the front of the building and the docks overlooking Briny Bay. A cluster of police cars idled near the entrance of The Westfall Crab Company, where a sign declared "Three Hundred Bottles of Briny Bay Spice Blend Sold Every Day!" An officer was talking to Rufus and her sister-in-law, Heather, who was the company's receptionist, near the water as a team of coastal police inspected the fishing trawler docked nearby. A small tent had been set up on the boardwalk, and a medical van hovered nearby. The lapel of Rufus's suit jacket fluttered in the breeze rippling off the Bay.

Sabrina called to him again and he turned toward the sound of her voice. Heather continued speaking with the police officer, her tight pink dress hugging her ample curves as she shivered despite the warm breeze.

"Darling," Rufus said as she made her way to him and the officer. "Are you all right?" He pressed Sabrina's hand into his large damp palm.

"Is it true about Albert?" Sabrina said, clutching his sleeve.

Jerry popped up behind Sabrina like a sand crab from a hole. "I found Mrs. Westfall like you asked."

Rufus glared at Jerry, his expression harsh. "I wish I'd been the one to tell you the details. I was hoping you could buffer some of the shock for Connie finding out about her father." He waved an arm at the police activity humming around the dock.

Jerry blanched and took a few steps back.

"Oh, the poor girl," Sabrina said, leaning into her husband. "And so close to the wedding. And the pageant!"

Rufus put an arm around her shoulders. "We'll do whatever we can to help her and Darius, of course," he said reassuringly.

A few of the contestants wandered over from the tent and huddled around the distressed Connie.

"Crazy, right?" Heather said, appearing suddenly at their side.

"The police are notifying Mrs. Eastman," Rufus said. "Why don't you keep an eye on Connie?"

"And what should I do?" Heather asked, her big blue eyes blinking in the sunlight. Although Rufus and his brother Cornelius were only a few years apart in age, Sabrina was at least twenty years older than her sister-in-law.

"Right," Rufus said. "If you wouldn't mind coordinating with the authorities. You know, mind the phone calls that come in. That would be great."

"And should I say there's a dead guy in one of our traps and to call back tomorrow or..." Heather began.

"No!" Rufus said abruptly, then softened his tone. "Let's not say anything specific. Just..."

"Take a message?" Sabrina offered.

"Exactly," Rufus said with relief. Heather gave a quick salute then turned on her high heels and went back inside the building.

"Sir," the officer said, tapping a pen on his notepad. "A few more questions?"

Rufus waved a hand at him. "Please, just a minute. We're all a bit...overwhelmed." He hurried over to the cluster of young women and opened his arms to Connie for a hug. "I'm so sorry about your dad." She nodded through her tears and leaned into his embrace.

Sabrina watched her husband console Connie and reminded herself how lucky she was to have Rufus Westfall for a husband. Their family meant so much to so many in their small seaside community, going back decades.

Finneas Westfall had founded the company in 1949 after he'd returned home from World War II, telling tales of heroism and glory. Rufus managed the company's operations now along with his brother under Finneas' watchful eye.

Rufus had proposed to Sabrina the night she'd won the Miss Crab Pageant, slipping a sparkling diamond on her finger with a slight tremor in his hands. She'd said yes, of course. She had been trying to catch Rufus' eye ever since their freshman year in high school. His good looks were a draw, although it was his kindness she really admired.

Rufus, with Sabrina by his side, and Cornelius, and most recently Heather, had brought the business nationwide with their popular spice blend. Sabrina thought how improbable that was, considering Finneas had started the company with a single broken down trawler and a small wooden shack of a warehouse he'd built himself on the Briny Bay docks. Back then The Westfall Crab Company was two people, Finneas and Jacob Eastman, his navy buddy.

Although well past retirement age, Finneas showed no signs of slowing down. His regular constitutionals on the boardwalk kept him fit, and his mind was still as sharp as the cheese he stirred into his shrimp and grits every morning.

Sabrina looked past the docks and out to the Bay and thought about the accidents that had happened over the years. Four fishermen had gone overboard from Westfall boats, their sodden bodies pulled from the water much too late for them to survive. Commercial fishing was a dangerous business, but the Westfalls had faced the challenges and strived to improve safety and working conditions for their employees. Sabrina admired how much Rufus cared for his staff, noticing more than once how he'd written checks from their personal account to cover medical or educational expenses for families in need.

Sabrina and a handful of volunteers worked all year long on the crab festival. Everyone who was anyone in town attended, and the population of Briny Bay swelled to twice its size for one weekend a year. Tourists came to feast on crabs, gamble during their casino night, and dress in gowns and black tie for the banquet gala.

She glanced again at the police tent on the dock and wondered what Albert Eastman's death was going to mean for the festival, the town, and her family. She also wondered why he'd been out on the Bay in the first place.

* * *

"You can't trust an Eastman," Finneas growled from his seat at the head of the table that evening. The old man's face was still handsome, despite the deep lines carved there by years of sea and sun.

"Dad," Rufus began. "It's time you quit—"

Finneas raised a hand to stop his son from speaking. "What? Darius isn't here. I can speak my mind."

"Must you, though?" Rufus said. "Tonight of all nights?"

"What do I always say?" Finneas continued, ignoring his son. "The Eastmans are liars. And now look. Old Jacob's son got caught up in one of our traps. Now, if that's not bad enough, your son," he glared at Rufus and Sabrina sitting next to each other at table, "wants to marry one of them."

"Really," Sabrina said quietly. "Must we discuss all of this over dinner? It's already been a very trying day."

"Rina's right," Heather piped up from her seat across the table. Sabrina gave her a quick smile. She'd never taken to the shortened version of the name her sister-in-law had graced her with when they first met a few years earlier but figured it was too late to say anything about it now.

Finneas shot Heather an annoyed glance, then relented, pushing a piece of flounder around on his plate with his fork. He'd taken to ignoring Heather for the most part, which was better than being outright hostile to her, Sabrina thought. Heather wasn't the sharpest harpoon on deck, but she meant well, and that was enough as far as Sabrina was concerned. She'd done wonders with the antiquated filing system at the office, and for that, Sabrina thought she ought to get a medal, or at the very least, Finneas' respect. He hadn't forgiven Cornelius for "dipping his pen in the company ink" yet, but they all hoped the old man would come around someday.

The stately dining room at the main house was where the family took their meals most nights before the two sons and their wives retired to their own homes on the Westfall estate, which overlooked the Bay. Sabrina's house sat closest to the water, and on a clear day, she could see to the other side of the cove, where the Eastmans' house perched on the cliffs. Sabrina wondered what was happening there now, how the family would have to go on after losing their patriarch so suddenly.

"Rina," Heather said, filling the dull silence that had fallen over the room. "I'd like to help with the pageant. Remember you said you'd think about it last year?"

Sabrina smiled again. "Oh yes, I do remember that now."

"She'd be great," Cornelius said, elbowing his wife gently in the ribs. "You're not the only beauty queen at the table. Heather won the spring break wet t-shirt contest three years in a row back in college."

"I've heard," Sabrina said with a gracious smile. "Several times."

Rufus cleared his throat and carved into the fish on his plate.

"She went to college?" Finneas muttered under his breath.

"Community. Office management." Heather smiled sweetly at her and pushed her shoulders back a nudge.

"You know," Sabrina said after a stern glance at her father-in-law, "I think it's a great idea. We should do more things together. We are family, and well, you never know when life might change suddenly—"

"What in blazes is everyone going on about?" Finneas shouted, slamming his fork onto the table. "Why are you talking about this nonsense?"

Sabrina took her napkin from her lap and dabbed the corners of her mouth before folding it and placing it on the table next to her plate. "Please excuse me," she said, pushing her chair back. "I'm feeling a bit...tired."

"Now look what you've done," Rufus said, raising his voice.

Finneas sat back in his chair, the candlelight glinting on his thick mane of silver hair. "This is still my house."

"Dad," Rufus said, regaining his composure. He placed a hand gently on Sabrina's forearm, urging her to wait a moment. "You have to let ancient grudges go. A man has died. Surely you can put aside your dislike of the Eastman family considering what's happened. Just give it a rest. Darius and Connie will be married, and our families will be joined. You certainly can't carry on this way for much longer."

Finneas' lips puckered as if he'd been fed a lemon. "I still don't see how you allowed that to happen. With all the girls on this beach, your son had to choose an Eastman."

"Dad, please," Rufus said. "Enough is enough. Whatever happened between you and Jacob happened a long time ago."

Finneas exhaled loudly and waved his hand. "You kids today don't understand. A man's word is his bond. At least it should be. Jacob Eastman was a no-good liar who tried to swindle me, and when that didn't work, he up and disappeared, left me holding the bag, not to mention his young wife and family. Briny Bay Spice almost collapsed, no thanks to him. Everything I worked for on the edge of ruin. You ingrates wouldn't be sitting at this fancy table if I hadn't worked—"

"Sixteen hours a day," Cornelius chimed in, mimicking his father's raspy voice. Heather tittered a laugh into her napkin. Finneas shot him a look that would spear a tuna.

"Spared the rod on you too many times," Finneas muttered under his breath. "I'll warn you once more. You're inviting trouble when you invite an Eastman into your life."

"Wonderful. Well, thank you for dinner. We have a lot of work to do for the festival tomorrow," Sabrina said.

* * *

"What do you think happened to Jacob Eastman all those years ago?" Sabrina said into the bathroom mirror as she rubbed her middle fingers in opposite directions on her cheeks. Her imported night cream worked wonders, but only if she applied it with precision and a nightly facial massage. She'd let down her long red hair and swept it away from her forehead with a pink headband to complete the bedtime ritual.

Rufus was propped against the headboard, reading a book. His pajamas still held fresh iron creases. "He probably got sick of my father lording it over him and headed inland. The story goes he went out for a pack of cigarettes and never came home."

Sabrina paused her massage and looked at him in the mirror.

Rufus twisted his mouth into a frown. "You've heard of those kinds of things happening."

Sabrina resumed her circles, the skin on her cheeks tingling under her fingertips. She shifted them to massage her forehead and chin. "It's very odd to disappear without a trace. With a young family and a business partner? Those are some serious anchors keeping him here."

"Dad says they had an argument, and then he just took off. A few postcards were mailed to the family. One was from Alaska, I seem to recall."

"So he went from fishing crab to king salmon?" Sabrina said. "What kind of man is okay with abandoning his family, but still feels the need to send postcards?"

"Jacob Eastman, presumably."

Sabrina finished up in the bathroom and turned off the light, sliding into bed next to her husband. "You'd never do anything like that, would you?"

Rufus shrugged. "Would I ever leave you and the kids and send you a postcard from Alaska? No."

Sabrina smiled.

"I'd send one from Hawaii. Much nicer weather there." Rufus' eyes twinkled.

Sabrina pulled a pillow from behind her and bopped him on the head with it. "You're the worst."

"I know," Rufus said, pulling her closer. "You know I'd never leave you."

"You had better not." Sabrina sighed and laid her head against Rufus' chest. "What made Jacob leave, I wonder?"

* * *

"Thank you all for getting here so early," Sabrina said, taking a sip of her coffee. Her volunteer Board sat around her dining room table and watched her expectantly. Everyone had heard about the death of Albert Eastman, and their usual lighthearted banter had been replaced with a quiet anxiousness. "The plan is to go ahead with the festival."

A few of the women looked at each other quickly, then turned their attention back to their leader.

"We will honor the passing of Mr. Eastman with a moment of silence," Sabrina said. "And Connie Eastman has withdrawn from the pageant, poor dear, as she is grieving the loss of her father."

A woman with tight tan skin and a tighter blonde bun sitting at the end of the table raised her hand. "Should we call up an alternate contestant?"

Sabrina thought a moment. "No, Fran, not in this case. We will leave Connie's space open for her. She will be with us in spirit." Fran owned

Brawny Bay, the gym on Main Street, which featured tanning beds in the locker rooms. Fran always looked like she'd just spent the entire day at the beach, even on Christmas morning.

Murmurs of agreement swept around the table. Sabrina trusted the four women on her Board, and more importantly she knew they rarely challenged her decisions.

Sabrina heard her front door open and the click of high heels on the marble floor of her foyer. Heather popped her head into the dining room, then scurried to the empty chair next to Fran. She'd swapped the pink tube dress from the day before to a magenta one of the same style. Sabrina thought she might have found them on the rack of the beach shop Kelli owned, the Board member at the far end of the table.

"Heather," Sabrina said. "Are you—?"

"Reporting for duty!"

"Great! I was worried you'd forgotten," Sabrina said. "Everyone, you all know my sister-in-law."

"Oh, I know all of you," Heather said, nodding. "You're Kelli," Heather said, sweeping her hand down her dress, confirming Sabrina's suspicion. "And Tan Fran..." Heather giggled. "You're Tiffany, from the jewelry store..." Heather flashed the large diamond Cornelius had given her on her left ring finger. "And Stella. Your husband owns that garage on Sandy Point. I used to take my 'vette in there, before I met Corny."

Stella eyed Heather up and down and her cheeks took on a rosy tint. Sabrina wondered if Stella's husband had a wandering eye, and if it had ever wandered over Heather.

"That's impressive," Tan Fran said with a laugh.

"I like to know what's what and who's who," Heather said.

"Right, well," Sabrina said, vaguely embarrassed by Heather's amateur detective display. "We're glad to have your help, of course. Maybe you can handle..." Sabrina leafed through the binder in front of her on the table.

"Whatever I can do," Heather said after a few moments of silence.

"You're great at keeping things organized," Sabrina said. "We can all use that."

The women around the table nodded in agreement, and Heather smiled, sitting back against her chair and crossing her long legs. "You should see the stuff I get to sort through at the office. Paper, records, junk shoved everywhere in every drawer. Like forty years of filing never done!"

"Wow," Tiffany said. "That sounds like a big job."

"I know where everything is now," Heather said confidently.

"Now, let's get an update on our committees," Sabrina said.

"Catering," Kelli chimed in, "is all set. Six local restaurants have their booth assignments, and they all know what to expect as far as crowds."

"The Town's Time Capsule opening is scheduled for noon on the second day," Stella said as she tapped her knuckles on the table. "It's a big one, fifty years, so we think we'll get a crowd."

"Perfect," Sabrina said. "That should work nicely with the timing of the other events. Speaking of which, what about the spice contest? How many have signed up for the shrimp boil to showcase their spice blends?"

"All in hand," Tan Fran said. "We have eight contestants."

"And who are the judges?" Sabrina asked, jotting notes in her binder.

"The three Westfall men and..." Fran said, then hesitated. "We need at least one more."

"I'll do it!" Heather said, clapping her hands.

"Now there's an idea," Sabrina said, nodding. "I like it. Why not have a lady Westfall on the dais?" She glanced at Tiffany. "How is press coverage going?"

"A reporter from the *Gazette* will be on hand all weekend covering the event," Tiffany said.

"Great news," Sabrina said. "Well, ladies, it's time to get out there and put on the best festival we can."

* * *

Sabrina watched her Board members head off in different directions once they arrived at The Westfall Crab Company and festival grounds. As she headed for the tents, a feeling of dread settled in her stomach. Were they wrong to carry on with a fun-filled weekend, yards away from where someone had lost his life?

A young man loitered near the main tent, jotting notes on a small pad. When he saw Sabrina approaching, he stopped writing and made his way over to her.

"Hi, I'm Ray Northam, from the *Gazette*," he said, sticking out his hand. "You're Sabrina Westfall, correct?"

"Hello, yes," Sabrina said with a gracious smile. "You're a bit early if you're here to cover the event. Nothing is happening until later on today."

"Oh, the crab to-do, right," Ray said. "Well, partly. I'm actually doing a story on a series of deaths in Briny Bay. The most recent one I'm sure you know about."

"Albert," Sabrina said, her chest tightening. "You said deaths, though. As in multiple."

"It's a funny thing around here," Ray said with a nod. "Every year that ends in a nine, like this one, somebody dies under suspicious circumstances. I think there's a connection."

"Oh my," Sabrina said. "That doesn't sound like the flattering piece about the festival we were told we'd get."

"I suppose not." Ray shrugged. "I'll be in touch, I'm sure."

"Who else have you talked to?" Sabrina asked.

"I'm not able to reveal that," he said. "Let's just say, I've been working on this story for a while." Ray glanced at his watch. "Sorry, I have to check in with my editor." He hurried away, pulling his phone from his pocket and pressing it to his ear.

"Years that end in nine," Sabrina muttered to herself as she watched him walk away. Her anxiety intensified when she noticed a pair of police detectives pacing the docks next to the tents, an overly tall man and a much shorter woman in suits the same dull brown color. What could they want? She thought as she walked over to them.

"Is there anything I can help you with?" Sabrina asked when they noticed her approach.

"Not at the moment," the taller one said. "We're just—"

"Investigating," the woman interrupted. "The murder that happened here yesterday. I'm Detective Southerland, and this is Middleburg, my partner."

"It's not common knowledge yet," Middleburg said, nudging her in the arm. He leaned over slightly to do it, to bridge the distance between their heights. It seemed to Sabrina he must do this automatically when talking to his partner.

"What? It's not like the news won't be all over soon anyway," Detective Southerland said. "And you are?"

"Sabrina Westfall. I'm sorry, did you say murder?" Sabrina looked over her shoulder to where she'd just been speaking with the reporter. "I thought Mr. Eastman had fallen in the water and drowned."

"Helped along by a bullet in his chest," Southerland said.

"Oh my," Sabrina said, pressing a hand to her own chest. "Who shot him? Why?"

"That's what we're here to find out," Detective Middleburg said.

"You're working on the crab feast this weekend, right?" Southerland asked.

"The Crab Festival," Sabrina corrected. "It's an annual event that draws hundreds—"

A scream erupted from inside the tent. Sabrina spun toward the sound so quickly she made herself dizzy. Middleburg's face froze in surprise momentarily before the two cops shuffled past her and dashed toward the tent. Another scream broke through the humid morning air.

"What now? What fresh hell?" Sabrina breathed, closing her eyes for a moment to stop herself from fainting.

* * *

Inside the tent, the detectives stood over Ray Northam's body, a boning knife sticking out of his neck.

"Dead," the squat Detective Southerland said. "Real dead."

"Is that your professional opinion?" Sabrina said. She immediately regretted speaking to the detective that way, but seeing the lifeless body of the man she'd just been talking to sent her into such intense shock she forgot her manners. "He's a reporter from the *Gazette*. I was just speaking to him."

Sabrina noticed the members of her Board huddled in the corner of the tent, Tan Fran shaking in her sundress despite the warm summer air.

"You all have to go," Middleburg said. "We need to call this in."

"Of course, they have to call it in," she said, waving the women away from the body. "Come on, ladies. Everyone back to my house."

* * *

Sabrina made a round of tea for everyone, setting the cups down with shaking hands on the wooden dining table where they'd met earlier.

"What in the world is going on?" Tiffany said. "Two people dead in two days. That just doesn't happen in Briny Bay."

"Except it does," Fran said under her breath. "That reporter was murdered. That knife in his neck? That's definitely not an accident."

"Maybe it was a suicide," Tiffany said earnestly.

"Oh, obviously," Stella said, an edge coming into her voice. "People are always shooting themselves in the chest and falling into the water and also knifing themselves in the neck in the middle of doing their jobs."

Tiffany cowered, her shoulders creeping toward each other as she attempted to make herself smaller.

The rest of the Board stared at her for a few moments before Tiffany spoke again. "How will I ever forget finding him like that?" No one answered.

"Who would want to kill a reporter? For what reason?" Sabrina asked, steadying herself with the back of her chair.

The group stared at her with various expressions of disbelief and shock. Sabrina stared back and noticed for the first time that someone was missing.

"Where is Heather?"

* * *

"Darling, are you okay?" Rufus said over the phone. Sabrina twisted the curly cord in her fingers as she stood in their kitchen.

"I'm okay," Sabrina said. "The ladies are here. We're not sure what to do."

"It's a real mess," Rufus said. "There are cops all over the tents, searching for clues."

"Clues?" Sabrina asked. She nodded to Fran, who pointed at the water pitcher on the counter.

"I guess," Rufus said. "Heather said you'd all come down to get set up for the day and then found that reporter."

"Heather? Wait, when did you talk to her?"

"Just before I called," Rufus said. "She's here now, talking with the police. I'm sorry, dear. I thought you'd told her to help, I just assumed."

"I'm...I don't know," Sabrina said. A headache was building above her eyebrows "Yes, she is helping. What is she saying?"

"I'm not sure. There are a couple of reporters here now too."

"Oh good lord," Sabrina said, alarmed. "She's not speaking on behalf of the festival, or me, is she?"

"I wouldn't know but I don't think—"

"Stop her from saying anything she shouldn't...or anything damaging," Sabrina begged. "Please."

Sabrina rushed to her front door, telling the committee to give her a few moments. Pulling it open, she found herself looking over the top of the head of Detective Southerland and mid-chest at Middleburg. She couldn't decide whether to look up or down and so nodded to greet the pair.

"Detectives," Sabrina said. "I'm surprised to see you here."

"We're now investigating two deaths. Murders."

"Cold-blooded murders," Middleburg said, wiping his nose.

"One of which happened right under your—" Sabrina said.

"We have a few background follow-up questions," Southerland interrupted.

Sabrina sighed. "Very well, come in then."

By the time Sabrina finished with the detectives, all she wanted to do was go upstairs and take a nap. The shock of the morning was finally wearing off, leaving only exhaustion and uncertainty in its wake. But she pressed on and headed out to her car to drive back to the festival tents. She'd sent her committee on their way when the interview ran longer than any of them wanted it to.

"Hey!" Heather called out to her as she stepped from her car. "Where have you been?"

"Don't ask," Sabrina said. "What is going on down here?" Her heart sank as her eyes traced over the tents, where yellow police tape flapped in the wind.

"They're about ready to remove the body," Heather said.

Sabrina eyed her curiously. "What are they saying? Do they have any idea who might have done this?"

"Something about a struggle, a fight of some kind," Heather said.

"This is truly awful," Sabrina sighed. "We're done for."

"Yeah," Heather said. "It seems like maybe we are."

"What could be so important to kill a man over? It's not like there is anything valuable lying around."

"Love or money," Heather said with a nod. "That's what they say it always is on the shows I watch."

Sabrina fought back an exasperated sigh.

"What did that reporter say to you before it happened? The police mentioned you were the last to see him alive."

"I know," Sabrina said. "They've been grilling me up at the house for the past hour. He was working on an article about the deaths in Briny Bay. He thought there was some kind of pattern. Years that end in nine."

"Whoa," Heather said. "And then he ended up being one of the deaths. I wonder if he knew that was going to happen?"

Sabrina squinted at her then shook her head. "I wouldn't think so."

"Right," Heather said. "If he knew he was going to be murdered, he would probably have called in sick today."

Sabrina put a hand over her eyes and wondered how much more she could take.

* * *

Sabrina sat at her dining room table and stared at the binder in front of her as the sun dipped lower in the sky, tinting her dining room in deep orange. She began flipping through the pages, leafing them over carefully and reading the minutes of all the meetings they'd had leading up to that weekend. Reaching the first pages of the binder, a thought struck her. She sat up straighter, then headed to the library off of the foyer.

In the far corner cupboard, Sabrina pulled out a few binders that looked exactly the same as the one on her table. Sitting at the antique secretary desk, she began flipping pages, pausing occasionally to read meeting minutes in more detail.

Twenty minutes later, Sabrina picked up the phone on the desk.

"Heather, it's me," Sabrina said. "Odd question for you. When you were clearing out those old files at the office, did you ever run across anything unusual?"

She pulled the phone away from her ear slightly as Heather's always louder than necessary voice echoed over the line.

"Well, that is very interesting," Sabrina replied. "Would you mind grabbing those from the office before coming to dinner tonight? I'd love to get a look at them."

Sabrina hung up the phone and stared at the receiver for several minutes before sitting down and making some notes.

* * *

That night at dinner, the Westfall family was subdued. The Crab Festival had been called off for the first time in fifty years. Sabrina was devastated, but she knew real strength meant not showing how upset you were, especially in front of others. She took her seat at the table and politely pushed pieces of crab cake around on her plate.

"First an Eastman and now a reporter," Finneas groused from his seat at the head of the table. "What the hell's going on?"

"What I want to know is who's out there killing the residents of Briny Bay?" Rufus said. He squeezed Sabrina's hand under the table. "You'd like to know your family's safe."

"None of us is safe," Finneas said. "I learned that in the war. I also learned you can only trust your family."

"That reporter thought the murders fit into a pattern. That they were related, maybe committed by the same person, I think," Sabrina said quietly. "What on earth could be so important, I thought to myself."

Heather twirled her silver fork in her fingers and winked noticeably at Sabrina. "People kill for lots of reasons."

“You would know,” Finneas sniffed at her. “Your lot would kill each other over a block of government cheese.”

“Really, Finneas,” Sabrina snapped. “I’m so tired of you treating Heather this way. Honestly, it’s unbecoming of a war hero like yourself, a man who built a company up from nothing. Can’t you show the woman your son chose to marry a modicum of respect?”

Rufus gazed at his normally quiet wife, then nodded in amazement. “Yeah, Dad. It’s enough.”

Cornelius slid over and kissed his wife on the cheek.

“Thank you,” Heather said.

“What has gotten into everyone?” Finneas huffed. “A man should be treated with respect at his own table.”

“It’s time for you to listen, old man,” Heather said. “Your lies are done. I know you’re not who you say you are.”

Finneas stared at her, then sputtered, “You know about—”

Sabrina sat forward, her heart racing.

“That Navy Cross you keep in your desk. It’s not yours. You’re no war hero,” Heather said.

Finneas exhaled as he glared at her. “Stupid little—”

“Dad,” Cornelius said. “Don’t.”

“What is she talking about?” Rufus asked.

“He’s a deserter,” Heather said. “I called and asked for your Navy record. It’s not hard to figure stuff out if you know how to ask. I’ve been waiting until just the right time to open up this particular can of worms.” She leaned forward and pointed a long pink fingernail at him. “You’ve disrespected me from day one. On day two I started finding stuff out.”

Cornelius put his arm around his wife’s shoulders. Rufus set his elbows on the table and dropped his head into his hands.

“I know what happened to Jacob,” Sabrina said quietly. Rufus lifted his head slowly and looked at her.

“It makes no sense,” Sabrina said. “A man leaving his family like that. A decent, respected man, from the way Connie tells the story.” Sabrina leveled a look at Finneas. “I figured out what you did.”

Finneas shifted in his chair and shook his head. “That bastard took off. That’s what happened.”

"I don't think so," Sabrina said, gaining momentum. "He disappeared, all right. But not the way you've been saying."

"I think your wife has the vapors," Finneas said to Rufus. "What's she going on about?"

"You killed him," Sabrina said. Her heart was beating so hard she was sure the others would hear it. "Jacob threatened to quit and take the spice blend he'd created with him. The Briny Bay Blend, the original recipe that earned you all of this." She waved at the large dining room, the antique silver, the crystal chandelier. "You couldn't have that. You got rid of him and told everyone he'd left town after an argument. Did you drop him out past the Bay, into the sea?"

"You're crazy," Finneas bellowed.

"And you're a ruthless, cruel man." Sabrina stood and pulled a notepad from her pocket, taking a quick glance at the scribbles she'd jotted down in the library. "In 1969, twenty years after the festival committee buried the town's time capsule, there was a break-in at city hall. The security guard was shot and killed. Heather found a stack of old newspaper clippings in the files at work."

Finneas sneered at her. "Bad luck for him during the Summer of Love. A bunch of hippies were camping out here then. One of them most likely was the culprit. I always save articles. What of it?"

"Because hippies are known for their violent tendencies and love of time capsules," Cornelius said under his breath.

Sabrina cleared her throat and continued, "In 1989, Briny Bay's cultural center was vandalized and the caretaker was hit over the head and later died. The coroner determined he died of a heart attack. The capsule was taken and never recovered. It was actually a replica, but no one knew that except the Crab Festival committee. It's in the archived meeting notes."

"Tell your wife to sit down," Finneas warned.

Rufus tightened his fists and glared at his father.

"Today, 1999, on the fiftieth anniversary of the capsule being buried, we have two deaths," Sabrina said, looking up from the notepad.

"Murders," Heather whispered.

"Yes, Murders," Sabrina said. "Thank you, Heather."

"How do you know these things?" Rufus asked, looking in awe at his wife.

"I thought about what that reporter said right before he died," Sabrina said. "And then went back through the minutes of all the committee meetings, and matched them up with the local news at the time of each incident."

"You're guessing," Finneas scoffed. "All of those incidents are unrelated."

"Dad," Rufus said, "what Sabrina is saying..."

"And then Heather found these," Sabrina said. She pulled an envelope from her other pocket, opened it up, and fanned out a stack of yellowing postcards with Alaska printed on them.

"They were in the old filing cabinet upstairs at the office," Heather said with a grin. "It's a shame when people can't keep themselves organized."

Finneas lifted from his chair as if to lunge at Heather, but then sat back down and began to laugh, quietly at first, then building to a roar. "None of you would be anywhere if it weren't for me and what I've done for this family. I went off to war...seventeen years old, and killed people. People who deserved it. Then I come home, and a man, this Eastman, who's supposed to be my partner, my brother-in-arms...he wants to go off and sell our spice blend to the first Tom, Dick, or Harry who shows him any attention. Three hundred dollars...can you imagine? We sell three hundred dollars of that spice blend every hour. What an idiot."

"So you killed him?" Rufus asked. "Dad, how could you do something like that? The man had children."

"How could I? You'd do the same thing in my shoes. All of you." Finneas pointed at Sabrina and Heather. "How dare you two...strangers...go poking around in my business."

Sabrina pressed on, undeterred. "When the time capsule was opened, what were we going to see? That it's not your recipe...it's actually Jacob Eastman's? The Briny Bay Blend, supposedly created by the Westfalls, that's made you millions? You stole Jacob's recipe and murdered him to cover it up. You knew his widow donated the recipe to the time capsule that inaugural year to commemorate the founding of the company you started together. Once you'd killed him, you had to worry every decade about your secret being revealed."

"How dare you judge me?" Finneas roared, weaker this time.

"The only judge you should worry about is the one you'll see in court when you're charged with murder," Sabrina said.

* * *

Finneas Westfall was arrested for the murders of Jacob and Albert Eastman and Ray Northam, the reporter from the *Gazette*. Albert had spoken with Ray about his father's disappearance and his suspicions he'd met with foul play after threatening to leave with his spice blend recipe. Finneas had agreed to talk to Albert out on the docks afterwards, after an entire lifetime of avoiding everyone in the Eastman family. During the confrontation, Finneas shot Albert, then rolled him into the water near the trawler, where he was snagged by a submerged crab pot. Police were also looking into the other deaths connected with the time capsule to see if Finneas Westfall would face additional charges.

Ray Northam had attempted to contact Finneas with questions about Albert's story, and had met with the old man, mentioning he'd keep digging until he uncovered the truth behind the Briny Bay murders. Then he turned his back on Finneas, to his misfortune.

Rufus finally took over the day-to-day operations of the Westfall Crab Company, and paid back-royalties on the spice blend to the Eastman family.

Connie Eastman and Darius Westfall were married the following summer, after she was crowned Briny Bay's Miss Crab.

Sabrina and Heather Westfall co-chaired the entire event.

* * *

**Shawn Reilly Simmons** is the author of seven novels in The Red Carpet Catering Mystery series and of twenty short stories. Shawn's stories have appeared in the Malice Domestic, Best New England Crime Stories, Bouchercon, Crime Writers' Association, Writers' Police Academy, and *Writers Crushing Covid-19* anthologies.

Shawn's short story, "The Last Word" won the Agatha for Best Short Story, and she also won the Anthony Award as co-editor of the anthology in which it appeared, *Malice Domestic 14: Mystery Most Edible.*

In addition to writing, Shawn also serves on the Board of Malice Domestic, and is Managing Editor at Level Best Books. She is a member of Sisters in Crime, Mystery Writers of America, the International Thriller Writers, and the Crime Writers' Association in the U.K. She lives in historic downtown Frederick, Maryland, with her husband and son. Website: www.shawnreillysimmons.com

FB: @ShawnReillySimmonsAuthor

TW & IG: @ShawnRSimmons

* * *

CRAB DIP RECIPE

*Ingredients:*

One 8-ounce package cream cheese

1/2 cup mayonnaise

1/2 cup sour cream

1/3 cup heavy cream

1 cup shredded white cheddar cheese

1 tablespoon lemon juice

1 teaspoon hot sauce

1 teaspoon kosher salt

1 teaspoon freshly ground black pepper

1/2 teaspoon seafood seasoning (like Briny Bay!)

1 1/2 cups shredded white gruyere

16 ounces of crab meat

Set out your dairy products for 20-30 minutes before beginning, to take the chill off.

Preheat the oven to 400 degrees F.

In a large bowl, or a stand mixer on low, mix together the cream cheese, mayonnaise, sour cream, and heavy cream until smooth. Stir in the white cheddar, lemon juice, hot sauce, salt, pepper, seafood seasoning, and 1/2 cup of the gruyere until well combined. Fold in the crab meat. Transfer to a 1-quart baking dish and sprinkle with the remaining cheese.

Bake until browned and bubbling, 30 to 35 minutes. Serve with a baguette and Sauvignon Blanc.

* * *

BRINY BAY SEAFOOD SEASONING BLEND

(created by the late Jacob Eastman)

*Ingredients:*

1/3 cup salt

1/4 cup garlic salt

1/4 cup celery salt

1/4 cup ground black pepper

2 tbs cayenne

1 tsp nutmeg
2 tbs thyme (dried)
2 tbs basil (dried)
2 tbs oregano (dried)
1/3 cup paprika
3 tbs onion powder
3 tbs garlic powder

# Frugal Lissa Needs a Break

## by Ritter Ames

"OH, I NEEDED THIS WEEKEND." I stretched luxuriously in my beach chair, digging my heels in the soft sun-warmed sand as I stared out at Galveston Bay. The smell of sand, salt, sea, and sunscreen filled my nose, and the bright shapes of the newly refurbished Pleasure Pier stretched high above and to the left of us, running more than three football field lengths over the water. Proving once again that everything was bigger in Texas. The crowds all around relaxed on blankets and beach chairs, doing exactly as my best friend, Abby, and I. Everyone enjoying the sunshine and the warm biting air. I sighed and said, "I love my boys dearly, but with Dek traveling almost constantly with his photojournalism job, there're only so many random elementary-aged questions one mom can handle before I want to cry out for help."

"Yep, Lissa, girls' weekends are like therapy with margaritas." Abby laughed, jostling my left elbow as she anchored her pop can in the sand, since neither of us would drink alcohol on a public beach—at least not since we came here for Spring Break in our senior year of high school. Especially at ten in the morning. No, not at all. Really.

"Remember the last time we were here?" I asked. "We were both chasing after the same guy."

"Carl Halper," Abby said, nodding. "What a waste of time and good beer."

"Oh, he didn't waste any of it. I think beer was all he lived on the whole week."

"And he stayed completely wasted. Whatever happened to him?"

I frowned. "He sells used cars now in Tulsa, and by the looks of him, beer is still his best buddy."

"You're kidding." Abby shook her head. "He had a full-ride football scholarship to the University of Oklahoma."

"Lost it after the first semester. We both dodged a bullet not landing him for a boyfriend."

She frowned. "Not that my record here in Galveston is too great anyway."

"What do you mean?"

"I came back a couple of years ago with a guy I thought was 'the one,'" she said. "Only to learn when we went to dinner at a steakhouse the first evening he was not only married, but he was a serial adulterer who had dated and dumped one of the waitresses who worked on shift that night, along with a few other women she'd learned of afterward. Which she reminded him about at top volume."

"See, these are the things I miss hearing about since you don't live in Rogerston anymore. Or you need to visit more often. We end up texting too much, and you're too busy working to tell me everything. Did you date long?"

"No, it was a whirlwind, but he knew all the right things to say. He traveled a lot, so joked he had to charm fast." Abby frowned. "I didn't even have time to tell my mother about him. Thank goodness."

"No kidding," I said. "Your mother wouldn't have handled it well if he seemed like a prince at the start. When did you dump him?"

"Before we even finished our salads. I caught the first flight back to Dallas."

"I'm sorry, Abs. Hopefully this trip will be better."

"How could it be worse?" She laughed. "This will be a man-free weekend for me. The only hope I have, I think. New rule! No more talk about any men this trip beyond your terrific husband and two adorable little boys."

"Adorable. Sure." I stretched to reach an errant blue beach ball heading my way and batted it back to cute twin girls in blonde pigtails and polka-dot bathing suits. "Did you miss the part where I said I needed a break from being an around-the-clock mom to the boys and their crazy questions?"

"I know the dynamic duo is a handful sometimes, but they're such a hoot." She waved away a gnat and asked, "What kind of questions have they asked lately?"

"Off-the-wall things you would never think of." I sipped my Coke. "Let's see, this past week's winner was a litany starting with 'Can astronauts fart in space? Or do the farts stay inside them because of there being no gravity? Or can the force of the fart shoot them across the capsule?'" I shaded my eyes with one hand to better watch a seagull nosedive for its brunch, then immediately take off again for the heavens. What a talent. "My boys are nothing if not inquisitive. I like to nurture their curiosity, but I have to admit I've looked forward to this weekend when they're on a travel assignment with their father in San Diego."

Abby chortled. "Dek will probably come back with some winners too. How did you answer on the fart front?"

"I googled it, of course. But I sidetracked them first with chores while I looked it up in secret, to keep my 'perfect answer-mom score'. Told them I wouldn't reveal any of my incredible wisdom until they were done."

"What'd they have to do?"

"Shovel up the dog poop in the backyard so I could mow. I figured the job should marginally be related to their question. Win-win."

"Might make them think twice before asking the next time."

I pictured my six-year-old, Mac, and nine-year-old, Jamey, and tried to imagine my boys with the ability to not say the first thing to pop into their thoughts. "Thinking before they speak? Nah... It'll never happen."

"Well, can you? Fart in space, I mean?" Abby was gorgeous, reclining with her eyes closed and her chestnut hair curling beautifully. She was already showing signs of a tan. She even possessed the confidence to wear a bright-red bikini on a public beach. I, on the other hand, wore a white cotton spaghetti-strap tee and khaki shorts to hide the baby fat I still attempted to rid myself of six years after my last pregnancy. If my best friend hadn't had the biggest heart in the world, I would hate her.

I loosened my ponytail holder to re-scrape my boring medium-brown hair out of the way and worried my skin was already freckling. "Yes, you can. But the force won't propel you anywhere. The smell just hangs around and irritates the rest of the crew." I wrinkled my nose. "Kind of like the dead-fish smell around here we can't avoid."

"You'll get used to it." Abby raised up and resettled in her canvas chair, so she was sitting upright again.

"That's what the astronauts say about fart smells in space."

She chuckled as she moved the brim of her sun hat. "You know I'll have to google it now. And you need to remember to grab a hat in a bit. The Texas sun gets too warm to stay bareheaded."

I shrugged. One more thing I never remembered. Then I pointed over her left shoulder at an older woman clad in a beige caftan and carrying a heavy walking stick, her attention seeming firmly rooted on each step she took. "Isn't she the same lady who sat in the lobby of our resort last night? The one who kept staring out at the parking lot like she was waiting for someone?"

Abby used a hand to pull her hat brim to better shade her eyes and twisted to look. "She's probably one of the residents there. The resort caters to older tourists and childless couples, and about half of it is rented out monthly to seniors who don't want to go to assisted living but want a place with maid service and amenities. I saw a flyer posted about a couple of walking groups and activities people could sign up for throughout the month."

"Another good reason for traveling without my boys," I said. "They'd have thrown us out otherwise."

"No, just not given us the reservation if we had kids. We would have had to use my reward points somewhere else."

"Thanks again for sharing all your points," I said. "I owe you a big one."

Abby waved a hand. "Forget it. I owe you millions."

This was our first morning in Galveston. I had left the Tulsa area yesterday morning after dropping my husband and sons at the airport. My family packed our Honda wagon the night before with everything I needed for a weekend away, including all the food, bowls, bed, and extraneous toys necessary for our family's Labrador retriever, Honey. The big pup and I hit Dallas just after lunchtime, and Abby's building super let us into her apartment to nap until she was able to escape early from the law firm which, in her words, "sucked the lifeblood out of everyone twenty-four/seven." Obviously, we both needed a little tequila and sunshine therapy. We'd left Big D ahead of five o'clock traffic, and a bit after ten p.m. we fell into our beds at the beachfront resort where we were staying. We could have made better time if we hadn't had to take unscheduled doggy breaks, but I'd spent just as many hours on the road as Honey, so I completely understood the need to get out and stretch. And do other necessary things.

"Not to belabor the subject—" Abby said.

"Yep, it's not anything like the questions you want answered in depositions. Right?"

"You'd be surprised." She shook her head. "But I honestly can't remember ever asking a fart question when I was a kid." Abby pulled her tote bag into her lap and dug around for sunscreen. I tossed her mine, and she smiled her thanks.

"Nope, those unknowns never crossed my adolescent mind either," I said. The warm sun felt glorious on my face. I closed my eyes. Heaven, even with the noise around us. "But my boys are notorious for intriguing bathroom-related questions. Especially if they can whisper them loudly in church."

"Embarrassing, much? Or do they just make most of the people in the pews around you laugh?"

"Usually the latter, unfortunately."

"Bet your group is a favorite with the minister."

"He was a little boy once, so he gets it. Thank goodness."

I thought about kicking off my flip-flops so the tops of my feet wouldn't show tan lines but felt too lazy to do more than think about it. Being a sloth sounded like the best idea. Happily sighing again, I grabbed my Coke and drank deeply, almost finishing the can this time. Such a luxury, not having to share a drink with a kid. Not that I didn't miss the boys. I did, believe me. However, squinting my eyes in the brightness, I could almost visualize my muscles relaxing as we watched the kids on the sand run back and forth and scream, simply because it wasn't my job to actually *watch* anyone in particular. "Gotta love mornings on the beach. All the people to make up stories about in your head. You have the body surfers, the sea birds circling to scavenge leftovers, the sand sculptures, and the big happy white dog with the red plastic shovel in its mouth getting chased by the kid—"

"Lissa, that's your dog getting chased by the kid." Abby pointed. "Honey stole the kid's shovel."

"Oh, no!" I whipped around to see where Honey's leash was looped on the short leg of my chair. The pink leather lead was still there, laying in the sand—with an empty collar. No dog. I dropped my Coke can and took off after my darn klepto blonde Labrador retriever, who was smart enough to figure out her neck and head were the same size, and if she got just one ear out of her collar, she could slip through and was home free. So much for a relaxing morning. "Honey! Stop! Get back here. Give the boy his shovel."

It took a good five minutes of chasing to catch my errant hound, as she ran the beach like an obstacle course. And success came only due to the quick-thinking of a middle-aged guy with a metal detector. Honey raced toward the hulking pier and its huge pilings and dunes. Nearby, the deeply tanned man stopped moving his sensor slowly back and forth and took in the sight of our chase. A moment later, he changed direction and swiftly cut ahead of the blonde Lab, corralling her with his detector in one hand, and the long handled sifting cup he carried in the other. His triangular roadblock worked. Which was a good thing, since the kid and I were both tiring fast and losing ground with every new step. Running in sand is hard work! The dog, on the other hand, was thrilled. She acted like she'd found a new friend, grinning and wiggling her tail even faster.

Honey loved men who took any notice of her. Such a tramp. Still, Honey flirting with her captor gave me time to come up behind her and put an arm around her neck, since I'd run off without grabbing the leash.

By the time I'd retrieved the slobbery shovel and returned it to the cute little owner, and apologized to the boy and his mother, who'd finally caught up, Abby joined us, wrapped in a colorful sarong and carrying the leash and our beach bags. I buckled the collar back on and warned the Lab for the millionth time she was inches away from getting a harness. Honey gave me her unrepentant grin and looked pretty pleased at all the attention she'd garnered. Then I turned and thanked the man for his help in capturing our canine escapee.

"I'm Lissa Eller and this is Abby Newlin, and I can't thank you enough for your help," I said, moving the leash to my left hand and holding out my right. "We might still be chasing Honey up the beach if you hadn't herded her to a stop."

"My pleasure," he said, shaking my hand, then using his forearm to wipe sweat from his brow, and moving us into the shade of the pier that stood high above. "Bill Winston at your service." He offered a half smile.

"We've disrupted your day, and I'm so sorry," I said. "Can I buy you an iced tea or a coffee as a thank you, Mr. Winston?"

He wore a canvas bucket hat with charms and pins on all sides, so it jingled a little as he shook his head. "Ah, call me Bill. You make me feel old saying, Mr. Winston. And thanks, but it's about time for me to leave. I've been out here since first light. I try to get ahead of the crowds to sweep the space between low and high tide. It's usually where I find the most swag. I do these cleanup areas at the end." He touched a relatively large canvas pouch hanging off his belt, where I assumed he kept the metal objects he found.

"Cleanup areas?" I asked.

"Those spots we go over at the end. Like here near the pier," he said. "A last pass in the spots we can't do wide sweeps as easily."

"Productive day?" Abby asked.

"Nothing too exciting." He looked away as he spoke, making me think he probably used the line a lot to keep people from knowing how good an area might be.

"So the best spot is between the two tide lines?" Abby prodded. "Quite a huge expanse. How do you cover it?"

He shrugged. "I do a zigzag sweep until the detector hits on something. Then I use my scoop to find whatever is hidden in the sand." He demonstrated as he spoke, running the sensor over the wet beach until a beep sounded, then scooped up a handful size of sand and sifted it back and forth until the treasure appeared. This time, a sand-encrusted penny. "Usually when there's a hit, you'll find more metal around the same spot. I just shift around a little more to see, then start zigzagging again until I find the next spot."

Honey started barking and pulling on the leash, wanting to get to the nearby sand dune, created when the wind and surf battered into the support walls and posts of the pier. I shifted so she could stretch closer. "Looks like my dog is on the hunt for something. Are dunes a good place to look?"

The curious Lab ignored our talk and began digging at a churned-up area of the dune. It looked like the sand had been stacking up awhile, then cascaded down in an avalanche along the outside edge.

"They can be good, but I've never had much luck with them. I've had better luck on flatter surfaces." He started walking away but stopped when Abby and I screamed.

Honey's digging had uncovered a man's body, the victim's head covered in dried blood. One look told me he was dead, but just in case, I pushed the dog away and brushed back the victim's longish fair hair so I could feel for a pulse. Nothing. His open eyes were pale blue.

Abby was already on the phone to 911 and our screams had alerted a bronzed lifeguard who ran up behind us. I dragged the persistent dog away from the body. Abby got her first look of the victim's face and made a choking sound and dropped the phone.

"What is it?" I rushed to her. She was shaking as I wrapped my arms around her.

"I-I know h-him." She buried her face in my shoulder. "He is...was...the cheater I was telling you about, Lissa!"

* * *

Anyone who didn't know my dog, and how much she mothered anyone who got hurt, would think Honey appeared far too happy with her find. I had to keep a firm hold on the leash to make sure the Lab didn't decide the victim's face needed a tongue bath. In a dog's universe, copious licking was all that was needed to make everything okay again. Labradors don't understand the concept of disturbing evidence.

Bill stayed with us, but he looked as unnerved as Abby and I felt. The police arrived quickly, thank goodness, but things took a turn for the bizarre afterward. When Abby explained she knew the name of the victim, and how she knew him, the officer decided she needed to be questioned by a detective and moved her away from the gathering crowd. I tried to follow.

"No, ma'am," the officer said, holding out a hand to stop me. "You need to stay and give your name and contact details, too, but I can't have y'all talking about this together."

"But my friend is—"

"No, ma'am," the officer repeated.

Bill touched my arm, then motioned with his head to suggest we should step away. We took a spot on the far end of the sand dune.

"I'll keep you company until they let you leave." Bill talked quietly out of the side of his mouth. I sensed his hesitation. "We can keep an eye on what happens with your friend."

"So nice of you. I appreciate it," I whispered, feeling a little shivery and wondered if I had a touch of shock. "This was supposed to be our fun girls' weekend. Who could have expected our finding a dead body?"

"I need to call my wife and tell her I'll be later than normal." He pulled a cell phone from his pocket.

"Oh, yes, I'm sorry. Do you need me to give you some distance?"

He shook his head. "You're fine."

His call was answered, and I heard a baby crying in the background as a woman spoke. I couldn't understand what she said, but he replied, "Some commotion here at the beach, Phyllis. I'll be a little later than usual. Go ahead and eat lunch without me."

There was a little more talk between them, but he didn't tell her what Honey had discovered. He hung up and returned the phone to his pocket, pushing his hat up his brow so thick gray-and-white hair broke free and moved with the sea breeze. There were still hints of blond hair among his silver. With a better look, I realized he was nearer sixty than I'd thought originally.

"She'd just worry if I told her what was happening here," he said, almost reading my thoughts.

"I figured as much. Sounds like you have a baby in the house." I smiled.

He returned my smile with a truly broad one for the first time and nodded. "My grandson. He's eighteen months. Davey is a special-needs baby, though, and he and my daughter live with us so we can help care for him. My wife is with him during the day while my daughter works in an insurance office."

"Is the father helping?"

Bill snorted. "Not someone who accepts responsibility for his actions. But we're better off without him in the picture."

"I'm sorry that's the case, but I'm glad your daughter and grandson can count on you."

He stuck out his chin and crossed his arms. "We'll always be there for her. Family is everything."

"Absolutely."

Another officer walked toward us, opening a notebook, and saying, "You're the other witnesses who found the body, right? I need your names and contact information."

We nodded.

"I need to see a photo ID, please."

After we furnished him with our drivers' licenses, he asked who found the body. I pointed to Honey. "My dog discovered him. When I realized what she had uncovered, I pulled her away as quickly as I could. Then I checked for a pulse, but he was already gone."

"Her friend called in the emergency, and we waited until all y'all arrived," Bill added.

Since we didn't have any other information to help in the investigation, he took down our cell phone numbers, and confirmed Bill's address was the one on his license. He turned to me and asked, "How long will you be staying in Galveston?"

"We just planned to stay the weekend. Abby's due back at work on Monday, and I told my family I'd be back in Tulsa on Monday evening."

The officer nodded. "A detective will be in communication with you by tomorrow. He'll let you know when it's okay for you to leave."

He then knelt down and took a closer look at Honey's paws. I hadn't even thought about her having blood or evidence on them, but he took several minutes to focus on the front paws. "She's a big Lab. Her feet are huge. It's amazing she didn't disturb the scene more," he said.

"Do I need to wait for a forensic person to look at her?"

"Probably not." He keyed a number in his phone. "But wait a second and I'll check."

He had a short conversation with whoever answered the call, then hung up, shaking his head. "No, they said my looking her over was enough. Nothing at the scene looks excessively compromised by her paws."

While this was all going on, I noticed a couple of other metal detectorists moving closer. Both were younger than Bill with ball caps on their heads. They wore cargo shorts and T-shirts, one a faded blue shirt advertising a long-ago chili cook-off, and the other a black Metallica one. The first guy had a well-worn machine resembling Bill's—cared for, but in steady use. The younger guy in black carried a much newer-looking detector and sift scoop, but he also wore a Rolex, so the newness wasn't surprising. Weekend treasure hunter, probably.

Like Bill, both were barefoot. As soon as the cop left, the pair surged toward us, only dropping back a little when Honey tried to rush them.

"It's okay, she's harmless," I said. "Unless you're allergic to dog slobber."

Faded Blue Shirt laughed, but Metallica remained wary.

"Was that the new guy in the sand? Just started coming here? He's dead, right?" Faded Blue Shirt asked Bill, jerking his head toward the dune now blocked off by emergency personnel.

"Didn't know him," Bill replied. Body language said he wasn't a fan of the younger men.

I saw Abby heading my way with a different officer in tow.

"Lissa, I'm going back to the station to see if I can answer some questions," she said.

"I'll come and—"

"No." She held up a hand. "I'll be fine. I'm just a witness who's helping with the investigation. Go have lunch and rest in the villa. I'll find you there later."

"You'll need a ride back. I'll wait in the lobby—"

It was the officer's turn to stop me. "Ma'am, someone will give her a ride back when all their questions are answered."

"How many questions can there be? She hasn't seen him in two years!"

Abby warned, "Lissa—"

The cop echoed, "Ma'am—"

I held up my hands in surrender. "I get it. But I'm going to time how long she's gone. And I better see her again soon." I pointed a finger at him. "And she's a lawyer. Don't think she doesn't have people who can help her."

The officer frowned. "I hear you, ma'am."

As they walked away, I muttered, "And stop calling me *ma'am*."

* * *

"Your friend's an attorney, huh?" Faded Blue Shirt asked.

His name was actually Jim, "call me Jimbo," but in my mind he remained tagged to his clothing. Metallica had drifted off seconds after Abby and the cop left. I don't think he ever said a word the whole time he was around us. Faded Blue Shirt, on the other hand, didn't know the meaning of quiet. He kept up a running monologue about the beach and what was going on in every direction as he and Bill and I ringed an outdoor table on the historic Pleasure Pier.

Actually, it was the newly historic pier. The structure had been rebuilt, refurbished, and reopened in 2012, taking the place of the original, but this was definitely not the same pier Abby and I visited our senior year in high school. Like the original, it was a place to get beachgoers to happily part with their money, but this version was full of bright new colors, updated rides, and yummy side shops to accomplish the feat. We were sitting at one of the white tables scattered in the area near the railing, looking around the big blue canvas "No Entry / No Jumping" signs, and watching the emergency personnel on the sand far below. The air was filled with the smell of sugar and salt, along with the happy screams of the people riding the speedy little roller coaster, and the playful music of the bumper cars. I'd gotten our drinks at an open kiosk, by a candy-inspired sweet shop with a hand-painted sandwich sign on the sidewalk out front proclaiming it open for business. It kind of felt like we were living in a fairy tale or the Candy Land game, as we tried to dodge all the people who came to have fun, while we attempted to get the best view of the dune below us.

Well, us humans tried, anyway. Honey, on the other hand, had moved on to a new audience and was paying too much attention to all the kids who kept coming by and petting her.

I should rent my dog out to politicians who needed to improve their likeability factor. No wonder most presidents ended up getting dogs for their time in the White House.

I was tired of Faded Blue Shirt's chatter, so I replied to his question to try to shut him up. "Yes, Abby and I have been best friends forever, and she's always wanted to help people. Going to law school was what she thought was her best option to accomplish her goal." What I didn't add was how bummed she was getting in her current career *option*, and how it had me truly worried about her. At least she knew people to call if she needed recommendations for legal representation in Galveston.

Our table was at the edge of the pier overlook, giving us a decent spot to watch the law enforcement activity on the beach directly below. When I'd offered again to buy Bill an iced tea or soda, the younger guy decided he was included in the invitation. I honestly don't think Bill would have agreed to come along, and he was on the verge of declining again before Faded Blue Shirt spoke up. But Bill seemed to not want to leave me alone with the other guy. If I could have figured out a way to rescind the offer without looking like a ditz, I would have, but my brain hadn't had enough caffeine yet to come up with an alternative.

"What do you do?" Bill asked Faded Blue Shirt.

"I'm an entrepreneur."

I almost laughed out loud when Bill raised his eyes to look upward and shook his head slightly. Obviously, we were of the same opinion about the guy.

"Are you a lawyer too?" asked Faded Blue Shirt.

"No, I'm a professional frugal mom," I said.

"What's that?"

"The only way I can be a full-time mom with two small boys is to recycle every dime until it's as thin as aluminum foil." I grinned. "If I lived around here, I'd probably take up metal detecting, too. I work every saving angle I can."

I noticed support poles and a large white awning was getting moved in around the sand dune area below. Seconds later, we couldn't see anything anymore from above. "Well, apparently our bird's-eye view is canceled."

Bill chuckled. Faded Blue Shirt laughed, then his eyes bugged out, and he said, "Hey, I've been looking for that guy." He pointed to the sand below, beyond the awning and the curious crowd. He jumped to his feet. "Thanks, Lissa, and nice to meet'cha!" Then he disappeared.

I wasn't surprised he left his empty plastic cup behind. It fell over, rocking across the flat surface after he shoved the table and jumped from the chair. I added the cup to the recycle bag in my beach tote.

"You're keeping his trash?" Bill asked.

"No, I'll recycle it when I see the right bin. I looked when we walked up here, but I only saw trash cans."

"There's some around, but I forget exactly where they are." He unhooked a refillable water bottle from his belt. "I usually drink this and go home when I need anything else."

"You live close by?" I asked.

He pointed toward the resort where Abby and I were staying several blocks away. "I live in the cul-de-sac behind the hotel structure. Our backyard shares their fence. It's easy to walk to the beach every day, and we like being able to bring our grandson here when it's not so busy."

"I'll bet he's a blast at a year and a half."

Bill grinned. "More fun every day. I just wish..."

As his words trailed off, I almost asked what was wrong with the boy, then decided for once to keep my mouth shut without Abby there to remind me. I have a real problem with talking too much, and being too helpful, and basically worrying my best friend by how open I am about everything. I think Bill's reticence might have been a good thing. I needed someone like him around more to rub off on me.

Instead, I changed the subject. "I take it you're retired."

"Yep, forty years in accounting." He shook his head. "Don't say it. Sounds boring?"

"Sounds like a good way to have made a living for your family and to plan for the future."

He let out a long breath. "It took care of all the 'planned for' things anyway."

Hospital bills for a grandson who may need help for the decades to come. Yeah, I could figure out what he wasn't saying.

"Still, you come out here each day and treasure hunt. Got to love your optimism, Bill. Does the hunt get better with experience, or is it always a real surprise when you get something good?"

He shrugged, then finished his drink and handed the cup to me so I could add it to my recyclables. "The finds are unpredictable, but the beach is predictable. The repetitive forces and laws of physics combine with plain old human habits to make beaches like this one a great spot for detecting. Plus, being able to get out under clear skies and walk on warm sand, well, it's something even a jaded old accountant has to put on the plus side of the balance sheet."

"Wow, you understand the whole science behind it." I jiggled my straw, then asked, "Maybe you could explain something for me. I know a lot of rings and watches and other jewelry are found by metal detectors. Why do people bring so many valuables to the beach? Or at least, why do they seem to lose so many of them?"

"Ah, there's more science in the probability numbers behind your question, too, Lissa. People wear rings and wrist jewelry to the beach without realizing their fingers and hands shrink in the water. Add multiple applications of sunscreen, and you can get some relatively slippery conditions. The jewelry slides off and people never know when it happens. They discover the items missing later but can't find the stuff when they try to retrace their steps."

"Which becomes a good day at the beach for you."

"Sometimes. But if an item is engraved, or if there's some way I can track down the owner, I'll reach out to them. I'd feel guilty otherwise."

"You are a very nice man, Bill Winston."

"I try to be."

I looked at my phone and willed Abby to call me. Of course, she didn't. But I did notice the time and figured I'd better move along. "I'm heading to the resort you pointed to earlier. We're staying there. Want to walk partway with my dog and me?"

"I'd like that. It's been a real pleasure meeting you and Honey, Lissa. Even under these circumstances."

"The pleasure is all ours, Bill."

* * *

Abby hadn't returned to the resort by the time we walked back. Honey immediately took up with the landscape crew who had plied her with treats when I'd walked her early in the morning, and I didn't know if I was ever going to get her away.

"Leave her with us," the head gardener said. "We have a lunch break coming up, and we'll give her our scraps and play fetch. She'll be ready to nap the afternoon away then, promise. We do this with residents' pets all the time. Keeps my crew happy."

I laughed. "Wish I could hire y'all to tire out my boys the same way, but then I'd have to take you home with me. But please don't feed her. She'll be happy enough with a game of fetch, and if you feed her, she won't eat the dog food I brought."

"Gotcha," he said. "I completely understand. I'll tell the others."

I gave him my cell phone number and asked him to call or have the front desk page me if Honey became a pest. The flirty Lab had already given her leash to one of the younger guys and was grinning at him. She'd likely forgotten I existed.

There was a sandwich and salad place on one of the terraces, and I wandered in to find something. But food didn't really hold my attention, as I was too worried about Abby. A phone call went to voicemail, so I tried sending a text. No answer, but at least my phone would alert me if something came from her later.

A smiling young thing with the kind of tan I'd always wanted was pulling hostess duties, and she seated me at a small table near a trio of seventy-ish women who seemed to be playing cards. Or at least arguing about playing cards.

"We need four people for it to work out evenly," said the tiny woman with pink hair. "This isn't any fun."

"Well, Susan has a migraine, and she's not coming down today," said the woman beside her who sported purple streaks in her white 'do. "Spades works fine with three."

The last of their group was the woman I'd spotted walking the beach earlier in the beige caftan. She kept quiet and frowned, then sipped her tea.

A waitress with "Sally" on her name tag came by, and I asked about the feta and strawberry spinach salad on the menu. We have an award-winning independent bakery near our house known for making those and a number of other specialties, and the salads are bought up each morning almost before the bakery staff can get them into the refrigerators for patrons to see. Forget about picking one up at lunchtime. I was interested in tasting the Texas version.

"Yes, I'll bring your food out in just a few minutes," Sally said, bowing her head closer so I could hear her over the other table's squabbling. "Would you like something to drink?"

"Water would be great. Thanks."

She whispered, "If you want to move out of the sun—"

"This table is absolutely fine." I grinned, and she winked and nodded as she moved to the kitchen to turn in my order.

Seconds later, the woman in the pink hair tapped on my tabletop. "Hello there. I'm Tiki, like the torches, and this," she waved a hand at the lady with purple streaks, "is Roxie. And over here we have Bette." She placed a hand on the shoulder of the woman from the beach.

"Nice meeting everyone. I'm Lissa."

"Well, Lissa." Tiki scooted out of her chair and took an empty one at my table. "We like to have a friendly game of cards at lunch, but we're used to a foursome, and one of our players didn't show today. We were wondering if you'd be interested in joining us."

Roxie rolled her eyes. "Tiki, can't you leave the poor girl alone to have her lunch in peace." She said it like a statement instead of a question, so I figured this wasn't the first time she'd said something like this to her friend.

"I'm just asking. I'm not holding her at gunpoint." Tiki huffed a little.

I recognized the only way I could stop the squabbling was to give everyone cards to concentrate on instead. "I'm kind of rusty on spades. Do you play pairs or individual hands?"

Tiki laughed. "Oh, spades is just our fallback game. We normally play poker. We start with jacks wild. Interested?"

I ran the suits through my head, trying to remember what beat what and when. "I suppose I could play a few hands."

She clapped excitedly, then called to Roxie over her shoulder, "See, it never hurts to ask someone if they want to join."

I moved to the empty chair between Roxie and Bette, and Tiki settled back into her original place. The cards were dealt, and I found I had a pair of twos. Then I learned they bet quarters. I had the feeling I'd been hustled. My salad arrived and it was glorious! I hadn't realized how hungry I was. I stole combo bites of the feta, spinach, and strawberries between betting and tossing away scrub cards for better tries. It wasn't very relaxing, but it did keep my mind off whatever Abby might be in the middle of at the moment, so it was definitely good. And I seemed to only be losing a little each hand.

Then Tiki got control of the deck and called for a game change. "Let's do Texas Hold'em."

"Ladies, what you're asking is beyond my talents. I'm out when you move away from the easy stuff. I'm sorry," I said, scooping up my dwindling stack of change and tucking it into my shorts pocket.

"Oh, don't do that, hon," Tiki said, patting my hand. "This game's fun. We'll help you. Let me deal you back in."

I shook my head. I'd tried the play-to-learn route one night when a bunch of us were together, and between all the rules and the margaritas, the game never got clear enough for me to know when I was winning or losing. I may have been sober right then, but my brain was still hung over from yesterday's travel and today's sad discovery. I said, "I haven't played it enough to know what to do each time. I'll just drag down your fun. My nine-year-old son is better at Texas Hold'em than I am. I don't know where he learned to play card games so well."

"Probably at school," Bette replied, keeping her eyes on her cards as she switched them around in her hand. "They don't just learn red rover and hide-and-seek on the playground anymore."

"Is he good at math?" Tiki asked.

"Amazing at it. And a chess master already," I added.

"There you go," she said, straightening the leftover cards before looking at her own hand. "He's probably a whiz at figuring the odds." She looked up and saw a waiter at the other end of the terrace. Tiki lifted her empty glass and called out, "Cabana boy! I need a refill, please."

He smiled as he took her glass, asking, "G and T, Miss Tiki?"

"Yes, sweetie. My usual. Light on the tonic water."

As he walked away, she pretended to slap his bum, then said, "I can't do that anymore. I got into trouble the last time. But he knows I'll tip him well."

I couldn't help but wonder how many gin and tonics Tiki had already put away. Before I could escape, Roxie touched my arm. "But you'll stay if we play spades, right?" She turned to Tiki. "You can't argue with us having four people now, can you? Since it's no longer an odd three."

"Tiki can argue about anything," Bette groused, discarding her hand, and stacking it on top of the deck.

"Well, it's not as much fun—" Tiki started.

Roxie crossed her arms. "Life is a bowl of cherries as long as you don't keep looking at the pits."

While they were trading arguments, I turned to Bette. "I saw you walking this morning on the beach. I loved your walking stick. When my husband

and I lived in London we had a neighbor who had a stick similar to yours. She called it a blackthorn stick."

Bette nodded. "It was my grandmother's, then my mother's. Now...now it's mine."

"Good and heavy. My neighbor said it was stout enough to always help her keep her balance. Does it help with the sand?"

The woman looked at me and sighed. Then got up from the table and said, "I'm not feeling very well. I'm sorry. I think I'll go lie down."

Tiki started complaining about the table being down to three players again as Bette disappeared. I forestalled the onslaught by saying, "I apologize. I shouldn't have brought up the beach. She may have been down there when the body was found."

"A body on the beach?" Roxie exclaimed.

"Tell us everything, doll!" Tiki cried.

I offered up the *Reader's Digest Condensed* version of the morning's events, and it was surprising enough to slow Tiki's tongue. Of course, the new G and T she'd downed almost immediately probably helped as well.

While I didn't talk about the nagging suspicion I'd been secretly harboring about Bill Winston, I did mention his family and my curiosity about his grandson. I truly did believe he was a nice man, but a tiny doubting concern in the back of my mind kept surfacing. He'd been adamant the father of his grandson was better left out of their lives. Given what I knew about the cheating habits of the victim, I couldn't help but wonder if he might not be the baby's father.

However, this hypothesis threw suspicion on Bill, and I didn't see him as a killer. At least I didn't want to. Yes, I hoped he wasn't the murderer. But I needed to do some sleuthing to find out anything I could.

My story had Roxie talking, and I tried to tune out the tiny negative voice again and listen to her instead.

"Yes, I know the family you mean. Your talk about the metal detector tipped me off. I can see their backyard from my balcony. I have a second-story room in the back of the resort. Cute baby, all dark-brown curly hair. Even from the distance I can tell his eyes are just as dark. He'll be a heartbreaker when he grows up. Poor little dear can't even walk, though, and he already has to wear braces on his legs. Hope he'll be able to someday. I wave at him, and his grandma and mama help him wave back to me."

"Bill Winston's hair looked like it was blond before he went gray," I said, trying to be casual. "Are his wife and daughter fair or dark-headed like the baby?"

"All of them are just as fair as can be, except for the little one. He must take after his daddy," Roxie added.

"My room's at the front." Tiki grumbled, "I can't see anything but who comes in and out of the parking lot."

"Get them to change your room."

"Don't want to. I like knowing who shows up, and when visitors are here."

"Nosy old biddy," Roxie muttered.

"I heard that." Tiki raised her empty glass to get the waiter's attention again. "And it's not true. I'm a curious sexy senior, thank you very much. Not a nosy old biddy. The stories I could tell you..."

"Oh, Tiki." Roxie laughed. "Please don't."

The discussion reminded me of the previous evening. "We checked in late last night, and I remember seeing Bette in the lobby. She was looking out one of the windows, like she maybe was expecting someone."

Roxie nodded her purple streaks. "Something about her granddaughter. The girl got a job as a lifeguard on the beach, but then something happened, and she hasn't been there for a few days. I think Bette was hoping she and her daughter would come by and talk. I hope it isn't anything serious, but Bette is keeping mum about it all."

"Hmmph." Tiki crossed her arms and leaned over the tabletop, whispering, "I heard the girl tried to kill herself. She won't be going back to the beach anytime soon."

"How—?"

"I heard two of the pool staff talking when I went down for my swim this morning." Tiki raised an eyebrow, then sat straight again in her chair.

Just then, my phone pinged with a text. It was Abby.

"My friend is in the lobby," I said, leaping from my chair. "I need to see how she's doing. Thanks so much for letting me sit with your group. It was nice meeting you."

"Of course," Tiki said, slurring a little. "Any time."

Roxie rolled her eyes and waved as I walked away.

Yet, I couldn't get Tiki's last revelation out of my mind.

* * *

Honey was standing with Abby when I reached the lobby.

"Look who I found playing with the flowers," she said, scratching my dog's ears.

"The crew was supposed to call if she got into trouble."

"Forget it," Abby said, laughing. "She had those guys wrapped around her paw."

As we stepped into the elevator, I asked quietly, "Are you okay?"

"I am since I see you're all right. I was worried about you being left with Bill Winston," she said. We exited the elevator and she added, "I have to tell you, I've had these worrying thoughts—"

"I've had the same ones, trust me," I said, inserting the keycard into the slot on the door of our room. "But no more. I have a lot to tell you."

I filled Honey's food bowl and gave her fresh water. Abby changed clothes, then ordered a salad on my recommendation and pitcher of tea for the room. Once everyone was happily eating, I launched into everything I'd learned and deduced since we'd found the body and the police decided Abby needed to go back to the station with them.

Roxie's revelation about the dark-haired baby and the fair-haired Winstons had her nodding in agreement to my conclusions. It was nice to know Abby and I still thought alike—both on why we worried Bill Winston could be guilty and how quickly the clues in Roxie's story told us the worries were unfounded. It was equally easy for her to jump to the same conclusion I had after hearing Tiki's gossip about Bette's family.

"She's really unnerved," I said, walking again to the window to look out over the garden. I'd seen Bette sitting there on a bench when we first arrived in the room, looking down at her lap. One glance, and I saw she was still there, twisting what looked like a handkerchief in her hands. "When we saw her last night in the lobby, I knew something was wrong. Then I forgot about her. Walking alone today—"

"What do you want to do?" Abby asked. "I have the number for the detective. Should I call?"

I shook my head. "I'd like to see if we can get her to talk first. I think she's going to need someone like you right away."

"Of course, I'll help her. But if she's dangerous? Maybe I'm worrying too much."

"Let's try talking to her, okay?" I looked out the window again. Bette looked miserable. "I think any fight she had in her is out by this point."

Minutes later, we approached the bench from a side angle, so as not to startle Bette when she saw us. She looked up, her face swollen from tears, and she held out a hand.

I sat beside her, and Abby remained standing.

"Bette, we don't want to bother you, but this is my friend, Abby. She's an attorney, and we wondered—"

The words flooded out of her. Bette cried and told us about her granddaughter, about how she approached the victim last night when he was using his metal detector at sunset. She said she'd tried to tell him about the damage he'd caused with his cheating. How he'd laughed at her heartfelt words.

"He just laughed," she sobbed. "He didn't care. I don't even remember hitting him with my stick. One second he was in front of me laughing and calling my granddaughter a fool. The next moment he was dropping against the dune, and some of the sand was falling down from the impact. I turned away and hurried back here. When you saw me this morning, I'd walked out to see if he was still there, hoping he'd walked away. But the dune apparently collapsed on top of him. I couldn't see him and thought he'd left. Thought all was okay. Prayed it was true. Until I heard someone was killed on the beach, and I knew. I must have hit him and killed him. I never thought I could do such a thing. I still don't remember. If I hadn't seen him fall..."

"You need to tell the police what happened," Abby said, sitting on the other side of the bench. "I can help you. Would you like me to go with you to talk to them?"

"If I turn myself in, it's better? Isn't that right?" Bette asked, dabbing her eyes again with the handkerchief.

"Yes, I'll be right there with you to help," Abby replied.

I gave Abby my car keys, and she and Bette left. I didn't want to risk running into Tiki and Roxie again, and because the beach no longer held the vacation allure it once had, Honey and I instead napped in our room. Well, Honey napped off all her gardening exertions, while I hid from the senior gossip girls.

Finally, it was late enough to feel sure my guys would be finished with whatever photoshoots Dek had on his agenda for the day. I called to get in a little FaceTime if I could manage it. He answered immediately. Seconds later with the magic of technology, we were all talking at once.

"How are my handsome men?" I asked, almost laughing when both boys fought over who was going to hold the phone. "Take turns. You don't want to break your daddy's phone."

"Mom! We were at the zoo! And we got to go back in some special places Daddy could get us in, but where regular people can't go!" cried Mac, my kindergartner.

"Wow! Cool beans. Your dad has some real cred there," I said, grinning at my husband's sheepish look behind the boys' heads. "How about you, Jamey. See anything exciting?"

My third grader started rattling off a list that seemed long enough to fill a week of days. I could only imagine how tired Dek was after doing double duty working and keeping the boys entertained at the same time. The look on his face, however, was calm, so I simply listened as the boys talked over one another. Finally, Jamey reached the point of the griping older sibling and said, "And please tell Mac again how we aren't taking the train to Legoland tomorrow. He won't shut up about it."

There's nothing better to a six-year-old boy than a train ride ending up in a dream park. When Mac heard there was a train from San Diego to Legoland in Carlsbad, he decided the rail route was the only one to take. Unfortunately, what was a half-hour drive by car became a four-hour excursion by train. No way either of my boys, not to mention my husband, would be able to spend so much time together in a train car and not be at each other's throats.

"Mac, you and I talked long and hard about this," I said. "I showed you the map and the timetable with all the stops you'd have to make. Going by train would mean you'd have less time at Legoland. Don't forget, it's four whole hours—like from breakfast until lunch."

He frowned into the screen. "I know, but the train sounds great."

"We'll find a way to book a train ride soon," Dek promised. "Maybe this summer."

"Okayyyyyy," Mac whined.

Jamie mouthed "thank you" at me.

I had to smile. Then I looked at my watch and burst their happiness. "It's time for baths, guys. I know you had fun today, but I'll bet you smell worse than Honey right now."

"But it's earlier here," Jamey said.

"You don't want to get used to Pacific Time when you're coming back to Central Time in just another day. Keep with the program, guys."

"Your mom's right. Move it," Dek said.

As the boys scampered off, he turned back to me, his dark-brown eyes soft with worry, and he said, "Is everything okay?"

"Can they hear me?"

He put in his earbud. "Not now they can't."

I told him how the day had progressed, how I was again waiting for Abby to get finished at the police station, and how I only wanted to go to bed and sleep without any dreams. I finished by adding, "Abby and I haven't really talked, so I don't know if she's riding back with me or flying home on Monday."

"I'd bet the latter," Dek said.

I shrugged. "If so, I'll probably leave out of here earlier, so I can get back home before midnight."

"You want me and the boys to fly there tomorrow and drive back with you?" Dek asked.

"I love that you offered, but no, I can't ask you to give up Legoland."

"For you, anything." He grinned. "Even spending twelve hours on the road with two easily bored boys and a Lab shedding all over everything."

"You are a knight among men." I was having trouble talking, because I was laughing so hard at the mental picture he'd created of fur flying all over the car and the boys constantly arguing. Ah, yes, what a great way to imagine the end of a weekend already falling far short of expectations.

"And you are a woman who always keeps me on my toes." He shook his dark head, then whispered, "If Abby doesn't drive back with you, the boys and I will meet you in Galveston. I'd rather they miss an extra day of school than have to worry about what kind of trouble you and Honey could get into driving alone on the way home."

I gasped. "Honey is offended you would say that."

"Hey, if she hadn't dug up the body, you'd have never known it was there—"

"Honey dug up a body?" Jamey squealed from the background. "Another one?"

"It's her superpower!" Mac shouted.

"She's a cadaver dog," Jamey added.

"The earpiece doesn't do any good if you say it out loud," I reminded. "Boys, go take your bath."

"Listen to your mother," Dek seconded.

"We can't hear her," Jamey said. "We can only hear you."

"Oh, the earphone," Dek muttered, then louder, he repeated, "She said go take your bath."

When they were finally out of view, I looked at my wonderful husband and said, "I love you. Take care tomorrow. Have fun and don't worry about me. You don't get enough fun time with the boys."

"And you get more than your fair share, I know." Dek laughed. "I love you too. Oh, and the boys got you a T-shirt at one of the zoo shops."

I was expecting something like "I come from a family of monkeys," but was surprised when he held the pink tee up to the phone's camera and I saw the words: "My mom knows everything. And what she doesn't know, she makes something up really fast."

Laughing, I told Dek the story I'd related to Abby on the beach that morning. He grinned and said, "Wait until I get home and tell you all the questions I've had to deal with this weekend."

"I can't wait."

A notification beep told me I had a call coming from Abby. "I need to take her call. See when she'll be back here to talk."

We hung up, but not fast enough. Abby left a voicemail message. Before I returned her call, I hugged the dog and counted my blessings Dek was having to explain things to the boys instead of me. It was his slip after all.

"However, Honey," I said, taking the dog's lap-sized blonde head in my hands so I could look directly into her dark eyes. "We're going to have to have a long talk about your new talent. I don't want you to make this a habit. You understand?"

She stretched her neck, and a huge pink tongue licked my chin and nose.

* * *

**Ritter Ames** is the *USA TODAY* bestselling mystery author who writes the cozy Organized Mysteries and the Frugal Lissa Mysteries series, as well as the light-suspense and caperish Bodies of Art Mysteries. She enjoys travel and trying new foods, and she loves to share her excitement of discovering places and different tastes with readers. Ritter considers travel a part of her research and feels there's no better way to translate settings to a page than actual personal knowledge gained from having been there. When she can take her blonde Labrador retriever along, too, it makes travel and writing that much more fun.

Ritter loves hearing from readers. Her website www.ritterames.com has more news and info, a page to contact her for questions, chapter excerpts of each title, downloadable coloring pages that tie to her series, and much more. Subscribe to her quarterly newsletter on the website or at http://smarturl.it/NewsltrSubcribe for subscriber-only extras like—free reads, first looks, inside scoops, reader gifts, cover reveals, alerts about bargain sales, info on characters, and series previews. If you're on Facebook or Twitter, you can follow her FB author page at https://www.facebook.com/RitterAmesBooks, and her Twitter handle is @RitterAmes.

* * *

10 Frugal Ways to Save Time, Money, and Frustration When Traveling—

**Clothes get wrinkled in your luggage**? Hang them in the bathroom and run a hot shower for five minutes, then be amazed at how the wrinkles disappear. Or for a quicker fix to a single item, get your hands wet and flick water on the wrinkles, then run a hair dryer over the area(s). Easier than ironing.

**Forget shaving cream**? Don't buy a new can. Use conditioner instead. Like shaving cream, conditioner closes pores and works as a quick and cheap substitute. Plus, your hotel probably offers sample sized bottles in your room.

**Can't sleep because there's too much light**? Pulling the curtains together can help, but often light still comes through the line where the curtains meet in the middle. Look in the closet and grab a couple of the hangers with clips for pants and use them to clip the curtains together. You'll be happily surprised at the difference it makes in the room's darkness level.

**Too much noise to sleep as people walk past your room at night**? Stuff a towel under the door to muffle a lot of the noise.

**Forget to bring your phone charger**? Ask the front desk if they have one you can borrow, or if there is one in their lost and found.

**Too many chargers for the number of outlets**? Unless you're traveling alone, trying to plug in everyone's phone chargers, laptops, and electronic devices can be a battle. Win the war by always carrying a mini power strip when traveling, so everyone can keep their phones and devices charged with ease.

**Need to wash out a few things in the bathroom sink and there's no drain plug**? Just line the sink with a large plastic bag and place a few coins over the drain area to hold the bag in place. You can wash your things with ease, and you don't even have to clean the sink before or after—just throw away the plastic bag.

**Have little kids, but your hotel room isn't childproofed**? Use duct tape to cover outlets and tape down any wires you're afraid might get tripped on. No duct tape? Band-aids are a great backup option to cover electrical outlets.

**Want to save money by cooking for your family**? Hotel and motel rooms usually have microwaves and refrigerators, but sometimes that isn't enough. Want to slow cook in your room or make shakes for the family? Ask the front desk if you can borrow a crock pot or a blender. You'd be surprised how accommodating many chains are today.

**Kids shoes—or yours—covered in dirt or sand and you need to pack them**? Grab the shower cap the hotel put in the bathroom for your use, wrap up the shoes, and stow them in your luggage without worrying they'll make a mess.

# Frog Days of Summer
# by Cathy Wiley

"ONE VIRGIN SEX ON THE BEACH."

I stared at the speaker, a tall man in khakis and a light green polo, offering me a garishly colored drink. While he was also dark and handsome, he wasn't my type...considering he was my brother. "A *Virgin* Sex on the Beach? Isn't that an oxymoron?"

Daniel Norwood smirked at me. "Who are you calling a moron?" When I laughed at his joke, he continued. "I know you wanted something non-alcoholic. And I thought all women liked Sex on the Beach."

"No way. You get sand in places you don't want sand." I knew this would embarrass him, and I wasn't disappointed when he blushed.

"Jackie!" He sputtered. "You know I meant the drink."

"Well, yes, but this was more fun." I raised the "mocktail" to eye level, inspecting it. "At least the alcoholic version did its job of making people look more attractive. But the virgin version?" I took a sip. "Blech. They've replaced the vodka, the schnapps, and the creme de cassis with generic grenadine. I've had lollipops with better balance, nuance, and less red dye Number 40." I glanced around at my surroundings. "I guess I shouldn't expect much at a beach bar, and a temporary one at that. But you can't beat the view."

Grenville Beach, our current location and the site of the food festival I was here to judge, was a prime example of the pristine beaches and sparkling waters of the Gulf Coast of Louisiana. After flying to New Orleans the previous day, we had driven through swamps, marshes, bayous—I wasn't sure which was which, but I was fairly certain we saw them all. Mostly, we had viewed flat, sea level Louisiana. No wonder the colorful houses here were on stilts. But the long drive had been worth it, since we were now surrounded by palm trees, tall dunes, and crashing waves. There were even dolphins jumping and playing in the surf.

I sipped the terrible drink, then reached up to make certain that my hat was secure on my head. While my brother had inherited our parents' Italian skin tone, I was a throwback to my grandmother's Scandinavian roots, with blond hair and skin that burned after two minutes of solar ray exposure. So, in addition to marinating myself in sunscreen, I tried to stay within the shadows as we walked between the twenty or so temporary booths. It helped, slightly, with both the sun and the blistering July temperatures.

Despite the heat, I shivered as I checked out the various chefs working on station prep.

One of the chefs must have noticed my discomfort at the type of meat being prepared. "Hey, Chef Jackie. Look, it's the Can-Can." The man—Richard, according to the apron wrapped around his muscular frame—set down his knife, then picked up two of the many limbs in front of him and started humming notes, kicking the gangly legs up in the air.

"Very funny, Chef. You have good rhythm," I admitted. "But you've disrupted my happy fantasy that everyone was working on chicken wings, and not frog legs."

Richard took the legs, tucked them below his armpits, and mimicked flying. "Is that better?"

"Better," I gave him a grin as we continued winding our way through the rows.

"See, the bad drink is going to come in handy," Daniel said. "It will numb your taste buds so you won't actually taste the frog legs."

"Tasting the frog legs is the entire reason I'm here. A desperate effort to restart my career, remember?" Oh, how the mighty have fallen, I thought. "Although I won't be doing that tonight. That'll be tomorrow." I pointed out a raised dais with two tables, where another chef and I would do the judging at noon the next day. "Tonight's just for loading equipment and a few hours of prep."

He raised an eyebrow. "Those things are little. Why do they take so long to prepare?"

I shook my head. "Daniel, your idea of cooking involves a microwave, so everything is quick for you. Do you see a microwave anywhere?"

He glanced around the beachfront parking lot, now repurposed as a multi-kitchen competition area. The booths were standard-sized, aluminum frames with a canvas roof and roll-down walls, each about 12 feet by 12 feet. Most of the contestants had raised their walls, so we were able to view the majority of the cooking area. The spaces were crammed with prep tables, portable cooking equipment, and generators, the latter of which provided a steady cacophony that, sadly, drowned out the sound of the ocean.

"No," Daniel admitted. "Definitely no microwaves."

"Right. The actual cooking of the froggies should be fast. But we chefs like to make it more exciting, zhuzh it up. Brines, marinades, dry rubs. Those take time."

One of the nearby chefs nodded her approval at my statement.

"I seem to recall soaking them in milk, too, in culinary school, which is probably the last time I had frog legs," I mused.

"Do they really taste like chicken?" Daniel asked, a dubious look on his face.

"Mostly. The texture is similar. I suppose you could say that it's fishy-tasting chicken, which tastes better than it sounds, trust me. My reluctance for tomorrow's tasting is that I keep thinking about the poor little frogs. In general, I'm fine eating just about anything. But for some reason, I just can't get the idea of the cute little animal out of my head when I eat frog legs. I had the same problem when I ate an emu burger." It didn't help that when we drove past the swamps, I kept picturing a banjo-playing Kermit the Frog, singing about rainbows and connections. That tended to dampen my appetite.

"If ze frogs didn't want to be eaten, ze frogs shouldn't be so delicious," a deep male voice said.

I reluctantly turned around, recognizing the voice as Henri Clement's, my fellow judge for this event. I had been trying my best to avoid him, but now he waddled my way, wearing a white toque and chef's coat that might have fit him twenty years and forty pounds ago. I knew Henri from my days as a celebrity chef, before the alcohol ruined things. Well, before I ruined things.

I had to be nice to him, since he was the reason I had secured this gig at the Grenville Beach Frog Legs Festival. It was only the second event I had attended since leaving rehab, but the less I thought of that first festival, the better. Starting over was hard.

In order to recover my career, I needed to be grateful and gracious to Chef Henri. Even if it was difficult.

"As my cousin, famed frog farmer René Clement, once said, 'The frog is like a woman: only their thighs are good.'"

His words were annoying enough, but they were made worse by the accompanying leer at my legs. I fought the urge to tug down my flowered sundress. As his gaze slowly moved up, I felt my brother vibrating in anger next to me.

I nudged Daniel, while reminding myself just how much I needed this job. "I see now why Frenchmen are known for being so romantic." Trust me, that was nicer than most of the things I was thinking.

Another competitor, Brenda Sterling, laughed and gave a thumbs-up. One of my first jobs had been as Brenda's sous chef, so I was glad she had my back.

Henri seemed less appreciative of her sign of support.

"Of course," Henri said, with a disgusted look in Brenda's direction. "Some women have too much in the thigh department, if you know what I mean."

Brenda stiffened. I knew her weight had always been a touchy subject. When I had started working in television, she'd been happy for me, but had admitted jealousy, wondering if her appearance held her back from similar opportunities.

I was instantly irritated for her. "And some men have too little in other departments, if you know what I mean." Part of me regretted saying that—I really did need this job—but I've never been good at keeping my mouth shut. The cooks in my kitchen had compared me to Gordon Ramsay, although much nicer and with 95 percent less cursing.

Henri spun on his heel and left the aisle. Daniel glared at his back as he retreated.

"Thanks, Jackie. I'm glad you put that man in his place," Brenda said, bending over her cutting board.

While she might not have appealed to Henri, I had always thought she was strikingly beautiful. Her dark skin was set off by her spotless chef whites, bright blue cornrows peeked out from under her yellow bandana, and her body was crazy strong from years of hard work as a chef. I wouldn't want to mess with her, especially when she had a knife in her hand, like now. She was mincing some garlic with great skill and, I suspect, some redirected anger.

"I've always admired your knife skills," I said, stepping around the edge of the booth to join her. I waved at Miguel Alvarez, her sous chef. "And your knives." I slid a large chef's knife out from a cloth knife carrier case and held it up to the light, admiring the edge. "I hate to admit it, but Japanese knives really do offer precision."

"That entire set is custom made for me, too. For my hand." She angled the knife to show the monogram on the side: SR.

I laughed as I realized that she used the initials from her restaurant—Sterling Reputation—rather than her own. I couldn't blame her.

She grabbed an onion and set it on her cutting board. "Here, try it," she said, stepping back from the cutting board. "I need some onions for the marinade."

"Minced?" I asked, setting down my barely touched drink. When she nodded, I balanced the onion in one hand and the blade in the other. I barely felt any resistance as I sliced the onion in half. A few seconds more and there was a pile of tiny onion cubes on the board. "Nice! As easy as, well, a hot knife through butter."

"And trust me, the custom fit means it's even better for me," Brenda said, taking back the knife.

"But I'm still not convinced to abandon my German knives." I had to defend my own cutlery.

"Getting help from the judges, are you, Brenda?" asked Richard, he of the Can-Can dance, from his nearby booth.

"You know we need some type of help, if we're going to beat you." Brenda set down her knife, placed her hands on her hips, and turned to me. "Chef Richard Hargrove here has been the Frog Legs champion the past three years. Also won the Rayne Frog Festival cook-off five years in a row."

He shrugged. "What can I say? I've been lucky."

"Well, I wish we could be lucky enough to get rid of Chef Henri," Brenda said, frowning down the aisle where Henri was leaning over a young female chef. "That man. Someone should go rescue Kayla Phillips from Handy Henri."

My brother immediately headed over three booths to save Kayla; he's just that type of person. Not anxious to deal with Henri again, I dawdled, even to the point of taking another sip of my drink, before following him to extricate the poor girl, or rather, poor woman. I had recently turned thirty, so I wasn't much older than she was.

Unfortunately, I had plenty of experience dealing with handsy cooks. There's something about those heated kitchens that makes everyone hot to trot. I often had to redirect kitchen employees from lust back to lunch, from sex back to sautéing. Usually, it was peer to peer and consensual, but I had known some executive chefs, like Henri, who abused their power.

Henri was scowling at Daniel when I arrived.

"Chef Henri, can I speak with you regarding our judging criteria? I just wanted to clarify a few things." While Daniel stayed with Kayla, I drew Chef Henri away, stepping onto the sandy beach. He appeared annoyed to be parted from the pretty young chef. She threw me a grateful look as she tucked her dark hair under her beanie.

Henri glared at me. "What could you possibly need to clarify about frog legs? Do they taste good? *Fini*. Alcohol hasn't killed all your taste buds, has it?"

I suppose he was getting me back for my size comment. "It has not. I haven't had a drop in over four months."

He peered down at the drink in my hand and raised an eyebrow.

"It's virgin." I realized this was a bad choice of word to use around him. "Non-alcoholic. And incredibly nasty." Since Daniel was distracted, I took the opportunity to pour my drink onto some beach grass. "I still have a chef's palate; I'm just not as experienced with frog legs."

"Then you are missing out, *mademoiselle*. Frog legs are so succulent, so moist and delicious."

I did my best not to laugh when he actually tapped his fingers to his mouth and kissed them with a loud *mwah,* like an effusive Frenchman in a silly cartoon.

"They are the epitome of French cooking, when treated properly." He sneered down the line, where some chefs were setting up a portable deep fryer. "That is *not* treating them properly."

"No, but it is Cajun. I assume these are Cajun frogs."

Henri rolled his eyes. "Yes, but I try not to hold that against them. They are, of course, inferior to French frog legs. But since the Cajun Catch Company is sponsoring the contest, they are providing the product for all the chefs." He pointed toward a large refrigeration truck parked outside the cooking area, with Cajun Catch Company in large letters, with each "C" being formed by a cartoon shrimp and the "J" in Cajun by an alligator tail.

"So, who is going to give Chef Richard some competition this year?" I asked Henri, gesturing at the other chefs around us.

"Ah." He rubbed at his chin. I suspect if he'd had a mustache, he would have started to twirl one of the ends. "I believe that Chef Kayla has a good chance; she is talented. And I have to admit it, Chef Gabriel has performed well in the past years. He might also have an advantage this year, since his daughter spent time under me and probably picked up many useful techniques. Chef Leonard came in second last year with his salt and pepper frogs—he is one to watch. Chef Frederick has a very good garlic frog with Herbes de Provence. Although I suspect that choice was him trying to cater to my taste." He sneered.

I couldn't help it. "So we could say he was toadying up to you? Pun intended."

Chef Henri stared at me, a blank look on his face.

"Get it? *Toad*-y-ing. Toad. Frog. Never mind." I frowned as I realized that Henri had skipped my friend. "What about Chef Brenda?"

He waved a hand in the air dismissively. "Yes, yes, of course. Chef Brenda caters to the local crowd with her Frog Legs Piquante. I find it too spicy, as the name suggests. Also, too many ingredients. Too complicated, much like a woman."

Henri's eyes brightened as he approached another table. At first, I thought he was interested in the food, then noticed the young chef's assistant in the booth. When she noticed us, her face flushed as red as her hair. She quickly spun on her rubber clogs and headed toward the portable bathrooms. She must have been desperate to take refuge there.

Henri quickly shifted his attention to the other person in the booth, an older man with a clean-shaven head and colorful tattoos covering every visible surface, including his scalp. "Bonjour, Chef Gabriel. It is good to see you once again."

"Chef Henri," he muttered in a manner that did not suggest delight. Gabriel glanced my way, then did a double take. "Wait. Chef Jackie, right? From 'Dinners, Drinks, and Decadence'?"

I nodded. "That *was* my show. Until the Gourmet Channel canceled it last year. And I recognize you as well," I rushed to add before needing to explain why it was canceled. "Chef Gabriel Zimmerman, right? Of Café Z? Your restaurant was featured in an article in my in-flight magazine."

"Really?" Henri said, his eyebrows raising to the level of his toque. "How much did you have to pay someone for that?"

I could see Gabriel clenching his jaw. "I didn't. They contacted me, said they wanted to showcase the best New Orleans restaurants." He paused. "Chef Henri's restaurant wasn't in that article, was it, Chef Jackie?"

I tried not to laugh as I shook my head.

"You will excuse me," Chef Henri said. "I am needed elsewhere."

I was relieved when Henri left, but I watched to make certain he wasn't after some other young woman. Richard seemed to be his target, so I sighed and turned my attention back to Gabriel.

"Well, I probably lost his vote," Gabriel said, not seeming too upset.

"Don't worry," I said. "I'll be fair, trust me. On another note, I hope your assistant is okay. It seemed like she wanted nothing to do with Chef Henri."

Gabriel's eyes darkened. "No, Taylor definitely didn't. I wish I knew why." He sighed. "She's my daughter. And since we wanted her to get a range of experience after culinary school, she started as a line cook for Chef Henri. I'm still not certain exactly what happened, but she quit suddenly and begged me for a job. I started her off as an *escuelerie*, to make certain no one accused me of favoritism."

I smiled, knowing that *escuelerie* was a fancy word for dishwasher.

"She's worked hard ever since and has been rising quickly. She'll soon replace me as executive chef." He held out an arm to the returning Taylor, who tucked herself into his embrace.

"No one will ever replace you, Dad, but thank you."

Gabriel introduced us, but Taylor's attention was distracted as she glanced around. I could tell the moment when she saw Henri. "Don't like Chef Henri, huh?" I asked.

"He's a great chef," Taylor said, obviously thinking more, but not saying it.

"No disagreement here," I said. "But not such a great person, and that's just my experience as a fellow chef. With his ego, I bet he was a lousy boss."

Taylor kept her lips firmly sealed.

I shot a glance at Gabriel, hoping he'd get my signal that I'd like a minute alone with his daughter. Catching on quickly, he released her. "Let me go pick up the frog legs from the truck." He ducked under a railing and jogged away.

"Real subtle, Dad," Taylor said to his retreating back. She turned to me. "Look, I know I've got a good set-up, working at my dad's place. Seems like I'd be safe enough to badmouth a former boss. But the restaurant business is small. And Chef Henri is powerful. He can make or break people. Restaurants, too. I'm not risking it just to get things off my chest."

"I get that," I said. "I probably should take that same advice, considering how precarious my own career is."

She furrowed her brow. "But you're Chef Jackie. You're a star."

"I *was* a star. Now I'm...I'm a meteor. Or wait, doesn't it become a meteorite after it falls on the ground? Or is it the opposite?" I shook my head. "Doesn't matter. My point is that I need to get up off the ground. I should also exercise caution. Still..." I paused. "That doesn't mean we let those in power get away with things. We, as women, are taught not to make a fuss, not to cause a scene. But that just helps those with power retain it."

Taylor nodded. "I totally agree, Chef Jackie. And if certain lines had been crossed, I would be telling everyone, including the police. But it was mostly insinuations, innuendos, and other things I couldn't prove."

"Understood." I glanced over at Henri. "That's usually the way, isn't it? So they can deny they meant any harm, or say you misunderstood their intentions."

When Gabriel returned, carrying a large box, I shook my head at his questioning glance.

"That's a lot of frog legs," I said, surprised. "How many do you have to cook?"

"We each have to make around 100 frog legs, enough for the judges and everyone who bought tasting tickets," Taylor said, taking the box from her father. "Thankfully, the legs are provided for us as part of the entry fee."

"And you have total freedom on how to prepare them?" I asked.

"Yes," Gabriel said. "You'll have quite a variety tomorrow. Grilled frog legs, Kung Pao frog legs, Provencal frog legs, stuffed frog legs, frog leg gumbo, fried frog legs—"

"Dad," Taylor interrupted. "You're starting to sound like that guy from 'Forrest Gump.'"

"How do you prepare them?" I asked, amused by Taylor.

"Firecracker Frog Legs. I hope you like spicy," Gabriel said, rubbing his hands together.

"Usually I do. Although I'm worried my definition of spicy might be different from yours. Good luck!" I said, and excused myself to catch up to Daniel, who was still with Kayla. I was surprised to see her wiping away tears. I glanced down—no onions in sight.

"Is everything okay?" I asked. Stupid question, since obviously it wasn't.

"It's fine," Kayla answered. She went over to the hand washing station, used a paper towel, and carefully dabbed at her face. "I was just telling your brother about some problems I've been having. But it's fine." She gave Daniel a long look.

After spending some time asking her about her preparation, we left her to her frog legs. "What was that about?" I asked Daniel the second we were away from her booth.

"She asked me not to tell you," Daniel answered, but being his sister, I could hear the reluctance in his voice. He wanted to spill. I bet I could get him to reveal it if I pushed hard enough. But out of respect for Kayla, I refrained. Plus, I suspected she had a similar story to Taylor's.

"Attention all chefs!" Henri bellowed from a few booths away. "You have two hours left to prep before we close down for the evening."

I felt the pace around me quicken at that announcement.

"People are getting excited now," Daniel commented.

"This is the most important time, really, as you prep for tomorrow, and the possibility of a grand prize." I shook some sand out of my flip-flops.

"How much is the prize?"

"Five thousand dollars!" I was surprised by the high amount until Henri said they had a sponsor. "Plus, if it's a restaurateur rather than an amateur, they'll get a special write-up in the *New Orleans Gourmet Guide* for best frog legs. That's probably worth more than the prize."

The next hour went quickly, as chefs raced to the finish, trying to get everything done and leave enough time to clean up. I was worried for a few contestants whose knife skills were slightly concerning. But, in the end, everyone seemed to have kept the same number of digits they came in with.

The closest anyone came to serious injury was Henri. A half hour before close, I noticed a commotion and ran over to find Henri involved in a pushy-shovey match. Since his opponent reminded me of The Incredible Hulk, minus the green color, Henri was losing badly.

Henri was attempting to escape from the booth, but The Hulk blocked his way and aggressively poked a finger into his chest.

Andrea Gomez, one of the contestants, tried to insert herself between the two combatants. I jammed myself into the middle with her, pulling Henri as she dragged away the other man. I managed to steer Henri out of the booth while Andrea tried to calm down The Hulk.

"Paul, stop it!" She grabbed his arm to hold him back.

It didn't work.

The Hulk—Paul—followed us out into the aisles. "Stay away from my wife," he yelled.

"I was only attempting to—," Henri protested, pivoting around and stopping in place.

"I *know* what you were trying to do," Paul interrupted, accenting his words with a slight shove.

Chefs' clogs are both comfortable and slip-resistant in a kitchen. They aren't, however, the best footwear for a wrestling match. Henri stumbled backwards, fell out of his shoes, and hit the ground.

I risked my life, got between Henri and Paul, and reached out a hand to help the fallen chef stand up. "Apologize, now," I whispered.

Henri's eyes flashed, but after a quick look at The Hulk, he cleared his throat. "My apologies for any misinterpretation of my intentions."

When Paul still stood there with clenched fists, Andrea smacked his arm. "Paul," she growled.

"Fine. But stay away from her." He stalked back to Andrea's booth.

I quickly muscled Henri away from the scene. "I don't suggest hitting on our contestants, but if you do, perhaps you shouldn't pick one with a husband massive enough to snap you in two. I don't think we want broken chef's legs on the menu."

Henri straightened his toque, which had gotten knocked askew in the struggle. "I wasn't 'hitting on' her. I was discussing her knife techniques. It is not my fault that her behemoth of a husband disagreed with my method of demonstration. I thought I could help her, as you say, 'get a feel' for it."

I thought he was the one getting a feel for it, or at least trying. "Of course, Chef."

Richard stepped out from his booth. "Is everything okay?"

"Yes, yes. Of course." Henri brushed at his jacket, then straightened it.

When he leaned over to wipe at his black and white houndstooth pants, Richard raised an eyebrow at me over Henri's bent form. I shrugged.

"Well, if you're okay, I've got some froggies to brine." Richard stepped back into his booth and stirred something in a stock pot resting on a metal counter.

Curious, I followed him. "What's in the brine?"

He tapped his finger to his nose. "Ancient family secret."

"Whatever he does to them, zey are exquisite." Henri's accent always got thicker whenever he talked about the frog legs. "Zey are so succulent, so tender, so moist and delicious. Reminds me of the frog legs of my youth. I don't know how you do it."

"It's the magic of the brine and the pressure cooker."

I peeked into the pot, which was filled with a brownish liquid. "Let me see if I can figure it out." I grabbed a spoon, dipped it in, and let the brine sit on my tongue a moment. "Salt, obviously. Brown sugar? That might get you some nice caramelization. Are those pink peppercorns? Interesting choice."

Richard nodded. "I find it gives a floral note, which pairs well with the cream sauce I create."

"It adds some type of magic," Henri added. "That I can tell you."

Richard poured the brine into a plastic bin, added in frog legs, closed the lid, and stored it all in a waist-high refrigerator. "Just need to clean up and I'm done." He placed the pot in a deep hotel pan already filled with dirty utensils and bowls.

"Thanks for showing me your ancient secret recipe, Chef," I said. "I look forward to trying it tomorrow."

"May I help you take everything to the wash station, Chef?" Henri asked, grabbing a cutting board. I'm sure that was a big help.

I took my leave from the two men to wander some more. After speaking with several other contestants, I settled down at one of the many picnic tables under the dining tent. It was mostly empty today, but tomorrow it would be overrun with people who would pay to taste the cook-off entries.

Pulling out my phone, I checked out the potential winning contestants Chef Henri had mentioned. Obviously, I was familiar with Brenda Sterling's eatery, a farm-to-table restaurant with amazing reviews and mouth-watering entrees, including the frog legs piquante I'd be trying tomorrow. Some of the reviews made me nervous, asserting how spicy the dish was. I could handle a certain level of heat, but I wasn't the biggest fan of kill-you spice as it overpowers the other flavors in a dish. Checking out the information on the website's About page, I was impressed to see she had two more restaurants in the works, in addition to a recent expansion of Sterling Reputation.

Chef Richard's site looked sleek and sharp, as did the photos of his restaurant, Délicieux. The description proclaimed that the restaurant 'combined the best of French and Southern cuisine, with a focus on environmentalism and sustainability.' The seafood items on the menu definitely fit that theme. There was no red snapper or grouper, two fish that were at risk due to overfishing. Instead, he featured hogfish, mackerel, and a variety of preparations for lionfish, which I knew was an invasive species.

His bio was impressive as well. Not just his cooking experience, but also his extracurricular activities. Notably, Richard had played running back during his college years at LSU.

Kayla was the sous chef at Louisiana in the Lobby, a hotel restaurant near the Louis Armstrong International airport. Even though people often sneer at them, I've had plenty of fine meals at hotel restaurants. The reviews were overwhelmingly positive, and an article about the restaurant mentioned Kayla specifically, saying she had been a saucier at The French Laundry. Impressive.

I wasn't able to find anything about Chef Leonard, making me wonder if he was an amateur cook. There were some amateurs at this cook-off, so that was very possible.

I hadn't yet met Chef Frederick; a few people had mentioned that he didn't bother showing up for prep day. I went to his restaurant's website next and was not impressed. Creole Kitchen was an uninspired and mundane name and the menu seemed to match. His bio listed every job he'd held, proving that he didn't stay in one kitchen for very long. In addition to many other assignments, he had been sous chef for both Henri and Richard. Obviously, the food world in Louisiana was as incestuous as in California.

I was already familiar with Chef Gabriel's restaurant from the airplane magazine, where they talked about his juvenile delinquency and how he turned his life around when he discovered cooking. Still, wanting to know more, I checked out Café Z's website and was further inspired by his story and his talent. Hopefully, I could be as strong as he was with my own recovery.

And the menu was intriguing, with a number of creative combinations that sounded amazing. I added his place to my hit list for this week. Since I wanted to thank my brother for his support, we had arranged to stay in New Orleans for a few days after the contest so I could show him the best Louisiana had to offer.

Daniel found me in the tent. "Are you about finished here, Jackie?" he asked, whipping out a brochure. "It says there's going to be a frog parade at seven on the boardwalk. We can't miss that!"

My brother loves oddities, so I knew he was sincere. I looked around and noticed most of the chefs were gone. "I need food first, though. Anything but frog legs."

Daniel and I grabbed an oyster po' boy and a shrimp étouffée from a nearby café. Then, we joined the crowd to await the festivities. Like many parades, this one started with the local high school marching band. They weren't too bad. Shriners drove by in their little cars, little girls in frog costumes twirled batons, and firefighters threw candy from their vehicles to waiting children. The parade ended with a float featuring this year's Frog Princesses, a bored looking teenager and a young girl dressed as a tadpole. Even the crowd was into the theme. I saw two teens dressed up as Prince Naveen and Princess Tiana from the Disney movie. Others wore frog hats, frog socks, and frog shirts. I hadn't seen this much green since last St. Patrick's Day.

One older man in frog overalls came by with an accordion. The crowd cheered. As he started playing a familiar-sounding song, everyone gathered in large circles to dance.

"It's the Chicken Dance," I said to Daniel. "Or at least a froggy version of it."

"Come on," Daniel said, pulling me into a nearby circle. "Let's do it."

"I'm not sure that I've ever danced sober," I said, as I let myself get dragged.

We caught on quickly. The moves were a little different from the Chicken Dance, starting out with bouncing, then some leaps, then the same twisting motion from the Chicken Dance, and then followed by frog hops.

While fun, the hops and jumps and squats were terrifyingly reminiscent of the killer workouts my former trainer would put me through, earning him the nickname Salvador the Sadistic. If they started doing burpees in this frog dance, I was quitting.

I had to admit it, Grenville Beach threw a good bash. After a spectacular sunset, we danced and partied into the night.

"Okay, I think we've earned ourselves some beignets," I declared. "Hopefully, there's a place open this late." I tapped the shoulder of a woman who looked like a local in the know. Ten minutes later, at her recommendation, we were once again near the competitor area, sitting on the boardwalk and enjoying Louisiana's excellent version of donuts.

"These are so good," I said. "Crispy outside, pillowy inside. Just as good as Café du Monde." When we had flown into New Orleans, that iconic restaurant had been our first stop.

Daniel stated his agreement around a mouthful of dough and powdered sugar. "Mmrrph."

"So well said, Daniel. Have you thought of a career as a food critic?" I laughed, then stopped suddenly, spotting a person-shaped figure walking through the booth area. "Who's that going into the competitor area?"

Daniel swallowed before answering this time. "I'm not sure. Maybe a security guard?"

"That makes sense. What with all that equipment." We watched as the dark figure walked confidently through the competitors' area, beaming a flashlight around. "You're probably right." I popped the rest of my beignet in my mouth, enjoying that last sweet bite. "It's late. Let's head to the hotel and get some sleep. As they say, the early bird catches the frog."

* * *

Sadly, even though the beignet bakery was right next to the parking lot, I had to resist stopping in for another one the next morning. The green sheath dress I was wearing was already a little snug. There wasn't even a single beignet's worth of room. I did grab a café au lait, counting that against my burned calories from the Frog Dance.

I was up bright and early, determined to make a good impression on Chef Henri. Only a few competitors were here already, but I was happy to see Brenda. Although she didn't look happy at all.

"Hey girl, want me to grab you a coffee or something?" I asked, since the other chef seemed to be busy moving around her booth.

"Coffee would be wonderful, but what I want more is my filleting knife." She bent over, checking under a table.

"It's missing?"

"Yes, and I need it to prepare the frog legs. Manuel must have misplaced it during clean-up." She scowled at her sous chef.

Manuel held up his hands, protesting his innocence. "I'm sure I kept everything together when I went to wash up."

Having faced Brenda's wrath as her sous chef before, I defended the poor guy. "You know how easy it is to lose track of things when you're at these outdoor events. Everyone's vying for the same sink."

"Yeah, yeah. I know. But it's pissing me off."

"Is anything else missing?" I asked, though everything else seemed in its place, as Brenda's kitchens always were. She was the poster child for *mise en place*. No wonder she was irritated at a missing knife.

"No." She frowned and grabbed a paring knife from her roll. "This'll have to do. I've got to get started. Can you ask around, see if anyone has seen it?"

"Sure. And I'll let Chef Henri know as well, so that he's aware."

Brenda glanced up, clearly distracted. "I haven't seen him yet, which is odd. He's usually first on site."

Great. So now I was looking for a knife *and* a pompous chef.

I checked in with everyone, which gave me the opportunity to talk to Gabriel and Taylor. I also made certain to greet Kayla, hoping she'd decide that I was just as trustworthy as my brother and spill the deets on Henri.

No one had seen the knife, or Henri. Making it to the end of the row, I came to a booth that was still closed.

"Whose booth is this?" I asked the competitor next door, who I recognized as Andrea Gomez, Chef Henri's latest victim. The Hulk, aka Paul, was hunched on a stool in the booth, clearly on wife-guard duty. From the scowl on his face, he didn't seem the forgive and forget kind of guy.

Andrea didn't even look up from her chopping, "It's supposed to be for Chef Frederick, who never deigns to show up until nine am. He claims the pressure on him transfers to the frog and makes it more tender." She raised her head. "Did you know there are some oddballs in our profession?"

"That's definitely true." I flipped open the tent flap, stepped inside. And screamed.

The good news was, I had found Brenda's knife and the missing Henri.

The bad news: one was embedded in the other.

* * *

*Brenda's going to need a new knife.* Probably not my best thought, but it's what came to mind, even as I realized I needed to call the police. I fumbled for my phone as Andrea and her husband came to see what all the screaming was about.

The emergency operator picked up immediately. Kitchen accidents happened often, so this wasn't the first time I had called 9-1-1, but I still stuttered for a few seconds before speaking coherently. "I'm at the Grenville Beach Frog Festival. In the cook-off area. I found a man who's been stabbed."

"Is the assailant in the area? Are you currently in danger?" The voice on the other end of the call was calm and quiet, which reminded me to take a deep breath.

I shook my head, then realized she couldn't see me over the phone. "No. I think he's been dead for a while."

"Are you certain that he's dead?"

"Oh yeah. I'm not a doctor, but I'm fairly certain that a person can't bleed that much and survive. There are multiple knife wounds on his body." Henri would have been upset with the bloody stains on his white chef's coat, but that was probably not a big concern for him now. "The knife is currently stuck in him. And his eyes are open, staring."

Paul crouched down and touched Henri's arm. "He's cold. I mean, not cold cold. More like room temperature. Well, not room temperature, but..." He cringed.

At least I wasn't the only one saying stupid things. I repeated his information to the operator.

I listened to her, then relayed her message to Paul and Andrea. "She says we need to leave the area, not let anyone else into it." Protecting the crime scene, I realized as I exited the booth. And it was definitely a crime scene. I doubted that Chef Henri had plunged the knife into his own chest, and even if he had, I doubt he'd have been able to do so repeatedly. The lyrics from "Cell Block Tango" kept running through my head, about running into a knife. Running into a knife ten times.

I saw Brenda, Gabriel, and Taylor among the group that had gathered around the booth. Paul was holding everyone back, arms wide. No one was getting past The Hulk. I walked over to Brenda.

"What happened?" Brenda's eyes were wide.

"It's Chef Henri. He's dead. Stabbed." I wondered if I should mention it was her knife but decided that would be cruel. Instead, I just finished with, "A lot."

She squeezed her eyes shut. "Please, please, please tell me that my knife was not involved."

See? She had figured it out on her own anyway. "I'd love to say it's not, but..."

"Oh hell. I've never had any trouble with the police in my life, but they're going to say I did it."

"Why would they think you did it?" Then I realized she might be worried, not because of her knife being involved, but because of her skin color. "You didn't have a reason to kill him, did you?"

She waved a hand toward the crowd. "Who here *doesn't* have a reason to kill him? He is—" She paused, took a breath. "That is, he *was* a jerk. Abused his staff, abused his status. Sneered at anyone who didn't have a French culinary background. I hated him, but not enough to kill him. Still, I'm going to get blamed, I know it."

"Do you have an alibi?" I asked.

"No." She cursed. "Jimmy usually attends this with me, but he stayed home this year. Tia had her freshman orientation at Tulane and we wanted one of us there with her."

Jimmy was her husband, I knew. It was hard to believe that their daughter was already starting college.

I saw Daniel pushing through the crowd and excused myself to get to him.

"Are you okay?" he asked, grabbing my arms. "They said someone was killed."

He looked distressed, so I didn't point out that it obviously wasn't me. "I'm okay. It's Chef Henri. I found him. And it looks like it was Brenda's knife that killed him."

Daniel flicked his eyes toward my former boss.

"She didn't do it, Daniel. I worked with her for years. She has a temper, but not that bad. And she'd never kill in cold blood."

I could hear the wail of sirens in the distance. Over Daniel's shoulder, I saw Kayla being comforted by Richard. They must have both just shown up. Neither had been around when I arrived. "What about Kayla?'

Daniel took a step back. "Kayla?"

"Could she have done it? She was obviously upset yesterday."

He bit his lip, a telltale sign. "No. She has no reason to kill Chef Henri."

"Daniel, I can tell when you're lying. This isn't a time for secrets. A man is dead. And I'm worried for Brenda." I could see police rushing our way. "Tell me quick."

"Henri promised her that if she came to his hotel room, he'd make sure she won the competition. She didn't want to do it, although she was tempted by the prize money. She's drowning in debt and doesn't get paid much, even though she does all the work at the hotel."

"Was she going to go?" I asked, stepping back for the rushing ambulance crew. I wanted to tell them there was no reason to hurry.

"I don't know." Daniel furrowed his brow. "I don't think so. I wish we could help her out."

"Me too, bro." In my flush, pre-alcohol days, I had loved being able to assist others.

But Kayla wasn't going to be winning the cook-off today. I strongly suspected it would be canceled.

* * *

It hadn't been too bad talking to the police officers about what I'd seen. Usually, I'd rather cook a gourmet meal for thirty toddlers than talk to the authorities, but at least they hadn't brought out any thumbscrews. Yet.

Now I was sitting in the same tent I'd been in the day before, when I was looking up all the information about the contestants. This time, however, I wasn't on my phone. The police hadn't taken our phones, but they had warned us that they could get a search warrant to review them, so anything we did now could be admissible in court. So I just sat there, with nothing to do other than watch my fellow tent mates. The police had separated everyone, placing one person at each picnic table, so we couldn't even talk to each other. I suspect that was the point.

Instead, I used my imagination.

Who could have done it? One of the victims of Henri's sexual harassment? My eyes flitted from Kayla to Taylor to Andrea. Or, of course, it could be a protective male. Taylor's father gave her a job to shield her from Henri; could he have taken things further? And, of course, I already knew that The Hulk was willing to resort to physical violence to defend his wife's honor.

My eyes met another caring male, but I knew this one was innocent. The phrase "he wouldn't hurt a fly" literally applied to my brother—he was the type that gently moved spiders and bugs outside rather than kill them. Daniel raised his eyebrows, then mouthed "are you okay?" I shrugged. As okay as one could be after finding a dead body and being interrogated.

Brenda sat at the picnic table next to my brother. She looked terrified. Still, I was as convinced of her innocence as I was of my brother's. I had worked under her for three years, and while I'd seen her angry, I'd never seen her make any physical moves. No, she preferred eviscerating people with her words. I'd seen grown men brought to tears by her razor-sharp tongue-lashing. Even when she was met by violence, like the saucier who threw an entire pan of au jus at her, she had effortlessly evaded the scalding liquid, handed him a mop, and then promptly fired him after he cleaned it up.

But now, she looked scared. When she glanced over at me, I copied Daniel's actions, silently asking if she was okay. She shook her head, held up her hand to demonstrate that it was shaking. Then she jerked upright when her name was called. I saw a brief look of panic, then she closed her eyes and seemed to collect herself. "Heard!" she called out.

I smiled at her use of that common kitchen acknowledgement.

We had all spoken to the police after they arrived, but then had to wait in the tent. Hours later, two plainclothes detectives had arrived, probably from the homicide department. I had hoped not to deal with their type again, I thought, remembering the crab festival I had judged.

After about thirty minutes, it was my turn with the detectives. I wasn't as nervous as Brenda, but it was close. A uniformed officer led me to a booth away from the cooking areas, which originally was going to be used to check in the festival attendees and was now being used for interrogations—I mean, interviews.

"Hello Ms. Norwood." The first detective, a dark-haired 40-something man wearing khakis and a blue polo shirt, welcomed me and waved toward a chair that had been set up across from a folding table. At the table was another plainclothes detective, this one blond and wearing khakis and a brown shirt. "My name is Detective Rodriguez, this is my partner Detective Paulsen. We understand you found the body?"

I swallowed hard. "That is correct."

"Can you go over the circumstances that led to you finding the deceased?" Paulsen asked.

I didn't want to, but I recited what had happened, from talking to Brenda, to looking for the knife, to finding the knife and the deceased.

Detective Paulsen shuffled through his notes. "This is Brenda Sterling? And you were looking for her knife when you found the body?"

I nodded, then realized that he was focused on his notes. "Yes."

"And you thought it would be in an empty booth?"

"I was just searching everywhere."

"Why would the knife have been there, since no one had used it?"

"Detective Paulsen, you would not believe what happens at these outdoor events. Things get lost all the time and turn up in the darnedest places. Like I said, I was searching everywhere."

"Had you met Ms. Sterling before this event?"

Hoping that Brenda had been truthful with the cops, I answered honestly. "Yes, I worked under her for three years as a sous chef."

"When was this?"

I wracked my brain for a moment. "About five years ago."

"And did you leave amicably? Or were you fired?"

"I left to be the executive chef at my own restaurant. Plus, I had an opportunity for a television show." I was slightly perturbed that they didn't recognize me. I assumed they were not the biggest fans of the Gourmet Channel.

Detective Paulsen held up a hand. "Wait. You're *that* Jackie Norwood? From the Gourmet Channel?"

Huh, maybe he *was* a fan.

He rolled his eyes. "My ex-wife loved cooking shows. That's all she watched, even though she never did any actual cooking herself. I think my favorite part of getting a divorce was that I don't have to watch that stupid channel anymore."

Or not. On the bright side, this probably meant that he didn't know that I had lost my show.

Detective Rodriguez spoke up. "Wasn't your show cancelled?" He furrowed his brow. "Something about you drinking?"

I sighed. "Yes. Seven months ago. A little later I entered rehab and have been sober ever since. Next question?"

"What was your relationship with Chef Henri?" Paulsen asked.

"We worked together on various food shows, judged a few episodes of *Sliced* together. He knew I had...well, nothing else to do and thought my presence here might bring some additional guests." I glanced around. "Sadly, the throngs of my fans never showed up."

"So, no personal relationship with him?"

I wrinkled my nose. "Good Lord, no. He's old enough to be my father. Plus, I'm married." More of a technicality, since I was in the middle of a divorce, but I wasn't going to tell them—

"I thought I read that you were separated?" Rodriguez said.

Great. I ended up with the only food show watching/gossip mag reading cops in Louisiana. "Yes, but that, like the show cancellation, is a recent development."

"Did you get along with the victim?" Paulsen asked.

I paused, considering. He was a jerk, a letch, a—

"I'll take your silence as a no." Paulsen scribbled on his notepad.

"Wait a second, I was thinking," I rushed to explain. "I can't say I liked the victim. He was sexist, misogynist, probably a few other -ist words. He'd hit on any young woman and insult any others who didn't fit his ideal. I wouldn't trust him with my kid sister." Not that I had one. "But I didn't *hate* the man." That was way more than I had planned to say. I suspected that had been the detectives' goal.

Neither of them said anything after my outburst. The silence stretched.

"I didn't kill him or anything." More silence. "Trust me, if I were to kill each annoying womanizer I came across, I could fill the Gulf of Mexico." I pointed to the water. Then cursed silently. They'd done it again, got me to say stupid things.

I met Rodriguez's gaze, trying to impress him with my direct eye contact. This time, when they let the silence continue, I let them. I started listing cooking techniques in my head: Basting, frying, sautéing, blanching, sous vide...does one say sous viding? Boiling, braising, simmering—

Rodriguez broke before I did. "If you didn't kill him, do you know anyone who might have had a reason to do so?"

I thought of all the names and motives I had come up with in the tent. I was tempted to tell them what I knew about Kayla, but that was hearsay. Even if it put Brenda in the clear, I wasn't going to throw Kayla under the bus. "Again, he was not a nice individual. I think I'd have a hard time coming up with someone who didn't have some motive. But I'm not sure who hated him. You'd have to hate someone to kill them like that, wouldn't you?"

Paulsen snorted. "You'd be surprised. People kill for some pretty minor things."

The detectives walked me through the timeline again. That was time number three now. I wondered if they were trying to trip me up.

"Thank you, Ms. Norwood. We appreciate your cooperation. Hopefully, you'll be staying in Grenville for a few more days?"

I nodded. "Yes, although I doubt the festival will continue. That's a lot of frog legs that are going to be thrown out."

"They've already started that," Detective Paulsen said. "We found what looked like an entire batch of frog legs thrown away in one of the trash cans. Any idea why a chef would have done that?"

"It's possible they overcooked them, so they decided to start over." I frowned. "Although it's rather early to have prepared them, since the tasting wasn't supposed to be until noon." I checked my watch and was shocked to see it wasn't even eleven.

Paulsen shook his head. "These weren't cooked. They were raw."

I raised an eyebrow. "That's odd. Do you still have them?"

"We do," Detective Paulsen said, with a nod toward Rodriguez, who left the booth. "We also found it unusual, so we kept them just in case."

"What temperature were they when you found them?" I asked, wondering if someone had tossed them after rethinking their preparation this morning.

"I'd say they reached the same temperature as the environment."

"Okay, so then they probably weren't thrown away this morning. Maybe last night. Where were they found?"

"In a trash barrel near the southeast corner of this lot." When I just stared at him, Paulsen turned and pointed. "That section over there, where the officer is standing."

I followed the direction of his finger. A policewoman was standing in the back, near Gabriel's booth.

Rodriguez returned with an evidence bag full of frog legs. Looked like a full batch to me.

"May I?" I asked.

He handed me the bag. I turned it around in my hands, inspecting the meat inside. "You're right," I said to Paulsen. "It does look like an entire batch of raw frog legs. Not sure why anyone would just throw away..." I paused, recognizing the pink hue of the peppercorns stuck to the meat. "Huh. These are Chef Richard's frog legs. There are pink peppercorns in here."

"Why would he throw them away?"

I shook my head. "I don't know. More importantly, when? I was there when he poured the brine on the legs, and I saw him leave after storing everything in the fridge. And he didn't show up this morning until after the police arrived." Confused, I stared at the legs. "Can we check his refrigerator?"

After I pointed out Richard's booth, Paulsen let me accompany them to search the refrigerator. Inside, still barely fitting, was the brining bucket. "Open it up."

As they did, I could see the brine, with pink peppercorns floating on top. "Let me fish out a frog leg, although 'fish' might not be the right word there." I grabbed a slotted spoon from Richard's utensils and 'amphibianed' up two legs. "This one is still full of legs." I inspected the froggy appendage. "These might be bigger than the legs I saw him brine yesterday. I mean, brining often plumps up meat, but..." He must have switched out the frog legs, but when? He couldn't have done it yesterday evening or this morning so it had to have been...last night.

I glanced over at the dining tent and caught Richard watching me. When our eyes met, he bolted to his feet and sprinted toward the exit.

"Grab him," I yelled.

The policeman guarding the tent tried to intercept Richard, but he demonstrated his collegiate running back abilities and sidestepped to the left, evading the tackle. He juked to the right to avoid another police officer, slipped out of a horse collar tackle from Gabriel who grabbed at his shirt, and leapt over a picnic table. I thought he was gone...

Until my brother, who had never played football, stuck out a leg and tripped him. Richard ended up face first, sliding hard, before being tackled by several police officers.

"Nice move," Paulsen said.

"Yeah, but that would have earned him a fifteen-yard penalty on the football field for unsportsmanlike conduct," I said, beaming at my clever brother.

* * *

"Richard killed Henri because of the frog legs?" Brenda asked, as we sat in the tent the next day chowing down. The cook-off had been cancelled, but rather than waste the product, all of the chefs—minus Richard, of course—had prepared their dishes anyway. While the majority of the food had gone to a local homeless shelter, the cook-off competitors had saved enough for themselves to enjoy.

I had just taken a bite of Brenda's super spicy frog legs piquante, so I grabbed some water, the only thing close by. "Yes," I said, before taking a deep swallow, wishing for milk. "Richard eventually spilled the beans. According to Detective Paulsen, Richard was bringing in his own frog legs rather than those supplied by the contest. And these frog legs were from France."

"Which, of course, Henri preferred," Andrea guessed. She and Paul were sitting across from me. I was happy to finally see him relaxed, acting more like Bruce Banner than The Hulk.

"He did. And evidently, Henri realized it and accused Richard at the end of the prep day, giving Richard the idea to grab Brenda's knife during the chaos of clean-up. Richard offered him money if he didn't tell anyone, and suggested that they meet in Frederick's empty booth at midnight and he'd pay him."

"Oh, that explains it," Kayla said, then blushed.

"Explains what?" I asked as I reached for the salt and pepper frog legs.

"I went to Chef Henri's room that night—not to do what he wanted" she added quickly. "But to tell him that I was going to tell the contest officials *and* the local press about his offer to award me first place. But he wasn't there."

"I'm sorry, Jackie." My brother jumped into the conversation, probably to take the attention away from Kayla. "But you're telling me Chef Richard killed someone because he was using the wrong kind of frog legs?"

"Well, yes. First of all, he's been winning the prize money from the Cajun Catch Company these past years, so they would probably have demanded back the money. And it was a pretty big chunk of change. But more importantly, it would have ruined his reputation if it got out. Not just because he was cheating, but because Mr. Sustainable Food was using smuggled-in French frog legs. It's been illegal to commercially farm or hunt frog legs in France for decades. In fact, frog poachers get a really hefty fine and a year in jail if caught."

Taylor, sitting next to her father, was engrossed. "How did he get the illegal frogs into the festival? Weren't there guards?"

I nodded. "Evidently Richard has been bribing them for years, so that he could go in and replace the normal frog legs with his ill-gotten ones. The guards just conveniently took a break at an arranged time. In fact, according to Detective Paulsen, it was the guards' confession that finally got Richard to spill everything. When they realized they might be charged with aiding and abetting a murderer, they admitted to this arrangement."

"I'm surprised Detective Paulsen told you all this," Andrea said.

I rolled my eyes. "Yeah, I suspect that he had an ulterior motive to tell me. That was confirmed when he offered to take me out to dinner and tell me more. But he was, at least, gracious when I told him no." I had sworn off men during my recovery.

"Well, I'm grateful that we mostly know what happened." Gabriel said, spooning some of his Firecracker Frog Legs onto my plate. "Here, try these."

I took a bite, and immediately reached for my water glass. It was empty.

"I'll get you a drink," Daniel offered. "Not Sex on the Beach this time though, right?"

"No," I croaked. "Although I suppose I'd prefer Sex on the Beach to this trip's Murder on the Beach."

* * *

**Cathy Wiley** lives outside of Baltimore, Maryland, with one spoiled cat and an equally spoiled husband.

She is a member of Sisters in Crime, Mystery Writers of America, and the Short Mystery Fiction Society. She's written two mystery novels set in Baltimore, Maryland, and has had several short stories included in anthologies, one of which was a 2015 finalist for a Derringer Award for best short story.

She is currently working on a series featuring Jackie Norwood, the former celebrity chef trying to reboot her career. The first novel, CLAWS OF DEATH, will be published in the fall of this year. For more information about this series and her other books, and to sign up for her newsletter, visit www.cathywiley.com. You can also visit her author page on Facebook at https://www.facebook.com/CathyWileyAuthor

* * *

KILLER FROG LEGS RECIPE

*Ingredients:*

1.5-2 pounds of frog legs (or chicken wings)

*For the brine:*

4 cups water

1/4 cup kosher salt

3 tablespoons brown sugar (optional)

1 ½ tablespoons pink peppercorns, whole

1 ½ tablespoons pink peppercorns, crushed

*For the sauce:*

1/2 tablespoon pink peppercorns

1 tablespoon salted butter

4 tablespoons shallots, finely chopped

1/2 cup cream

1/4 cup brandy

1/4 teaspoon salt

Directions:

1. Purchase frozen frog legs (we found them at an Asian grocery store) or you can order them online. Defrost them in the refrigerator overnight.

2. Prepare the brine. Pour water into medium-sized pot, add salt and sugar. Heat mixture until salt and sugar dissolve. Cool mixture, pour into gallon bag. Add in the peppercorns, lightly crushing about half of them (in your hands, these are more fragile than regular peppercorns).

3. Zip up bag and place in a container in case of leaks. Place in refrigerator for 6-18 hours. (Please note, the longer they are in the brine, the saltier they are.)

4. Remove frog legs from the brine and discard the brine. Rinse thoroughly and pat dry with a paper towel. Coat with olive oil.

5. Turn the grill on to medium heat. (I used a gas grill, but charcoal would be fine, or even an indoor grill pan.)

6. While the grill is heating, prepare the sauce. Melt butter, then add shallots and cook until they are soft, about 3 minutes. Remove pan from heat and carefully add brandy. Return pan to heat and cook for 1-2 minutes. Add cream, peppercorns, and salt. Reduce heat, simmer for nine minutes. While the sauce is simmering, begin to work on the frog legs.

7. Grill frog legs over medium high heat, covered, 3-4 minutes per side. Cook until the meat is no longer pink and begins to separate from the bones. (If using a meat thermometer, the temp should be 145 degrees F.)

8. Plate the legs with the sauce and enjoy.

# Beach Party Body
## by Lucy Carol

CRASHING WAVES RUSHED OVER SMOOTH WET SAND, splashing against Madison's lower legs. She tried to hold still, her dark hair dashing about her face. The sea breeze carried a salt spray that cooled her skin, but the feel of the water at her feet, pulling back into the Pacific Ocean, gave her mild vertigo.

Madison's job at the moment was to stand just inside the water's edge, holding a reflector to bounce light at four gorgeous models. With the right illumination, Spenser's camera could work its charms. But the mild vertigo caused Madison's arms to shift, losing the correct angle no matter how hard she tried.

Her best friend, Spenser, had needed a last-minute assistant for this photo shoot to handle odd jobs, including holding the reflector.

"I'm sorry, Spenser. I never thought this would be so hard."

Spenser patiently instructed her. "Lift it higher a few inches. Now to the left."

Madison tried to follow instructions. "After all the times you've helped me out of a jam, I was hoping to return the favor."

"You are! I knew I could count on you. And for a beginner, you're doing great."

"I'm not great."

"You're fine."

"Not fine."

"Better than nothing?"

"Okay. I'll take that."

Spenser lowered her camera and smiled. "Let's just say my regular assistant has nothing to worry about." She let her camera hang from her neck as she approached Madison, then gently but firmly repositioned Madison's arms.

Madison let her arms be moved. "How is she, by the way? Any word?"

The models standing in the shallows held their pose, their sarongs whipping in the breeze, revealing colorful bathing suits underneath.

"Doc says her foot is just fractured, not broken. Now, don't move!"

Madison held ramrod still, keeping the reflector aimed at the models' faces as Spenser took her shots. Another wave splashed Madison's lower legs, than slowly retreated into the ocean, bringing that mild vertigo again. But she managed to hold still.

In the distance behind the models, Madison could see another wave building, slowly rising to a peak. But before it curled over into its musical crash, a surfer on his surfboard flew across it. His sunset-colored trunks stood out against the blue water. Madison admired the way he dominated the wave in a casual flight.

The sea breeze now chose to wreak havoc with a model's hair. Mindy's long red tresses blew sideways, slapping repeatedly at Babe's flawless, dark-skinned face. Babe tried to hold still, her eyes and lips closed to the red-hair onslaught, giggling through her nose as her tight black spiral curls waved gently in the wind. The other two models, Keiko and Kursey, saw it happening, and struggled not to smile.

Then a salt spray slapped everyone, exploding into a scattershot of cool fat drops. The models screamed and laughed, their sarongs flying with the wind and spray. Spenser captured the moment, shooting several shots in rapid succession. She looked happy, which pleased Madison. Things were finally going well.

A young man bearing a bar tray filled with colorful drinks stepped up to the water's edge near the little group, breaking the moment. He wore an apron over black clothing. Clearly, he came from their beach-front hotel.

Spenser straightened, her camera still clutched high in her hands, strands of blond hair waving aimlessly in the breeze. Madison could see surprise in her face. Spenser shared a glance with Madison, but Madison shrugged, not knowing what the man was doing there. The shrug threw off the angle of the reflector.

Kursey, one of the models, waved her arms in the air. "Woo-hoo!" Her light brown hair tossed in the wind as she left the group of models, dancing through shallow water right past Spenser toward the man.

Spenser lowered her camera, the lens aiming nowhere. "Kursey? Where are you going? We're not done." Her head whipped back to the remaining three models. "What is she doing?"

Mindy and Babe shrugged, their beachwear sarongs dripping at the hems. Kursey's roommate, Keiko, shoved her long dark hair from her face as the wind changed course. "It's Kursey," she said. "So who knows?"

Kursey took cocktails from the bartender's tray, returning to pass them out to the other models who hesitantly accepted them.

Spenser's gaze went from Kursey, back to the man with the tray. "What's going on?"

"Maybe the hotel sent us drinks?" Madison tucked the reflector under her arm. "I'll go talk to him."

"Maybe Lon sent them," said Spenser. "But I asked him to bring water bottles, not booze."

Lon was the other assistant, here to carry heavy gear and set up equipment. Madison felt sure he wouldn't confuse water bottles with cocktails.

She looked across the dry sand at Lon. He had a shaved head and tattooed arms, and he was presently working on the finishing touches of a tall, upright tent, the portable cabana for tomorrow's shoot. He pulled the tent door flap to the side, trying to attach it to a pole to hold it open. As Madison watched him, Kursey approached Lon, giving him a drink and a kiss on the cheek. He looked at the drink in his hand, confused.

Perplexed, Madison said, "Whatever it's about, I'll find out."

"And tell Kursey to get back here."

Madison walked through ankle-deep water to the young man from the hotel. "Excuse me. May I help you?"

He cocked his head, his brown hair moving slightly in the wind. "I have your drinks, ma'am."

Madison knit her brows. "What is this for?"

Matter-of-factly, he said, "Cocktails for your party."

Kursey excitedly shoved a drink into Madison's hand. Several bright red cherries shone on top of the ice. The arrival of drinks seemed odd. It wasn't even noon yet. But perhaps the management was thanking them for booking the shoot at their hotel.

She gestured to the models and told the server, "We're just working here. It's a photo shoot, it's not a real party."

"I'm sorry, ma'am," he said. "I meant your party, as in, the number of people in your group." He picked up the check and a pen from his tray. "I need a signature, if you'd be so kind..."

"Wait." Madison tried to sort this out, but it didn't make sense. "I assumed this was from management. On the house, so to speak?"

He looked mildly puzzled. "I was not informed of that, but perhaps there's a memo I haven't seen. Were you expecting management to send you cocktails?"

"Well, no, especially not this early in the morning. But we never ordered—"

"I called it in," said Kursey, bouncing on her toes with a big smile. "Gotta liven up those boring cows I work with." She slapped her hand over her mouth, giggling. "Oops. I meant to say, models."

"Ah-ha," he said, with a nod. "The mystery unfolds."

"This is Brant." Kursey put her hands on the man's upper arm, her head on his shoulder. "But I call him Mr. Metropolitan. Isn't he the cutest thing?" Brant smiled at her, but when he glanced at Madison, he cleared his throat, then studied his tray.

Madison shook her head. She should've known this was Kursey's doing. That girl kept pushing every boundary, stretching every rule; arguing one moment, sweet and playful the next.

Kursey winked at him. "Just charge it to my room number."

"Very good, ma'am."

"Ma'am?" Kursey punctuated with a giggle. "He called me 'ma'am.' So adorable!"

"Kursey, we need you back with the other girls, please," said Madison. "And I'll need to check with Spenser to see how she feels about you girls holding drinks in the photos."

Kursey pouted. "Party pooper." She left to rejoin the other models.

"I'm happy to wait," said Brant. "There's no one else in the bar at this time in the morning. I can take the glasses back if you need."

Madison hurried to Spenser, then filled her in. Spenser grudgingly admitted the colorful drinks looked good on camera. "We may as well use them as props," she said quietly, "but Kursey is really pushing the limits of my patience." She studied the girls in the changing light. "At least I don't need the reflector this time. Just stay nearby."

Madison heard a different man's voice call out, "Wow! Looking good, ladies! Hey there, Kursey."

Kursey twiddled her fingers in a cutesy wave of greeting.

Madison turned to see the surfer with the sunset-colored trunks. While walking by, he had stopped on the wet sand, holding his surfboard under one arm. His deep tan set off long sun-bleached blond dreadlocks, dripping water. He was well muscled, with calluses on his knees, and looked older than Madison had expected.

Taking them all in, he shook his head. His gaze drifted to include Madison and Spenser. "Damn." He grabbed his heart, pretending a near faint. "I'm going to have me a heart attack with all this beauty around." He stumbled comically in the sand as a wave hit his feet.

The models laughed, his flirting so over the top, they were having fun going along with it. A small wave whapped them from behind and they fell into girlie laughter, giving each other playful shoves, their cocktails adding color. Spenser caught it all on camera, then turned, coolly appraising the surfer.

Madison took that as her cue to stop him from distracting the girls. She asked, "Weren't you the one surfing out there a little while ago?" She moved closer to him, but stood so he'd have to turn his back to the girls to answer her.

"Yeah. That was my daily dawn patrol."

"Dawn patrol?"

"Have to get up early to catch the best waves."

"That was amazing, seeing you out there." It was actually fun having this chance to meet him. Watching him on the waves was truly impressive. "You must love surfing, to be getting up so early every day."

"Well, you ladies are a bonus. I don't usually see many people out here so early. But tonight will sure bring 'em out. There'll be a lot of folks cramming together to see the water. And with no moon tonight, it'll look extra cool."

"What's so special about tonight?"

"Water's gonna be lit. Starts tonight."

She stared at him.

"You know..." He shrugged. "The red tide. Phytoplankton."

Madison blinked.

He adjusted the surfboard under his arm and squinted at her. "Haven't you ever heard of bioluminescence?"

The term sounded vaguely familiar. In fact, yes, she'd heard someone say that word in the hotel lobby this morning. But she'd had no clue what they were referring to.

Just then, Brant's voice came from behind Madison. "Move on, Eddie. No one needs your commentary."

Eddie's face dropped to deadpan. "I'm just saying hello to the pretty girls."

Brant held a hard gaze, the tray hanging at his side. "You said it. Now go."

"What's the matter, Brant? Afraid I'll mess up your sandbox again?"

"Yeah, you'd like that."

"You belong back inside."

"Not going."

"Then watch yourself." Eddie hefted the surfboard a little higher under his arm. "Next time it'll be your face."

"You'd like that, too."

Eddie slowly smiled. "Yeah." He nodded. "I would." He resumed walking down the beach, his long blond dreadlocks still wet down his back.

Madison swung her head to Brant. "What the hell was that about?"

He shook his head. "I'm sorry about that. He's a local. We can't legally keep him off the beach, but we try to shoo him away when we can. They call him Crazy Eddie."

She watched Eddie walk further and further away, down the beach. "Where'd that name come from?"

Brant was watching Eddie, too. "Used to be some surf champ or something. Had a head injury. Lives off his winnings now."

Madison slapped her forehead. "Oh, geez, I forgot. I was supposed to tell you Spenser okayed the drinks."

"No problem," said Brant. "It was worth the wait just to chase off Crazy Eddie." As he walked away, he held his tray underneath his arm the same way Eddie held his surfboard.

Madison knew bad blood when she saw it.

* * *

*Two*

She stopped at the cabana where Lon stood with his hands on his hips, giving the tent flap dirty looks. Loose sand clung to his tattooed arms.

"Something wrong?" she asked.

He shook his shaved head. "Not really. I'm just annoyed the assembly directions didn't match what they actually sent us. I had to figure it out as I went along."

"You'd never know that. It looks great."

Madison saw the water bottles inside the cabana. Outside the cabana, she eyed the drink that Kursey had brought him, tilted in the sand. It looked mostly full.

He picked it up, tossing its contents well away from the cabana. The wet red cherries reflected the sun while the liquid quickly disappeared into the sand. "I wish Kursey would take the hint. I'm not into her. I'm trying to be polite, but she comes on strong."

"Want me to talk to her?"

"Nah, you'll be too nice about it." He gave her a wry smile. "I'll tell her to back off. I just don't want Babe getting the wrong idea every time Kursey hangs all over me."

Madison's brow lifted. "Babe, huh?" She slowly smiled. "I didn't know."

It was cute to see this gruff young tattooed guy get suddenly bashful. "Well...yeah." He shrugged, hiding a smile.

"Does she feel the same way?"

He thought. "I don't know yet. I think so." He nodded. "I hope so."

Spenser trudged up to the cabana, with Mindy, Keiko, and Kursey in tow. Their sarongs looked as tired and worn out as they did. Babe wasn't with them.

"That's it for today," said Spenser. "We're still behind schedule, but we'll catch up tomorrow. Great job, everyone." They all went inside the cabana.

"Water!" Tossing her wet red hair behind her shoulder, Mindy rushed to the water bottles, handing one to Keiko before opening her own. They drank the water as if it were the nectar of the gods, then began flicking water into each other's face in silly fun.

Lon looked around. "Where's Babe?"

Spenser opened her own water bottle as she looked around. "She was with us a minute ago."

Mindy and Keiko stopped playing. "She went back to the water," said Mindy.

Kursey tried to give a water bottle to Lon, but turning his back on her, he said, "No thanks." He faced the opening, looking out toward the breaking waves. Madison assumed he was looking for Babe.

Kursey giggled, and put her hand on his shoulder, rubbing down his arm. "You need to keep up your strength so—"

He pushed her hand off. "Stop it."

Kursey stared at him, then pouted. "I was just being nice."

"I'm not interested, Kursey," he said, firmly. "Let it go."

With a frosty gaze, she left the cabana.

Spenser looked up and around at the cabana, nodding her head in approval. "Lon, you pulled off a miracle. I love it. This will look good tomorrow."

"Thanks. All that's left is the volleyball net. I'll put that up in the morning."

"Sounds good," said Spenser. "But for now, I'd rather you all went inside the hotel. Make sure you stay out of the sun for the rest of the day. Clean up, get lunch, take a nap, whatever. Just stay out of the sun."

"Oh, I wanted to tell you, once it gets dark tonight," said Madison, "there's supposed to be a display of glowing water out here. That surfer guy was telling me about it. I'm going to check it out."

"I heard something about that," said Spenser. "I'll join you. Maybe I'll see you all out here tonight."

As they stepped out of the cabana, Spenser added, "And someone please tell Babe—"

Lon cut her off. "I'll do it." He jogged out to where Babe stood by the water's edge, watching the waves break. But when Lon reached her, she looked down at the ground. She turned suddenly, hurrying away.

Madison could hear Lon's confused voice calling out, "Babe? What is it? Talk to me."

"Uh-oh..." Madison murmured.

Spenser stepped close, quietly asking, "What?"

"Later." Madison waved her hands at the girls, shooing them away. "Everyone inside the hotel. When you see Kursey, please tell her we want her to stay inside, out of the sun."

* * *

In her hotel room, Madison put the finishing touches on her fresh makeup. With the prolonged sun exposure sapping her energy, she'd taken a long nap, showered, and was now getting ready to meet Spenser for dinner.

The skin on her shoulders felt tight and tender. Her shoulders definitely hadn't looked that pink an hour ago. She leaned closer to the mirror, pushing a shoulder forward to examine the tender skin. Annoyed with herself, she realized she hadn't reapplied the sunscreen as she should have, and it must've worn out before—

Loud pounding sounded from the corridor. She looked up. Someone had urgently knocked on a neighboring door. It sounded nearby.

The pounding resumed, harder, more determined. She heard a man's voice demand, *"Kursey!"*

"What the hell?" Madison hurried to her door. This did not sound good, whatever it was. She threw her door open, looking into the hallway in time to see Keiko open her door as Lon's fist gave it one more pound.

"She's not here right now, Lon," said Keiko. She wore a robe, and her long dark hair dripped as if she'd hurried out of the shower. She clutched a towel, rubbing it over her head.

"WHERE is she?" he yelled.

"I don't know!" Keiko sounded distressed.

"I did NOT hook up with Kursey last night! She was with that asshole on the beach and she damn well better tell Babe the truth! Or maybe she was so drunk, she doesn't even remember who she was with!"

Keiko winced as he got louder.

Madison had enough. *"Lon!"*

He jerked around to face her.

"Stop yelling at Keiko!"

He pressed his lips together hard, punched the wall next to the doorframe, then stormed down the hallway.

* * *

Spenser's eyes rounded as Madison recounted the whole incident from the hallway. But Madison zipped her lip when the hotel waitress showed up to remove their finished dinner plates. It wouldn't do to let word get out that Spenser's team displayed drama in the hallways. As soon as the waitress left, they resumed their discussion.

"Wait, wait," said Spenser. "I'm trying to wrap my head around this." She touched her fingertips as if she were counting. "Kursey said she'd been with Lon, as in, slept with him?"

Madison shrugged. "That's how I took it, yeah."

Spenser touched another fingertip. "He denies it..."

"Vehemently."

Another finger. "...and says she may have been too drunk to know who she was with."

Madison grimaced. "Not something you'd want on your resume."

"It's not a good look." Spenser blinked. "And I had no idea about Babe and Lon. How long has that been going on?"

"I don't think it had a chance to start. Lon was telling me just this morning he didn't know if Babe felt the same way, but he hoped she did."

Spenser rolled her eyes. "So many things have gone wrong before this shoot even began, and now I have a model who acts like she's from a mean-girl movie."

"We shoot again tomorrow, then fly home the next morning," said Madison. "I'll help you get through it the best I can."

Spenser sighed. "I'm so glad you're here. You're helping me stay sane."

"Wow," said Madison. "I usually have the opposite effect on people."

"Weird, huh?"

"Just don't get used to it. I don't know how long I can sustain it."

Spenser took a deep breath. "Well, before we go any further, I'd better talk to Lon and..." Her brows rose, her gaze focusing behind Madison. "Speak of the devil."

Lon approached their table. "Madison," he began, looking at the table, the floor, the distance, anywhere but in her eyes, "I want you to know I apologized to Keiko." He sounded uncomfortable but resigned. "And I'm apologizing to you, too." He finally lifted his gaze to her face. "I'm sorry I lost it."

Madison studied him. Clearly, apologizing was hard for him, probably because he still felt the sting of being falsely accused. "Okay." She nodded. "I accept."

"And Spenser, you don't have to worry. I'll do the job tomorrow with no other problems."

Spenser looked thoughtful. "Let's forget about it. You've been doing a really good job. I'm sure everything will be fine."

He pursed his lips, gave a brisk nod, and quickly walked away.

"By the way," said Madison, "Kursey charged all those drinks this morning to her room number. She's already way over her daily food and drink allowance."

Exasperated, Spenser released a heavy sigh. "I keep hoping she'll straighten up. I still need the cabana and volleyball shots for the client." She took Madison's hands, squeezing hard. "I *need* her to be professional tomorrow. Can you give her some kind of inspirational pep talk?"

"How about I threaten to beat her with a chain?"

"Less severe, please."

"A garden hose?"

"No."

"An old T-shirt? C'mon, I can get somewhere if I threaten to beat her with an old T-shirt."

Spenser smirked. "I won't ask how you do it."

Madison swung a fist through the air. "*Yes!* Who's the client, by the way?"

"Beach Dream Travel. A start-up with money. I got lucky."

"Luck? Not with your talent."

"Says the gorgeous talented unemployed actress across from me. Sometimes it doesn't matter how good we are. We still have to jump when a decent offer comes along."

"Good point."

Spenser sighed. "I have one more request. If Kursey pushes me too far tomorrow, I want you to take her place."

Madison slumped in her seat. "Please, no. I'd have to shave my armpits."

"Take one for the team."

* * *

*Three*

Madison cried out, "Oh my god!" Her mouth hanging open, she watched the waves crash in the dark night. The part of the wave that would be the crashing white water in the daylight was now a brightly lit neon blue.

"Look at the water, Spenser. I mean, *look at the water!"* Her footprints made iridescent circles, larger than dinner plates, everywhere she stepped.

A small wave rushed over Madison's shins, the neon blue light of the water splashing and tumbling around her. As her steps took her further from the water toward drier ground, the glow on the sand diminished until it no longer lit up. She hurried back to the water's edge where the lights were the most intense. The wetter the sand, the brighter the lights.

It felt to her like a fairyland ocean filled with magical lights in shades of blue and green. She'd never known the bioluminescence of plankton could enthrall and fascinate her so.

Spenser had her camera, shooting like mad at the wondrous sight. Madison used her cell phone to take photos.

"All you have to do is disturb the water, and that makes the lights fire off for a few seconds." Madison bent down to brush her finger through the wet sand. A blue neon light followed everywhere her finger went. She tried writing her name in neon, but the lights in the first letters faded before she could finish writing her whole name.

They sat on the wet sand together, worn out from the day, their camera and phone in the tote bag nearby. Laughter and chatter sounded from all around as the beachfront hotel guests strolled by or played in the shallow end of the water.

Madison stared at the dark ocean, unable to separate the dark water from the dark sky on the horizon. But anywhere a wave curled over and crashed, a magnificent frothy blue or green light developed, rushing toward the shore before slowly dissipating.

Spenser marveled. "They said it hasn't happened on this beach in years and it'll only last for a few days. I'm glad we got to see it together." She playfully bumped Madison's shoulder.

"Ow." Madison pulled her shoulder away. "I got sunburned today." She delicately touched the skin on her shoulder. "It seems to be getting more tender by the hour."

"Oh, no. I'll give you the aloe gel I brought. That'll help. And make sure you're slathered in sunscreen tomorrow morning."

Laughter nearby pulled their attention. It was Mindy and Keiko, squealing in delight. The surfer was there with them, showing them how to make snow angels in the wet sand. His long blond dreadlocks looked like dark ropes in the watery sand. In spite of their pretty clothes, Mindy and Keiko had laid down in the wet sand, waving their arms and legs with Eddie to make snow angels.

A few feet away, Babe and Lon sat together in the sand. Babe leaned back into Lon's chest, his arms around her waist. Their quiet conversation erupted into laughter at the electric blue snow angels that Keiko and Mindy made.

Madison sighed happily. "Looks like Lon worked it out with Babe."

As if she'd heard her name mentioned, Babe's head turned toward Madison. Then she stood, walking to where Madison and Spenser sat in the sand.

"Have you decided on the shoot time tomorrow?" asked Babe.

"I know I said it might be at a later time," said Spenser, "but I'm afraid it'll be 6:00 a.m. again. We're behind schedule."

"That's fine with me, I'm a total morning person," said Babe. "Everyone teased me last night for leaving the party so early."

Madison smiled. "What'd you do last night?"

"Oh, we all wandered out here after dark. Turned into a beach party where everyone's dancing in the sand. But the only music was from Mindy's tiny cell phone. So, there we were," she laughed, "all crowded around the phone, trying to dance to music we could barely hear!"

Madison chuckled.

"We must've looked ridiculous, but it was so much fun!" Babe's expression turned shy. "That's how Lon and I got to talking."

As Babe returned to sitting with Lon, Spenser watched the snow angel activity, then leaned in, quietly asking, "Hey, what about the surfer guy over here? Didn't you say they call him Crazy Eddie?"

"Um...yeah. That's what Brant said."

"Who's Brant?"

"The bartender guy. Kursey introduced me to him when he brought the drinks this morning." Madison hunched her shoulders. "Honestly, I was a little uncomfortable with the way she flirted with him, hands all over his arms. She even gave him a nickname, calls him Mr. Metropolitan." Madison shook her head. "I mean, we're here on business. It wasn't appropriate, but he didn't seem to mind."

"Huh," said Spenser. "She doesn't waste any time. And didn't I hear the surfer say, 'Hey there Kursey,' when he walked by this morning?"

"Yup, he sure did. I've been thinking about that. I'm wondering if that's who Kursey was really with last night, but she told Babe she was with Lon."

"But...she'd barely know him. And he has a rep for being crazy?"

"It worries me."

Spenser cocked her head, watching Mindy and Keiko with Eddie. "Should we chase him away?"

"I'm not sure we can. Brant said they can't legally chase him off the beach. But I'll tell you one thing, those two did not like each other."

"Who? Crazy Eddie and Brant?"

"Yeah. Eddie said Brant belonged inside, but Brant said he wasn't going. Then Eddie threatened him, saying, 'Next time it'll be your face.'"

"Whoa." Spenser looked concerned as Eddie demonstrated another glowing snow angel. "I take it they had a bad encounter at some point."

Madison watched as the girls laughingly messed up each other's snow angels so they'd have to start over. "Eddie's just showing them how to make the wet sand light up. Seems harmless enough."

"I'm actually glad the girls are having fun. They needed a break. We're probably worried over nothing."

Madison agreed. "How about we just keep an eye on them?"

At that moment, Kursey stumbled into view, weaving unsteadily toward the water. "What the hell is this?" she demanded to know, her words slurred.

Madison stared in disbelief. "Are you kidding me?"

"What?" asked Spenser.

Madison nodded her chin in Kursey's direction. "She sounds hammered."

Kursey steadied herself, swaying but standing upright. "I've never seen water like that." She suddenly threw her arms out wide. "I love it!" She waded into the water, going deeper, and deeper.

Madison's eyes widened. "What is she doing? No!"

* * *

*Four*

Madison jumped up from the sand, running into the dark surf. Kursey was already hip deep in the water and still going, leaving an iridescent trail behind her.

Splashing through the waves as fast as she could, Madison tried to catch up. The water hit her waist level. She paddled with her arms to help herself move forward, faster. "Kursey! Kursey, that's far enough!" she cried.

A dark wave headed for them rose higher, then curled overhead. The wild crash of neon water slammed into them, throwing Kursey's body into Madison. Madison fumbled an arm around Kursey's waist and held on as they went under in the rush and tumble of the surging wave. She held her breath, her body thrown and spun, losing the sense of where gravity was, wondering how long the tide would hold them under.

But the longer they tumbled, the closer to shore they were thrown. When the tumbling suddenly stopped, Madison found herself in knee-deep water. She and Kursey rose to their feet, sputtering saltwater as the tide rushed back into the ocean.

*"Woot!"* Kursey whooped, punching her fist into the air. "What a ride!"

Still shaken, Madison parted the sopping wet curtain of dark hair from her face, wiping the water from her eyes as best she could. "What the hell were you thinking, Kursey?" She grabbed Kursey's hand, leading her out of the water.

"Why didn't you tell me everyone was out here having fun?" Kursey demanded, her feet kicking the shallow water. "Why didn't *anybody* tell me? You're all bitches!"

"Oh, come on! It wasn't intentional. You left the cabana before I made the announcement."

"If I hadn't been cut off at the bar, I wouldn't have wandered out here. I wouldn't have seen the pretty lights. I would've missed it! You all hate me!"

Madison stopped. Putting her hands on her hips, she said, "Did you just say the bar cut you off?"

"Yeah, that metro jerk. His boss was there, so he suddenly gets all judgey on me, pretending I've gone too far. What a hypocrite."

"You have no business drinking so much that the bar has to cut you off. You're supposed to be here professionally. Your actions reflect on Spenser and everyone else."

"They should fire that guy and—" Kursey's eyes widened. "Eddie!" She ran toward Eddie and the girls on the sand. Eddie caught her as she threw her arms around him.

While Eddie taught Kursey how to make neon snow angels, Madison returned to Spenser. "I hate babysitting drunks," she said, wringing water out of her hair.

"I hate taking pictures of them. As pretty as she is, at this rate she's going to look like hell in the morning."

"If we can get her to go to bed, right now, she could still look okay tomorrow. Besides, it's getting late," said Madison. "We have the perfect excuse to send everyone to their rooms to get some sleep. That way we don't have to play bodyguard with drunks, crazy surfers, and drama in general."

"Sounds brilliant. I'll make the announcement." Spenser strode over to the group playing in the sand. Within moments, Babe and Lon took off for the hotel. Keiko and Mindy waved goodbye to Eddie, joining Madison and Spenser as they trooped into the hotel, carrying their towels and sandals.

Madison retrieved her cell phone from Spenser's tote bag. Then she walked backwards, watching Kursey take her time saying goodbye to Eddie. It became apparent that Kursey wasn't actually coming with them.

"Is she coming?" asked Spenser.

"Nope," she sighed. "You guys go on. I'll handle it."

Spenser sounded tired. "You've already run into the ocean for her."

"Hey, this is serious. If she doesn't get her act together, I may have to shave my armpits."

Spenser smirked. "The world will come to an end."

"Not the world, just my plan to not have to shave for a week." She gave Spenser a hug. "Go sleep. I've got this."

Madison headed back toward where Kursey and Eddie stood in the sand, hugging. "Kursey!" she yelled.

Kursey and Eddie jerked, breaking their hug. Kursey rolled her eyes with a dramatic slump of her shoulders when she saw it was Madison. As Eddie stood by, Kursey crossed her arms defiantly and strode toward Madison.

Madison met her halfway. "You heard Spenser ask all of you to please go get some rest."

"What's it to you?" said Kursey, her expression sour. "You're just an assistant. Go assist something."

Madison fought not to rise to the bait. "I'm assisting you right now. If you drink lots of water to counteract some of the alcohol, and get lots of sleep, you'll still have a chance to look good in the shoot tomorrow. Looking good in the photos is why you've been hired." Madison's gaze held Kursey's, pleading with her. "Come on, Kursey. You can do this."

"Oh my god." Kursey snickered. "What is your problem?"

Madison had little patience left. "You. You're my problem. We need you to act professionally."

"Yes, Mommy!" Kursey laughed mockingly.

Madison stared hard at the immature woman before her. "You know what? Let's skip the pep talk. Let's get straight to the consequences."

"Oh, I am so scared."

Madison felt the cell phone in her hand. "If you like your agent, you should be." She poked a few buttons on the screen.

"What? Now you're going to call my agent and lie to her?"

"I won't have to say a thing." Madison held up her cell phone and took a quick photo of Kursey. "A picture says a thousand words."

That got Kursey's attention. "Wait. What are you doing?"

Madison used her calm voice. "No drinks, no drama, just good old-fashioned sleep. Oh, and don't forget about drinking water. Chug it."

"What...are you blackmailing me?"

"How do you think your agent will react to your drunk face? Worse, how do you think she'll react to your early-morning face, because so help me, if you show up looking hungover I sure as hell will send photos to her."

Kursey was silent.

"We need you looking your best, and out here on the sand by 6:00 a.m. like the rest of us. Got it?"

*"Fine!"* Kursey used both hands to flip her hair behind her shoulders.

"Oh, don't you flip your hair at me!"

Kursey huffed. "Calm down. I'm going."

As Kursey stormed back to the hotel, Crazy Eddie called to her, "I'll see you later."

Kursey called over her shoulder, "Count on it!"

Madison faced the surfer. "Did you two make plans to meet up out here?"

He shrugged. "She's an adult. She can make her own decisions."

"She's an employed adult. Not everyone can live on their winnings."

His stony face gave way to a half-smile. "Not everyone has winnings big enough." He turned and left, leaving neon circles fading in his wake as the darkness swallowed him along the water's edge.

Hopefully, going home.

* * *

Madison sat up in bed, checking the time. Three in the morning. She groaned.

Damn sunburn woke her. All she did was turn over in her sleep, and the skin on her shoulders sent a pain message to her brain, loud enough to wake her.

She yawned, swinging her feet to the floor. Where had she put that aloe gel Spenser gave her? She sleepily stumbled into her bathroom, found the aloe gel on the counter, and poured some into her palm. As she carefully spread it all over each shoulder, she thought about her confrontation with Kursey earlier this evening. She was glad she'd walked Kursey all the way to her room. Kursey's roommate, Keiko, had to open the door for them when

Kursey couldn't find her key card. Madison had said goodnight to them and left.

Done with the aloe gel, she turned the bathroom light off to return to bed, but the gel was still wet on her shoulders. She didn't want to chance that it might rub into her sheets, so she tried to find something to do while it dried. Looking out the sliding glass door of her fourth-story balcony, she saw the dark water with its occasional lovely color burst when waves broke. Perfect. The warm summer air would help the aloe gel dry faster. She slid the glass door open, then stepped outside onto the balcony.

She bent slightly, resting her forearms on the wide railing, looking down at the black beach. The rhythmic sound of the waters gently rushing to shore felt like a lullaby, shushing the world to sleep. In the darkness, she could not see the line between water and sand unless a wave broke, causing the phytoplankton to light up in the breaking water. Her eyes followed the blue florescence of a crashing wave as the water rushed toward the shore, the iridescent foam slowly dissipating as it spread thinly across the wet sand.

She looked to the drier sands, to the spot where the cabana should be. It was too dark to see it distinctly. Then faint lights caught her eye.

She saw small circles of gentle illumination. One faint circle in front of the other slowly made their way toward the water. As the circles got closer to the water, the illumination grew a little brighter.

She smiled, remembering how her footprints made circles of light the size of dinner plates everywhere she stepped in the wettest sand. Someone must be walking on the beach, enjoying the empty expanse. Except...she peered closer. What was that smear of light following them? A florescent line, like a wide groove, pursued the round circles. The groove was about the width of a surfboard.

"Eddie," she whispered. She'd heard surfers never drag their boards. He must be feeling lazy, dragging his surfboard to the water instead of carrying it. But 3:00 a.m. seemed early for what he'd referred to as his dawn patrol. And with no moonlight, how safe was it to surf in the dark waters? She shook her head. They did call him Crazy Eddie, after all.

She watched the florescent lights go all the way into the water, creating a muddled light as the waters were disturbed with tiny splashing.

The soft illumination gently died as the waters stilled.

She yawned, wanting to go back to sleep. But just then, the circles returned from the water, crossing to drier sands where they gradually disappeared. Madison wondered if Eddie had managed to lose his surfboard in the darkness, because the florescent groove was gone.

She touched her shoulders to check the aloe gel. It was dry enough to return to bed.

* * *

*Five*

Madison collected the paper coffee cups from the models, taking the cups into the cabana where she added them to a paper trash bag. The small table they'd brought inside the cabana held the last fresh coffee cup, the one waiting for Kursey. And of course, she was late again. Madison gazed at the lone coffee cup, wondering how Spenser would handle the situation.

Through the open flap, movement caught her eye. Down by the water's edge Eddie passed by, his long blond dreadlocks dripping water again. He carried his surfboard under his arm, just like yesterday. He must've just finished his dawn patrol.

Remembering Eddie's words last night about seeing Kursey later, Madison hoped Kursey did not keep whatever date they had arranged. Or maybe she had, and that was why she was so late this morning. Probably overslept.

Spenser stormed inside the cabana, fighting with the back of her camera, fiddling with the battery. "I just recharged this thing last night. Why can't it hold a lousy charge?"

"Let me get you another battery." Madison pulled Spenser's leather gear bag up onto the table to dig around for the spare batteries. But the jostling accidentally knocked over the paper trash bag, and the last fresh coffee went with it.

"Oh—" She tried to grab the cup in time, but it spilled onto the sand. "Dammit! Sorry for making a mess." She squatted to gather the trash, picking up coffee cup lids, wadded napkins, and stir sticks, shoving them all back into the paper bag. The spilled coffee made a brown wet sand puddle that she tried to cover with drier sand. As she pushed the sand around, something orange caught her eye. She pulled it from the sand. It looked like half of an orange pill capsule. There was nothing in it except a little sand, and she vaguely wondered where the other half was.

"Your mess is so small of a problem, it's cute," said Spenser. "It may be the last day, but things are still going wrong. Did you see the portable volleyball net?"

"No, why? Is there a problem?" Madison stood, wadding the top of the trash bag so it couldn't spill again.

"It was a big tangled ball when we opened the box this morning. Unbelievable! Lon's working on it now."

Madison finally handed Spenser a fresh battery, then followed her out of the cabana. "I hate to add to the trouble, but Kursey still hasn't checked in." She followed Spenser around the corner of the cabana to where the models waited in a little group.

"Keiko?" Spenser waved her over. "Was Kursey close to being ready when you left your room?"

Keiko shook her head, her long dark hair shining like silk. "I haven't seen her this morning. I had to stay with Mindy and Babe last night."

"What?" Madison blinked. "What do you mean, you had to stay with Mindy and—?"

Lon stepped up. "Spenser, sorry to interrupt. I got the volleyball net untangled but it's full of holes. Do you still want it set up?"

"Holes?" Spenser's eyes widened. "They sent us one with *holes*?" Spenser stared from Lon to the net he'd spread out on the sand nearby. "You've got to be kidding me!" She stormed over to the holey net, inspecting it.

Madison turned back to Keiko. "Tell me what happened."

"Kursey was arguing on the phone with room service, trying to get more drinks brought up." Keiko shook her head. "I was sure I wouldn't get any sleep with her in the room."

"Why didn't you call my cell and tell me what was going on?"

"I didn't want any drama, I just wanted sleep. So, I stuffed a few things in my purse, like my PJs, and got out of there."

"Did you tell her where you were going?"

"No, I didn't want another fight with her. She probably thought I was coming back. I just hurried out while she was in a good mood."

"Good mood? I thought you said she was arguing on the phone."

"Well, yeah, she started out furious. But just before I left, she was sort of laughing." Keiko rolled her eyes. "It was that cutesy giggle she likes to do around men. I heard her say, 'I can bring that' and 'I'm totally up for that' or something." Keiko shrugged. "I hurried out. I went to Babe and Mindy's room and asked if I could bunk with them."

Madison nodded. "Sounds like you did the smart thing."

"All my things were still in the room at that point, so I had to go back this morning to get ready for the shoot," said Keiko. "She was already gone. I assumed I would see her out here."

"Is it possible she got in so late this morning, you just missed her?"

"I guess. And if she did, she saw my things are gone. I moved the rest of my stuff into Mindy and Babe's room this morning before coming down here. I'm staying with them again tonight." As if to prove a point, she gave Madison her room key card, saying, "You can have this. I won't need it anymore."

Madison shook her head. "I don't know what to do with her. Her behavior is, well..."

Keiko's response was blunt. "She has a problem. Remember when Lon was yelling in the hallway about Kursey not remembering who she was with, the night before?"

"I sure do."

"He was right. She really didn't remember. I had to tell her what she did."

"Are you referring to the party when you were all dancing to Mindy's cell phone?"

Keiko blinked, seeming surprised that Madison knew about the impromptu party. "That party started out fun. I'd even say, cute. But then Kursey's drinks kept arriving, she kept going, next thing she's all over the men..." She shook her head. "She likes to party beyond anything I'm comfortable with. I'm done."

As Keiko left, Spenser returned from mourning over the volleyball net. She looked irritated, but calm. "Lon's repairing the more obvious holes in the volleyball net, so we have some unexpected time on our hands."

Madison held silent, not wanting to tell her what she just found out from Keiko.

Spenser studied her. "Don't tell me." She closed her eyes tightly. "It's Kursey, isn't it?"

Madison nodded.

With her eyes still closed, Spenser said, "Are you nodding? If you are, I can't hear you nodding."

Madison nodded again.

Spenser opened one eye. "You're messing with me."

"Yeah." Madison smiled, sadly. "Just trying to lighten the mood."

"Good news will lighten my mood."

"Sorry, I got nothing. Except, well, I shaved my armpits."

"I'll take it. You're hired."

"I guess I'll go slap some makeup on."

"Well, you have all the time in the world, because everything is so screwed up I can't shoot until we fix multiple problems." She rubbed her temples. "I'm going to stay here and fight with my camera batteries, Lon will fight with the volleyball net, and you can go fix up. Be back here in an hour."

"I'm on it."

* * *

After she got herself ready for the camera, Madison stood in the hotel bar. She had extra time, and lots of questions. "Can I talk to you for a minute?"

Brant finished drying a glass, setting it down on the bar top. "Sure. Can I get you anything?"

"No thanks, I just wanted to ask if you've seen Kursey this morning."

"One of your models?"

"I'm sorry, I just assumed you knew her name. She spent so much time with you at the bar last night."

"Ah. The one I had to cut off."

Madison sighed. "That's the one."

"She's also the one who called in all those cocktails early yesterday morning."

She nodded. "Afraid so."

"I remember because of the cherries. Every drink I hand her always has to have at least five long-stemmed cherries in it."

Madison smiled, wryly. "I've seen that. She must really love them."

"I haven't seen her since last night." He smiled apologetically. "I don't think she likes me now. She'd had so much to drink, I had to cut her off. It's hotel policy for the bartender to make a judgement call on things like that."

Madison chuckled. "She said you cut her off because your boss was here."

He rolled his eyes, sharing a laugh with her. "*Especially* because he was here! I couldn't serve her in her condition in front of my boss. I'm still on probation and could lose my job if I made exceptions for her. I tried to explain it to her."

"I completely understand." After a thought, Madison asked, "Would it be all right for me to use the bar phone over there? I'd like to call room service. I just want to know if she was okay when they last saw her."

"No problem." He lifted the old-style phone with its long cord from the back of the bar, setting it on the counter in front of Madison.

She pressed the Room Service button and made her inquiry. After a brief chat, she hung up, disappointed. "I guess she never completed the order. They said there's no record of sending anything to her room."

The bartender tilted his head. "Well, why did you think she'd called room service?"

"Because she was arguing about getting more drinks. Wouldn't that be room service?"

"It would," he nodded. "Any food or beverage delivered to the rooms has to go through room service. The kitchen sends me drink orders, I make the drinks, they pick them up to deliver to the room number on the order."

"Could we look at the checks from last night?"

"Sure. See for yourself." He handed her a stack of white paper slips.

Madison looked at every single one. Nothing for Kursey's room. "This is frustrating. After arguing with room service, she suddenly got happy, saying she was up for that."

"Up for what?"

"That's what I want to know." She got off the barstool, taking a few steps heading out of the lounge, then stopped. "Brant? Have you ever seen Crazy Eddie surfing at night?"

"Eddie?" He shook his head. "Can't say that I have. Why do you ask?"

"It's probably nothing, but I saw someone out there late last night. It was dark. At first, I thought Eddie was out there to surf, but now I wonder if that's where he and Kursey agreed to meet."

He shrugged. "If she was with Crazy Eddie, anything is possible."

* * *

*Six*

Madison knocked on Kursey's door, hoping she was back in her room. No answer. Kursey's behavior was increasingly erratic, unafraid of consequences, and it made Madison nervous. She knocked again, louder.

Still no answer.

Maybe she was in there sleeping it off.

Then a frightening thought occurred to Madison. What if she's unconscious and needs help?

Using the keycard Keiko gave her, she let herself in.

No one was in the room. If Keiko moved all of her own things out of here as she'd said, that meant anything left in the room was Kursey's. Madison looked around, seeing plenty of items left here and there. Okay, so Kursey hadn't checked out of the hotel. The closet door was open, showing hanging clothing, and shoes on the floor underneath. The sandy beach sarong from yesterday's shoot lay rumpled in the corner.

She wandered into the bathroom, seeing makeup and hair products scattered on the counter.

And something else.

The corner of a small plastic baggie stuck out of a makeup bag. Madison used that type of baggie to hold her vitamins when she traveled. But these weren't vitamins. These were orange colored capsules. Tiny print on the capsules read, Adderall.

Madison sighed, feeling guilty for snooping. She told herself Kursey probably had a prescription for the pills, and she carried them in plastic baggies the same way Madison carried her vitamins. No one ever questioned whether or not Madison had a prescription for her vitamins. But then again, no one ever used vitamins as a recreational drug, like Adderall.

The bigger issue remained. Where was Kursey? Madison had personally escorted Kursey here to her room last night. Keiko said Kursey was on the phone when Keiko left to go stay with Babe and Mindy. After that, Kursey could've gone anywhere.

Madison left the room and hurried down to the beach to take Kursey's place in the shoot.

* * *

The volleyball flew in Madison's direction. She tried to hit it but connected painfully on her thumb. The ball rolled down the wet sand into the water, but the wave rushing to shore brought the ball with it. She snatched the ball and brought it back. The other models shouted encouragement as she returned, but she knew her performance sucked.

"Sorry, Spenser," she called. "I was never good at this."

Spenser lowered her camera, coming closer to the volleyball net. "I don't need any of you to be good at volleyball," she laughed. "I just need some beach party bodies to play in the sand." She played back some shots in her electronic viewfinder. "It's looking fantastic." She fiddled with her camera's menu as she said, "Let's have Madison serve it this time. I want you all to react as if she's just hit the most magnificent serve you've ever seen."

"Oh, I get it. You want fantasy now," said Madison.

Spenser laughed but didn't correct her.

Madison served the ball, surprising herself that it flew pretty decently. Excited, she turned to Spenser, shouting, "I did it!"

The ball hit her in the head. She hadn't paid attention for just a second and that's all it took.

As she staggered to regain her balance, Babe ran to her. "Are you okay?" She suppressed her laughter, a hand on her mouth.

"I'm fine. But my pride is in cardiac arrest."

The ball flew over the wet sand, back into the water again.

"I'll get it," cried Mindy. Her long red hair bounced as she ran, trying to grab the ball in the frothy water.

Madison put her hands on her knees, trying to catch her breath, scolding herself for not paying attention. That's when she heard Mindy scream.

All heads snapped toward Mindy. She was staring at something, her hands on her mouth, her feet quickly backing away from the water.

Next to the volleyball bobbing in the water, Kursey's body washed up on the shore.

* * *

All was quiet at the table in the lounge. A paper happy hour menu, rumpled and stained, fell to the floor. Soft music filtered in through overhead speakers as Madison gazed at all the empty glasses still sitting on their table. Every glass had cherries, or cherry stems, in memory of Kursey.

Everyone involved with Spenser's shoot had gathered this evening, taking up the private table in the back corner. Still in shock, they tried to understand how a young life could so easily be lost. But tomorrow they would fly home, and the hour was late. Everyone except Madison and Spenser left for their rooms.

The police were long gone, the body removed, and the reason for this tragedy seemed obvious. Kursey went swimming when she was too drunk, again. But this time there was no one to stop her, and she drowned. Open and shut case.

"There's nothing more you could've done, Madison." Spenser held Madison's hand, trying to get her point across.

"But it doesn't make sense." Haunted by something, Madison kept going over it in her mind. "Why was there an orange capsule, or rather, half of a capsule, in the cabana? I mean, I saw the Adderall in her room, but half a capsule? That means it was opened, and the contents spilled out."

"That's how some drug users do it," said Spenser. "They empty the capsules into a cocktail and drink it. It hits them faster and harder that way."

"But why in the cabana? She had them in her room, she could've taken it anytime." She wadded a napkin in her fist. "And all that fuss about Kursey saying she was with Lon that first night, but both Lon and Keiko said she was too drunk to remember what happened. Have you noticed, no one has told us exactly what *did* happen? In fact, no one except Babe ever acknowledged the beach party that happened that first night. I mentioned it to Keiko and she acted surprised that I knew about it."

"It sounded harmless," Spenser shrugged. "Dancing in the sand. Why would they keep it to themselves?"

"Remember when Babe told us she's a morning person, and they teased her for leaving early? That means whatever happened, happened after Babe left. But when I asked Keiko about it, all she would say was that Kursey kept drinking, and that she was all over the men."

"Man, or men?"

"She said *men*. Good catch," said Madison. "There had to be another man there besides Lon."

"Maybe that's when Crazy Eddie entered the picture. Because the next morning he walked by and knew Kursey's name."

"That's what I'm thinking. But why the secrecy? He boldly said hello to everyone."

Spenser's phone sounded an alert. She picked it up, scanning the message. "Kursey's agent says she personally knows Kursey's family. She'll be the one to break the news to them."

"Can you imagine getting news like that?" Madison shook her head, her eyes closed.

Another alert sounded from Spenser's phone. "It's the client. I sent them the news about the drowning. They agree with my plan to remove Kursey from the shots." A heavy sigh escaped her. "It'd be too heartbreaking not to."

The bartender, Brant, came to their table with a tray. Quietly, he said, "I'll clear this away for you." He put the glasses on his tray, shuffling to make room. "Are you okay?"

Madison nodded, then closed her eyes and shook her head, no.

He gave her a sad smile. "Can I get you anything else?"

"A new brain." Madison leaned back in her seat. "Mine's worn out from trying to make sense of this."

He shook his head. "You know, she talked about swimming in the beautiful lights. I just assumed she'd wait until she was sober." He fit one last glass on the tray, then left.

"It is beautiful," she barely mumbled to herself. "Kursey marched right into the water and I had to stop her because—"

It finally hit her. She shut up as her mind calculated, everything thrown into a new light. Her certainty warring with her doubt, she didn't want to say anything until she knew for sure. Murder was not a thing to take lightly. She had to find out, and she knew where to look.

Spenser was busy trying to pick up the pieces and salvage what she could of this job. Madison's heart went out to her, but for now it was convenient that Spenser was distracted.

"Can I leave you here for a few minutes?"

"Sure." Spenser stared hard at her phone while she typed. "I'll be here awhile."

Madison slipped out of her chair, then hurried through the lounge to the exit to the sand outside. The warm air caressed her as she quickly strode across the dark beach, breaking into a run.

In the dark she rushed inside the cabana, pulled out her cell phone, and hit the flashlight button. Her cell phone threw bright light onto the sand. Madison dropped to her knees where she'd spilled the coffee earlier, where she'd found the orange half-capsule. Holding the flashlight phone with one hand, she sifted through the sand with the other. She found another orange half. Then five more, then two more... but it was something else she sought.

There it was. Cherry stems. At least a dozen or more cherry stems mingled with Adderall capsule halves in the sand.

"Why are you out here?" A man's voice from the opening flap of the cabana made Madison whirl around.

* * *

*Seven*

She cursed herself for acting thoughtlessly. Of course Brant saw her rush out of the bar, and followed her outside. How could she be so stupid?

His gaze fell to Madison's light in the sand. "The cherry stems?" After a clipped laugh, he said, "I never thought of that."

"She never called room service, did she? That was you on the bar phone, arguing with her that the bar was closed. You didn't agree to sneak all those drinks to her until she offered to bring Adderall. But when she overdosed, you had a problem on your hands. You had to choose between running for help, or keeping your job."

"Oh, believe me, the choice was easy. She was about to ruin my life."

"So you *killed her*?"

"Give me a break! She was already killing herself. I just helped her get on with it. I'm not going back inside because of her, are you crazy?"

Madison stared at him. "Eddie said, 'You belong back inside,' and you answered, 'Not going.' What..." She blinked at the implication. "You mean...prison?"

"Metropolitan Prison. It's no secret. I even told you I was still on probation."

She could hardly breathe. "I thought you meant your job probation."

He shook his head. "You couldn't just fly home and forget about it. It's like you're obsessed. Why did you have to come out here?"

"Because you lied! She never told you she wanted to swim in the lights. Out here on the beach she said if you hadn't cut her off at the bar, she wouldn't have wandered out here. She was angry that no one told her about the lights."

He snickered. "She knows about them now."

Madison threw sand in his face, then sprang forward. She dropped her cell phone in the sand, plunging the tent into darkness. She got in a lucky shot, landing one really good punch to his throat. With his brief shock, she was able to scramble past him and run out the opening of the cabana.

But he tackled her from behind. With one arm around her waist, his other hand covering her mouth, he cut her scream off so quickly, she doubted anyone could've heard the short yelp over the crash of the waves.

She struggled as he manhandled her down to the water's edge, the wind slapping sea spray into them both. Dinner-plate-sized circles of illumination lit their footsteps in the wet sand. But the circles she'd seen from her balcony were accompanied by a wide neon groove. She knew now that groove was not made by any surfboard. It was Kursey's body, being dragged to the water.

She fought and scratched, hoping at the very least he'd have a hard time explaining where all the deep gouges came from.

The iridescent tide seemed so wrong in this context. It wasn't supposed to be beautiful when you were fighting for your life.

She saw the lovely blue muddle of the water as he dragged her in, deeper into the tide, knowing this was what she had witnessed in the middle of the night when Brant murdered Kursey.

And as he plunged Madison's head into the water, she wondered how long she could hold her breath while the waters lit up around her.

But just as suddenly as he'd plunged her under, she felt movement near her legs in the water, and Brant's hands came off her. Her feet found the sand at the bottom and she jerked upright, water running down her face.

It was Crazy Eddie. He was smashing his fist repeatedly into Brant's face.

With a loud growl, Crazy Eddie cried, "I told you next time, it'll be your face!"

* * *

In the early morning, multiple suitcases sat together in front of the hotel. They all had a flight to catch. Taxies came and went, but Spenser's group wanted to travel together in a van that would take all of them to the airport. The trauma of the last twenty-four hours made them want to stay close to each other.

Lon and Babe stood off to the side, their carry-on items at their feet. They were in deep discussion about staying in touch. They'd said earlier they had decided to try a long distance relationship until they could work out a way to live near each other.

Mindy and Keiko looked through the photos Spenser showed them as she held out her camera's electronic viewfinder. These were the dozens of photos Spenser took of the iridescent waters, and the neon snow angels Mindy and Keiko made while their infectious laughter filled the air.

"Wow!" said Keiko. "These are amazing."

"Ooh, look at this one!" Mindy's eyes grew wide. "That's my favorite."

Madison marveled at how lovely the photos were. "And you said the client likes them?"

"They *love* them!" Spenser beamed. "They want the whole batch. They're considering the contract fulfilled after all, and these shots are giving them ideas for their next advertising campaign."

Keiko nodded. "I can see why." Her eyes lifted to Spenser's face. "I want you to know I loved working with you and Madison."

"Me, too," said Mindy. "I'm so sorry for what happened to Kursey, but I hope you both know you did all you could. Her problems had nothing to do with you."

They were all surprised to see Eddie step up at that moment. "I'll second that," he said. "That poor girl had some problems that I'd like to think she would've overcome if she'd had the chance."

"Oh, Eddie!" Spenser threw her arms around Eddie. "Thank you, oh my god, thank you for saving Madison. I'd be lost without my bestie."

Madison smirked. "You might have less trouble to deal with. Just saying."

"Worth the madness. Every minute of it."

Keiko hugged Eddie next. "Thank you for doing the right thing at the party that night. I was so uncomfortable I was just going to leave. But you stepped in and stopped it."

"Speaking of that party," said Madison, "what exactly happened that night?"

Mindy pushed her red hair behind one shoulder. "Kursey got all hot and heavy on Brant, and he went along with it—with enthusiasm. I was wishing they'd get a room. When her clothes started coming off, Eddie stepped in and shut it down hard. He grabbed Brant, threw him down on the sand, and walked Kursey into the hotel."

Keiko said, "Then Brant told the rest of us he was worried what his boss would do if he found out. We didn't want him to lose his job because Kursey was taking her clothes off, so we all agreed not to say anything."

"It was hard to know," said Mindy, "whether Kursey knew what she was doing. She walked the edges that way. But the next day her memory was messed up. That's when we knew Eddie's instinct to step in was right."

Madison shook her head. "You must've known about Brant."

Eddie sighed. "I did. But the hotel has always had a Second Chances program for guys trying to start their life over. It's helped a lot of people. Now Brant has marred the good reputation of the program."

"Well, the police have Brant now," said Spenser. "He was still wet when they led him away in cuffs." She smirked. "But he'll be dry long before his face heals."

Eddie smiled. "Happy to oblige."

"It all makes sense now," said Madison. "But I have one last question. Eddie, how did you happen to be there when Brant pulled me into the water?"

"That night you asked me if Kursey and me made plans to meet up?" He shrugged. "We did. But I told her I wanted to wait till the next night, same spot, extra points if she's sober. I didn't know if she could do it, but I wanted to give her a chance. But when I arrived to meet up with Kursey, I saw you trying to fight off Brant."

Madison released one final heavy sigh as she hugged Eddie. "Thank you. Because of you, the people who love me back home will get to see me again."

"And that's a wonderful thing. People who love you." He patted her back, maybe a little too long, trying to break out of the melancholy moment. "You ever want to learn how to surf, you come back here. Bring some of those folks of yours."

"I'd love that."

The van pulled up and the porters loaded luggage into the back while everyone climbed inside the van, finally heading to the airport. As the van pulled away from the hotel, Madison watched Eddie waving goodbye. She pictured him out there on the water, dominating the waves, his sun-bleached blond dreadlocks flying in the wind. Once his image disappeared, she watched the ocean along the side of the road until the road swerved away, and the ocean turned to a slim blue line in the distance, fading out.

* * *

**Lucy Carol's** top priority is to entertain you, and keep you turning pages. She writes mysteries for those who like it fun, fast, and don't mind losing a little sleep. Living and writing in the Pacific Northwest, she loves martinis, flowers, dancing, a good lipstick, and cake.

To find out about sales, giveaways, or her latest book release, sign up for Lucy's newsletter on her website at lucycarol.com.

Start reading the series with Boyfriends & Bodies (Madison Cruz Mystery #1)

Secrets, spies, sexy guys. Staying alive is hard!

Happy reading!

# Coast Busters
## by Karen Cantwell

WHAT I WANTED, WAS A VACATION. A *mom* vacation.

Family vacations are not relaxing. They do not restore sanity in any way, shape, or form. The planning and packing involved to get two adults and three kids anywhere, whether it's across town or across the country, creates so much anxiety that a vacation is necessary to get over the vacation. Because it's the moms who do all of the planning and packing. Dads and kids pretend to help, but who are they kidding?

What I wanted, nay, *needed*, was the kind of getaway with girlfriends where a mom can act like a teenager again and throw caution to the wind. Be wild and crazy, be the first on the beach and the last at the tiki bar. *That* was the kind of vacation I proposed to my best buds, Roz Walker and Peggy Rubenstein. They heard the word beach and jumped on it like cheese to macaroni. Well, except for a brief moment when Peggy worried that wet t-shirt contests would be involved.

"I mean, I'm not a prude, Barb," she said, "but my body looks better dry."

Peggy is very Irish in appearance—wide hips, bright red hair, pasty skin that's never managed to tan. Quite frankly, I worried more about how her body would look after a day under a blazing hot sun. Sun screen. We'd bring lots of sun screen.

"Definitely no wet t-shirt contests," I agreed.

Sweet, super sensible, forever-on-the-PTA-board Roz was surprisingly zealous about the tiki bar. And she wanted a cabana too. "With a cabana man," she said. "Not a cabana boy—that sounds very wrong. I want a cabana man."

I doubted her husband would think that sounded any better, but that wasn't my problem and I loved her enthusiasm. "It sounds like we have a blueprint," I said. "Let's start building a vacation."

Peggy's third cousin four times removed told her about a great deal on a newly opened resort in Florida, and Roz researched flights until she found us rock-bottom prices on round trip tickets.

Now, you're probably reading this and thinking, oh boy, these ladies are going to have the time of their lives. Good food, great drink, fun in the sun, cabana men...

Well, here's the problem. I'm Barbara Marr and in the simplest terms, I am a disaster magnet. When trouble wants company, it looks for me. It's a mystery as to why. I mean, for a good period of my life, things were calm. I was married to my college sweetie who looked like George Clooney, I had three beautiful, smart, kind, creative daughters. The dream life was mine. Then at the age of forty-five, something went terribly screwy and I started finding dead people. Not "seeing" them like that kid in *The Sixth Sense*—*finding* them. Or almost dead. And there was that time when a famous movie director keeled over on top of me and died. And if all that wasn't enough, I nearly ended up dead myself a couple of times. We're talking kidnappings, helicopters crashing, hand grenades detonating. Some truly hair-raising, life-endangering calamities. You know it's a problem when the police have you on speed dial. Then, for seemingly no reason that I can pinpoint, the chaotic episodes ended. A couple of years went by without a dead body. I could actually go for a walk in the woods and not worry about stumbling upon human remains. Excepting the occasional bad hair day or unexpected visit from my overbearing mother, my day-to-day existence was relatively dilemma-free.

Then I went to the beach. Oh well. The serenity was nice while it lasted.

* * *

Sunny Delray, Florida, May

I will say that none of us saw the metaphorical shipwreck coming. Our arrival at Quirky-Chic Seaside Resort was even better than we had imagined it would be. When the airport shuttle van dropped us off at the front door, three young, bright-eyed porters scurried up like a trio of eager sandpipers and whisked our bags away even before all six of our flip-flopped feet had hit the pavement.

As the driver accepted his tip from Peggy, Roz and I gazed in wonder and amusement at the resort's lush, elegant tropical landscaping ornamented here and there with fun and unconventional features like the life-size Bigfoot sculpture peeking out from between two taller banana trees. Near the street, a retro motel-style neon sign flashed the resort's name for all to see.

"I'm in love," I said on a sigh.

A lanky woman breezed through the automatic sliding doors, greeting us with a toothy smile and multi-hued leis. Her Caribbean-blue eyes twinkled. "Welcome to Quirky-Chic Seaside Resort where relaxation and recreation abound. I'm Willow, your hospitality and recreation coordinator. Which one of you is Barb?"

I stepped forward, speechless at the unexpected greeting. I was not accustomed to this sort of reception. My last experience was at a one-star hotel where the front desk clerk referred to me as Mr. Marbarb and informed me I would have to heft my luggage up three flights of stairs because the elevator was being repaired after an "unfortunate incident."

Willow draped a lei over my head so it rested prettily on my shoulders. "Are your curls natural?" she asked.

"They are," I said, beaming. At that moment, a porter appeared in front of me as if by magic. He held out a cocktail in a tall glass with a lime green paper straw. I accepted it eagerly.

"Frozen strawberry daiquiri is your favorite, correct?" Willow asked.

I tested the icy drink, remembering we had filled out a questionnaire designed to help us have the best vacation experience possible. "Perfectly delicious, thank you."

Another porter arrived with a margarita for Roz and Peggy was handed a limoncello martini.

We were flowered-up, liquored-up, and ready for a cabana.

Willow ushered us into the bright, airy lobby. To the right, an empty reception desk. Straight ahead a two-story wall waterfall emptied into a brightly lit concrete pool. Very chic. In front of the waterfall, two patchwork quilt couches faced each other. I'd never seen couches upholstered with patchwork quilts, but I adored them immediately. They added the quirky to the chic as did the purple paper mâché elephant hanging from the ceiling.

To our left, floor-to-ceiling windows provided a view of a garden with tables and chairs and a tall Grecian fountain. Near the windows, a woman with bobbed, jet-black hair talked with a man who towered over her by at least a foot. She wore vintage black slacks, a yellow striped blouse, and chunky shoes Katharine Hepburn style, while the man sported basic jeans and black t-shirt. I couldn't hear words, but their expressions and postures didn't give me the impression it was a happy conversation.

"Mika wants to meet you personally and thank you for your patronage," Willow said as she stopped just short of the couches.

"Who is Mika?" I asked.

"Mika Huraki, the owner and proprietor." Willow waved her hand to catch the dark-haired woman's attention.

Mika caught the signal, cut the man off mid-sentence, and moved in our direction. He stalked away, fuming.

Though small in stature, Mika carried herself with the confidence of a giant and the grace of a gazelle. This impressed me, since I carry myself with the confidence of a chipmunk and the grace of a giant three sheets to the wind. She had discarded any indication of annoyance and was all smiles by the time she reached us. "Welcome to Quirky-Chic—or as we like to call it, The QC. I'm Mika. Hopefully your first impression is a good one."

Peggy seemed as dazzled with Mika as I was, maybe more. She thrust her hand out to shake. "Peggy Rubenstein. This is the best limoncello martini I've ever had. And your resort—true, I haven't seen it all yet—but so far, it is *bellissimo*!"

Roz and I introduced ourselves as well, but we kept the fawning to a minimum.

"Willow," Mika said, "I'm going to show these ladies to their suite now. I still haven't had a chance to welcome our newlywed couple. See if you can make that happen while honoring their privacy, would you?"

Willow nodded with a retreat.

Roz, Peggy, and I followed Mika as she walked down a bright hallway flanked by the wall of windows on our left. The lush green gardens, visible through the glass, appeared endless. "I gave you ladies the Coast Busters Suite. It's fun, but luxurious."

Happy as a clam in a tide pool, I hummed a few bars of the *Ghostbusters* theme song.

Mika laughed, then continued. "As you know, we are in soft-open mode right now. Given that it's May, we should have already had our grand opening and been fully booked, but we had some setbacks. Then more setbacks, unfortunately." She had stopped momentarily in front of a glass door that led to the garden and onto a path. She pushed that door open, gesturing us to follow the path. "One of the setbacks was with our security system installation. I apologize. We currently have no functioning camera surveillance, but a security guard will do rounds twice each night. Also, I'm on the premises twenty-four-seven as is my partner, Roger, so please know, you are very safe." We turned a corner where a funky, colorful crossroads sign pointed the way to various locations, including the Pool and Tiki Bar, Honeymoon Cottage, Suites 1 – 3, Main Building, Key West, and Narnia. Behind the sign, four bikes were parked in a rack. "This weekend the pool and the tiki-bar will be open, although the pool area décor isn't quite completed. That will be done by tomorrow, even if I have to do it myself." She laughed, but there was a hint of tension under the laugh, I could tell. "The restaurant, I am sorry to say, is not open for business yet. But Delray is filled with great restaurants and Willow can get you reservations at any of them. The mini-bar in your suite is fully stocked and to thank you for coming despite the lack of full amenities, all items in them are gratis. Our way of saying thank you for being one of the first guests at Quirky-Chic Seaside Resort." We had turned yet another corner and stopped in front of a wooden gate connecting two sides of a yellow stucco wall. "Here's the patio entrance to your suite. Each suite, is designed in a unique Quirky-Chic theme. Soon we'll be opening Sunny-Side-Up and A Shore Thing. This, I admit though, is my favorite." She pointed to the ceramic name plate on the wooden gate, which read, *Suite 1, Coast Busters*.

"Who ya gonna call?" I shouted like the true movie geek that I am. "See, Coast Busters rhymes with *Ghostbusters* which is a movie," I explained to Roz who knew nothing about American cinema at all.

"I know that," she said, almost sneering. "With Eddie Murphy."

I considered correcting her since she had *Ghostbusters* confused with Eddie Murphy's *Haunted Mansion*, but I didn't. I wanted to keep drinking my daiquiri and see the suite. "Yeah, with Eddie Murphy," I agreed.

Mika pressed the latch, swung the gate open, and stepped aside, allowing us to enter first. Flowering vegetation surrounded the patio from the ground to far above our heads. A soothing urn fountain bubbled near a table and chairs. I pictured myself drinking coffee and eating a chocolate croissant there the next morning. Sigh. Was this the best girls' getaway or what?

While we oohed and aahed, Mika swiped the suite door open. She was handing each of us a keycard when her phone rang. Looking annoyed, she said it was important, made her apologies, and left us to explore on our own.

The suite design was a lively surprise: classy hotel luxury mixed with *Ghostbusters*-themed decor, like a fire house pole in one corner, Stay Puft Marshmallow Man pillows on each of the beds, and a portrait of the green ghost, Slimer. There was nothing quirky about the bathroom—it was hotel spa-chic from top to bottom. Conveniently separated into two rooms connected by the bathroom, one room had a king-sized bed and a large seating area in front of a widescreen TV, while the second room had two queens and the mini-fridge. The icing on the cake: the porters had already placed our bags on free-standing luggage racks. For a soft-open, they sure did have their service down pat already. I'd give a five-star review for sure.

Peggy pulled back the curtains to let the sunshine in.

Roz did a little dance and her blond hair danced with her. "It's cabana time, it's cabana time!"

We threw on our swim suits, beach wraps, and sunglasses, snatched complimentary beach towels from the bathroom, and hiked back to the lobby where we found Willow assisting a hand-holding couple make dinner reservations at a seafood restaurant. I scanned the area for signs of blooming jasmine since I was sure I smelled some. One of the glass doors to the garden was held open, so I figured the breeze must have been wafting it in for me to enjoy. Meanwhile, Peggy and Roz whispered to each other about the female half of the romantic duo. They both thought she looked familiar, but were not sure why.

Finally, Willow finished with the reservations and we were next. "Newlyweds. Aren't they so cute?" she said.

"How many guests are here this weekend?" Roz asked.

"Five. You three and them. We had hoped for more, but only two suites are completed to Mika's satisfaction. And then there's the whole restaurant debacle. And other debacles..." Willow shook it off. "She's a perfectionist. You gotta love her."

"She's impressive," I agreed.

Peggy got to more important matters. "When I registered, I reserved a cabana on the beach. Which way do we go to find that? And," she added, "can we take cocktails onto the beach with us?"

Willow winced. Nothing good ever comes after a wince. "Let me answer the second question first. That might make the answer to the cabana question a little easier to take: drinking alcohol on the beach is illegal in Delray. No open containers. I'm not saying people don't do it, but the fine is hefty if you're caught."

"What about the cabana?" Roz addressed the wince head-on.

With a sigh, Willow offered up the bad news. "So, Mika had an agreement with Bob of Cabana Bob's to provide our guests with beach cabanas. Then, don't ask me why, but last week he backed out of the agreement. Mika is very upset about all of this, so she bought a cabana for the poolside and it's yours for the weekend. It's just not on the beach. But you can drink all of the cocktails you want by the pool. The tiki bar is right there and Joaquin will see to your every need."

"Is Joaquin a cabana man?" Roz asked.

Willow seemed puzzled. The term cabana man probably threw her off. "Um, no. He's the bartender."

I whispered in Roz's ear. "You can pretend he's a cabana man."

"Poolside cabana, here we come," Roz said with renewed vigor. "Point me in the right direction, please."

I motioned my buds to follow me. "It's back toward the suite. I saw the sign."

We found the pool and were soon reclined in lounge chairs under a royal blue cabana, waiting for Joaquin to bring us our next round of cocktails. I noticed two plastic bins stacked one on the other tucked into a corner by some folded chairs. From the looks of it, I guessed they contained the awaiting décor that Mika had mentioned.

Peggy pulled a book from her beach bag. "Finally, time to read. I joined another book club and my first meeting is next week. This should be a good one, though—*Evil Under the Sun*. I've never read an Agatha Christie before. And so perfect to be reading it at the beach!"

If there was a Book Clubs Anonymous for book club addicts, Peggy should join.

"Exactly how many book clubs are you up to now?" I asked her.

She paused to count. "Technically, eight since joining this Women Who Kill club. But four of the six members in my money management book club are being investigated for tax evasion, so we haven't met in a while."

"I just caught the movie version of *Evil Under the Sun* on the Classic Movie Channel last week," I said. "Great cast."

"Don't tell me whodunit," Peggy said. "Unless I don't finish it in time, in which case, I'll ask you for a synopsis."

Roz didn't care about books. "Joaquin can't bring me my drink soon enough," she said. Then she lowered her sunglasses to glare at me. "And Barb, stop what you're thinking right now. I love Peter. I'm not ogling another man. I'm merely basking in the luxury of having someone bring me fruity drinks while I do absolutely nothing PTA-related."

She'd read my mind. "Fair enough," I said. "I feel the same way. Except, of course, I love Howard, not Peter."

"And I love Simon," Peggy added.

Yes, we loved our husbands deeply.

At the same time, it was easy to pretend that Joaquin was a cabana man, because *man*, was he sexy. He had this whole smoldering, Mediterranean stud thing going with the olive-tanned skin; dark, brooding eyes; wavy black hair that fell to his shoulders; tight polo shirt that emphasized the bulk of his biceps; and the perfect Kirk Douglas dimple right in the middle of his chin. Maybe it was rude to stare, but we did anyway. From across the pool, we watched his every move as he poured and stirred and shook and poured some more and stirred some more. Finally, he brought us our drinks on a tray.

"Thank you, Joaquin," we purred in unison.

"You are most welcome, ladies. I am so happy to have work to do. Sitting behind the bar all day in the heat with no guests to serve can make Joaquin a very dull boy, no?"

"Don't be dull," Roz said while stirring her margarita, and playing unusually coy. "Pull up a chair and tell us about yourself."

He pulled a lounge chair over and sat. "There is not much to tell, I am afraid, but I am glad for the conversation. Is there anything I can recommend in Delray? A restaurant perhaps? Fun things to do like the sand sculpture contest on the beach this weekend or an Everglades airboat tour? The airboats are quite a thrill. I highly recommend."

"I love your accent," Peggy said, "where are you from, Joaquin?"

"Espana," he said.

I sighed. "Spain. Lovely country."

"You have been?"

"No. I wish. The closest I've gotten is on my TV when watching *House Hunters International*."

"I am from Malaga. It is the most beautiful city in Espana, but I am, you know, um... prejudice to my home. In Malaga, we are on the coast, and the magical blue waters of the Mediterranean cannot even be compared to the brown, murky waters here of the Atlantic." He shook his head. "No comparison."

"What brought you here then?" I asked, eager to know more about him. And not because he was sexy, but because I was genuinely interested. In him. As a person.

"Why did I come to the United States, you mean? Yes, I met a very handsome man and he swept me off my feet and soon we will be married."

"Oh," we ladies said in unison, not purring this time.

He pulled his wallet from his back pocket. "I show you a picture."

We crowded around to see an image of Joaquin and a slightly taller man with rich, dark brown skin, and happy eyes. The two posed for a selfie on the beach in front of a rising sun. Their smiles spoke volumes of their love. "Oh," we ladies said again in unison, purring once more.

Joaquin replaced his wallet. "Emmanuel. He is from Haiti originally, but he come here many years ago. Look at that! You have finished your drinks already. Another round, yes?"

Roz accepted the offer like a baby boomer accepting free tickets to a Rolling Stones concert. "Definitely. But can I try a mai tai this time? I've never had one of those and I just love how the words rolls off the tongue. Mai tai. Mai tai."

Uh-oh. Roz was usually wound tightly. She sounded fairly un-wound at the present. I wondered if a mai tai might not loosen her screws too much. "And maybe a glass of water too—for all of us."

"I'm sticking with the martini, Joaquin," Peggy said, pointing to her nearly-empty glass. "Can't get enough of these babies, am I right?"

Peggy sounded four-fifths of the way to Tipsy Town as well. Crazy that I didn't feel a thing, except the need to use the bathroom. "Surprise me with a new drink, Joaquin. And, can you direct me to the...facilities?"

Luckily, the facilities were only a few steps behind the tiki bar. On my way back to the cabana, I thought I'd give Joaquin company while he whipped up our drinks. I sat on a stool facing the main building of the resort. I realized there was a second gated entrance to the pool. On the other side of the gate and several feet back, Mika and Tall Man were conversing again. "Hey, Joaquin, who's that guy talking to Mika?"

Giving Roz's mai tai a toss in the shaker, he rolled his eyes. "That is Roger, her business partner and—get this—ex-lover." The word *lover* rolled off his tongue with the sensuous elegance of a Latin tango.

"I'm detecting tension between them."

"*Si.* The tension is as obvious as the curls on your pretty head. Those two, in my opinion, should not be partners in any way. Not on the ledger sheets, not between the sheets—you understand what I am saying? Although, the lover business was a very long time ago from what I hear." He poured the mai tai into a tall glass and garnished it with an orange slice and a sea-blue rock candy stick.

"Interesting," I said, my curiosity growing. "Mika was complaining about all sorts of set-backs. Is he the reason?"

"Not entirely. He is a *culo*, but she has, um, what you call tall expectations. She, too, can be very difficult."

I was sure he meant high expectations, but I needed help with another word. "Culo?"

"It is a curse word and I do not like to curse in front of a lady. One could say nicely: a donkey. Or a rear-end."

I nodded. "Gotcha. Well, she seems so together and yet very friendly and approachable."

"She does seem that way..."

"You mean she's not?"

"Do not get me wrongly, Mika has been very good to me. Her fiancé, Rahul, is my fiancé's friend and she give me this job for that reason. I say no bad things about her." He shook his head adamantly to prove his point. "But I cannot say that about everyone here. Roger even once joked to me that if Mika died, he'd be doing much better because he would collect the insurance moneys and use it to run this place right. I did not think this a funny joke."

"I agree. Not funny."

"The words of a *culo*." He shrugged, then poured an orange icy concoction into a frosty glass and plopped a sprig of mint on top. He slid it my way and raised an eyebrow.

I sipped the mystery drink and my taste buds rejoiced. "Joaquin, you're a master craftsman. What's it called?"

"This is my own creation that I have named, 'Murder on the Beach.' Like a Long Island iced tea, only much, much better. And stronger. Pace yourself. Could be deadly." He winked. "Now, shall I tell you more about Mika?"

I always tell my girls not to gossip, then turned around and indulged in the nasty habit myself. *Bad, hypocritical mother*, I chastised myself silently. Do not go there, Barb. Don't poke the hearsay bear. Alas, I was not strong. "Yes, do go on."

"Willow, your genuine Hospitality and Recreation Coordinator," he started on Peggy's martini. "She is not so much of the genuine character and does not like our boss."

"Get out!"

"I will stay in. It is true. Ask the porters." He wiped his counter with a towel. "She chitters about Mika to them all of the time. Like a chicken in the chicken yard." He did a clucking chickens thing with his fingers. "Chitter, chitter, chitter. 'She's a witch,' 'She's a cow,' 'She's a shrew.' That last one is Willow's favorite. I had to look up this word—I had never heard it before. I hear it a lot now. And, I have to say, sometimes, Mika can be one. A shrew, I mean." He picked up Roz and Peggy's glasses and I followed him with mine. He continued giving me the scoop as we made our way to the cabana. "And there is Bob, you have heard of Bob?"

"Of Cabana Bob's?"

"He is the one. He says he is going to sue her."

"Willow told us she doesn't know why he backed out of a deal to provide guests cabanas on the beach," I said as we arrived back at the lounge chairs.

"That is Willow not being truthful. Everyone knows why—Mika lied to a city official, saying Bob does not correctly run his business. A whole permitting scandal that shut him down."

"Why would she do that?" I slipped my sunglasses under my chair, then with great care, lowered myself back into the comfy lounge. I managed it brilliantly, not spilling a single drop of Murder on the Beach.

Joaquin handed Peggy her martini. "To swoop in, get her own permit and take over his stretch of beach, of course." His eyes widened and he gestured with a small head nudge toward Mika and Roger. "Speaking of the devil, there he is now."

I swung my gaze over to catch a very tanned man in a yellow t-shirt and matching sun visor approach the business partners. A large black logo on his shirt advertised Cabana Bob's. He wasn't greeted by smiles or handshakes. After a very brief and seemingly stern discussion, the three disappeared around a cluster of small palm trees. Darn. I wanted to see some drama. "Debacles, disgruntled employees, and law suits. Sounds like a soap opera in the making."

"What are you two talking about?" Roz asked as she traded Joaquin her empty glass for a full one.

"Some very juicy gossip," I explained. "And no, I am not proud. Still, very juicy."

The newlywed couple entered the pool oasis and took side-by-side seats at the tiki bar. They slid their stools closer together and nuzzled.

With a lowered voice, Joaquin whispered. "I hate to leave you ladies now, but they were here last night and tip like Rockefellers. Must run." He gave us a wink. "Remember, don't drink and drive."

"Peggy," Roz said, watching Mr. and Mrs. Newlywed. "I think I've got it."

"Got what?" Peggy finally put the book down, giving up on the pretense. Apparently, martinis and reading don't mix.

"That lady's face," Roz said. "I've seen it on a refrigerator."

"That's shilly," Peggy responded, slurring the 's' in silly. "A refrigerator." She giggled. "You know what isn't shilly? Cabana by the pool. It's the besht. I don't mish the beach at all. The beach is shandy. I don't like shand."

"You are so right, Pegs," Roz said. "Can I call you Pegs? I'm going to call you Pegs. Oh, you know what? We should go out to eat. Fancy, expensive restaurant. And after we eat, you know what we should do Pegs and Barbs? We should paint the town red. Let's put the red in wild and crazy."

They were *both* silly, drunk women. Couldn't hold their liquor. Unlike me. I was fine. Maybe a tad hungry though, as I considered the idea of restaurants and food. "When *did* we eat last?"

"I just ate a shliver of lemon rind, does that count?" Peggy hiccupped then laughed. "Oopsh. The lemon rind must have given me the hiccuppsh."

My world began to spin while I slowly calculated our food consumption to alcohol consumption ratio. The math was too much for my inebriated brain so I ordered another Murder on the Beach. I sort of remember Joaquin and the newlyweds eventually helping me and my friends back to our suite while I hummed the *Ghostbusters* theme song and Peggy periodically asked "Who ya gonna call?" with Roz replying far-too-loudly, "Eddie Murphy!" And as the three of us crawled into our beds, still in our bathing suits and cover-ups, we agreed that if we ever formed a rock band, we'd call ourselves Joaquin and the Newlyweds.

All in all, it was a fun first day as Coastbusters at Quirky-Chic Seaside Resort.

Unfortunately, the fun was about to end.

* * *

When my eye lids unrolled slowly to the up position, all they viewed was darkness. I would have sworn the sound of voices woke me up, but the room was dead quiet, so I chalked it up to a dream. I blinked a couple times and located the window. The curtains were still open and I could tell the sky was lightening ever so slightly. Morning was on its way. My head and stomach, in the meantime, were in a battle to prove which was more disgusted with my choices the day before. Joaquin's Murder on the Beach had proven murderous to many of my brain cells, that was for sure.

Barely able to unpeel my dry tongue from the roof of my mouth, I figured some hydration was necessary. I managed to feel my way to the bathroom where I clicked on the light, cursed the light, then found a glass and filled it. Oh, that water tasted so good. I downed two full glasses before setting out to find my phone. The flashlight option helped me search for ibuprofen in my carry-on bag. Peggy stirred in the bed next to me, but she didn't awaken. Roz was in the room on the other side of the bathroom, but I doubted she was awake yet either. I texted Howard good morning, then as the room began to lighten with the rising sun, set about to organize my items. I always did this on vacations after I once left my favorite sweater at a hotel in Choccolocco, Alabama. I didn't discover the loss until a week after we were home. By then, Hotel Choccolocco said I was out of lucko.

Purse, wallet, home keys, room key, watch that Howard gave me for our tenth anniversary, charm bracelet my daughters gave me when I turned fifty, phone in my hand, phone charger in the wall...something was missing.

Peggy stirred again and this time she mumbled. "Can't take the sun. Close curtains, please."

Sun. That was the missing item. Not the sun, but my sunglasses. I remembered taking them off in the bathroom by the pool and then I didn't put them back on because I was so engrossed in Joaquin's tell-all. From the tiki bar, I had returned to my lounger and I...put them underneath so they'd be safe from me accidentally stepping on them when I got up again. Bingo. They were likely in the same spot. I rarely spend a lot of money on vanity items, but those sunglasses made me look like a movie star and I practically needed the salary of one to afford them.

Peggy moaned. "Make the throbbing stop. Head not bongo drums."

Roz hollered from the other room. "How can I feel hungry and nauseated at the same time?" She was quiet a moment, and then with a lowered voice, added, "Ouch. Should not have yelled. Did I mention my head feels like it might explode?"

I slipped into a pair of shorts, threw on a t-shirt, and closed the curtains. "Water and drugs help ease the pain. Hang on ladies, Barb is coming to the rescue."

Two minutes later, they both had a large glass of water in one hand and two pain killers in the other. "I'll be right back. Left my sunglasses by the pool last night." I grabbed my phone and room key before pulling the door behind me.

As I followed the circular path that led to the pool oasis gate, I was wowed by the color of the sky in the east. The horizon glowed orange and pink as the sun crept upward. I loved a good sunrise, but rarely had time to enjoy one. This moment need to be remembered—I lifted my phone, hit camera mode, and clicked a perfect picture. I did a second one just to be sure. Somehow, I accidentally shifted into video mode. What the heck, I thought, if a picture is worth a thousand words, then a video must be worth a million. After several seconds of recording the sunrise, I panned down, catching footage of the nicely manicured grassy lawn. Still in video mode, I eventually continued on the path to the gate, figuring I could show Howard and the girls the pool. As I did so, I narrated for them. "Now I'm coming up to the pool and tiki bar where we rested under a cabana yesterday." Somewhere behind me I heard leaves rustling and a door slam. Hm. Someone must have been up early like me. The familiar scent of blooming jasmine tickled my nose again. As I reached the gate I noticed a male figure kneeling on the concrete pool deck. "Oh, and someone is at the pool already," I said for my future audience viewing the video. Hearing my voice, the man pivoted, his face was horror stricken. Mr. Newlywed. "I found her like this," he said, his voice shaking. "I...I don't think she's breathing."

"Oh my God!" I shouted, lowering the phone as I realized he knelt over a woman's body. "Who is it?"

"Mika!"

People always say, "It happened so fast," and I know why. The time it took me to see the blood and register that Mika Huraki was probably dead felt like a millisecond.

"Help!" I screamed as I dropped my phone and scrambled to unlatch the gate. "Someone help!" I fumbled. The gate just wouldn't unlatch. Definitely operator error, I was in a state. "Help! Help!" I screamed louder. "Call 9-1-1!"

"I don't have my phone with me," the man shouted. "Don't you have one there?"

Of course, I did. I bent over, scrambling in the grass to get my shaking hands on it.

My screams had roused others. As I eventually managed to dial, Roger arrived, followed by Roz, Peggy, and Willow.

After two long rings, a 9-1-1 operator answered. I gave him our location and the fact that we'd found a woman unconscious and possibly mortally wounded.

Roger unlatched the gate where I had failed, and was beside Mika, giving me answers to the operator's questions as I shouted them out. The bottom line, according to Roger: she had marks on her neck, there was a lot of blood from her head that looked crushed against the concrete, and she had no pulse or breath.

Willow wrung her hands and paced on the grass, unwilling to enter the pool area herself. "Please, please, please" she mumbled in what seemed to be a prayer.

I hung up the phone when there was no more information to give. "The operator said to wait for the police and paramedics to arrive," I told everyone. "We're not to touch or move anything. You two," I said to Roger and Mr. Newlywed, "it's probably best if you leave the pool area. Wait on this side of the fence with us."

Mr. Newlywed rose right away to leave, but Roger lingered a few moments. Then he raised his head with dark, angry eyes focused on the other man who was at the gate by now. "Hey, who are you? Did you do this?" He leapt to his feet and was practically tackling the guy by the time he'd passed through the fence. "I asked you a question."

"I found her like that, man," the groom said. "Get your hands off me."

Willow got into the middle of the scuffle. "Roger, stop it. This is Craig Bonner. He and his new wife are guests in the Honeymooners Cottage, for crying out loud. Maybe we should all be more concerned about a killer who is now on the loose."

Roger's violent outburst had me wondering if the killer wasn't among us. I pulled Peggy and Roz aside. "I think he might have done this," I whispered. "Watch him closely."

"Well you had to go and do it, didn't you?" Roz complained to me. "You couldn't stay in the room and leave well enough alone. You had to go get yourself right into the middle of a crime scene. This is giving me a headache."

I felt that last statement needed clarification. "Don't blame me. Two margaritas and bottomless mai tai's gave you the headache. This just..." my thought wandered off topic as I watched Willow and Roger argue. "What is she doing here?" I wondered aloud.

Peggy looked confused and rightly so. "Willow? Um, she works here."

The cogs of my suspicious mind turned. "This early, though? Maybe she did this."

"Whoa, whoa, whoa," Roz said, her bloodshot eyes boring into me. "Pull back on those amateur sleuth reins, Miss Marple. Right now, we're safe and the police are on their way. No one has tried to kidnap us or obliterate us with hand grenades or hidden incendiary devices, so please keep it that way and don't go sticking your nose where it shouldn't be stuck. I'd like to get home in one piece."

"But something isn't adding up. Joaquin told me yesterday that Willow bad-mouthed Mika behind her back to everyone. Called her a witch and a shrew."

Peggy narrowed her eyes while observing Willow more closely. "Really?"

Roz rolled her eyes. "That's enough evidence for me. I mean, we have to take Joaquin's word to be true. Never mind, we only met him yesterday."

"Willow, when did you get here?" I asked, raising my voice loud enough for everyone to hear.

She pulled Roger away from Mr. Newlywed. "I'm sorry, what?"

I repeated my question. "When did you get here?"

"I came down when I heard the sirens."

So, she was already here. Interesting. "How early do you come to work?"

"I never left last night," she said. "With only five guests and limited staff, I figured it would be easier if I just stayed in the Sunny Side Up suite."

Strange, I thought. "But you said there were only two rooms ready for occupancy."

"Only two that were up to Mika's standards. Most are ready enough." She sniffled. "I never thought... Oh, I'm sorry. I just can't believe she's gone, you know? Such a wonderful, smart, kind woman. And the best boss I've ever had."

I scoffed under my breath. "Or the best boss she's ever killed," I whispered to my friends. "Roger said Mika had marks on her neck. She could have been strangled by Willow."

"I don't know," Peggy said. "She doesn't look like she has it in her. Look at those arms. They couldn't strangle a gnat."

"True. Maybe she had help. Maybe she and Roger did it together. They look awfully chummy right now. What if they're lovers? He'll collect the insurance money, and off they go, rich, happy murderers."

"Insurance money?" Roz asked. "Where are you getting all of this?"

"I told you—Joaquin. He gave me the 4-1-1 while mixing drinks at the tiki bar."

"Maybe Joaquin is guilty," Roz said. "He is suspiciously absent from the scene. And he set the stage nicely for you with all of these 'clues.'" She punctuated the last word with finger quotes.

"Good point, Roz," I agreed. "I like your thinking. He made me his special drink: Murder on the Beach. He could be one of those brilliant killers who like to mess with people's minds. Yup. He needs to be on our list."

"I'd argue, though, that his absence is not suspicious," Peggy interjected. "As a bartender, I doubt he stays on site twenty-four-seven. And in all fairness, this could have been a random attack."

Sirens sounded in the distance. Soon we'd be separated and they'd bring an investigator in who would figure all of this out. Roz was right. I should just let the professionals worry about it all.

Mr. Newlywed, or Craig I guess, made a move to leave.

Roger grabbed his arm. "Where are you going?"

"To check on my f—" he stopped to correct himself. "My wife. The sirens might worry her."

I shook my head. "No. The operator was adamant we all have to stay right here until police arrive." Of course, I suddenly realized Mrs. Newlywed *was* suspiciously absent. Why hadn't the screams worried her, but the sirens might?

Two distinct sets of sirens whirred loudly now and within seconds both stopped in what sounded like the driveway in front of the lobby. Guided by our shouts, a uniformed police woman plodded across the grass followed by two EMT's. Roger pointed the EMT's to the pool deck.

"I'm officer Daniels," she said. "Who—"

Officer Daniels was rudely interrupted by Mrs. Newlywed who finally descended upon the scene, all frantic for herself. "Craig? Craig? Are you alright? Oh my, God, what's happening?" She ran past me and into her husband's arms.

Blooming jasmine wafted up into my nostrils, but not the real thing, I realized. Perfume. Mrs. Newlywed's perfume was jasmine scented. That's what I had been smelling all along.

Daniels attempted to gain control of the situation. "Ma'am—"

"I found Mika by the pool," Craig said. "Sweetheart, she's dead."

Mrs. Newlywed gasped. All too showy for me, given my red flags were now raised higher than the Rocky Mountains. The last time I smelled that jasmine scent was at the gate of the pool when I first walked up. She had been there, what, maybe a minute or less before I showed up? It couldn't have been very long considering how strongly I detected the fragrance.

The breathy bride hugged her husband tightly, then turned to Officer Daniels. "I was taking a walk a while back and saw a man running from this direction. He had a yellow shirt and visor. I think the shirt said Cabana Tom or something like that. Do you think he could have done this?"

"Wait," Roz said, at the end of the newlywed's spiel. "I have it now. She's in a picture on your refrigerator door, Peggy. In the picture, her hair is in a ponytail like it is now."

"Ma'am," Officer Daniels put a hand up to stop Roz from talking.

The hand didn't stop Peggy though. "Yes! The picture of my cousin, Janet. Well, she's my third cousin four times removed, but that doesn't make her any less loved. She told me about the deal for this weekend stay."

"Ma'am, I must ask you—"

More sirens were headed our way.

Peggy isn't one to stop once the tongue starts flapping. She addressed the familiar-looking woman directly. "You must be her friend in the picture—Nancy?"

Mrs. Newlywed didn't answer. Instead, she gave Peggy a blank look. But I could tell the innocent act was contrived.

Sirens whirred to a sudden stop. I figured another one or two suits would be walking up any minute.

"You have her confused with someone else," Willow intervened. "This is Tanney Bonner."

"Ma'am—" Poor Officer Daniels said.

"No," Peggy shook her red head vehemently. "I'm sure Janet said her name was Nancy. I have a very good memory—"

Scowling heavily, Officer Daniels appeared ready to pull her gun out and fire it off to stop the chatter. Instead, she bellowed, "I need everyone to stop talking right now."

As police officer number two approached, his accoutrements jingling, someone's cell phone began to ring. It didn't take too long for everyone to realize it was coming from Craig's pocket.

"Can I answer it?" he asked Daniels.

"You said you didn't have your cell phone with you," I blurted. "And she was at the pool." I pointed to Mrs. Newlywed whose name was either Nancy or Tanney. "Whatever her name is—I smelled her jasmine perfume. It's very strong. I walked up to the gate, I smelled the jasmine, then I saw him."

"Ma'am—"

"Nancy," Peggy said. "I'm telling you it's Nancy and she was engaged to someone, but his name wasn't Craig. Oh, what was his name? I should call Janet..."

"No one is calling anyone or answering phones or anything," Daniels said. "And if I don't get some cooperation here, I'm hauling all of you down to the precinct."

"Rahul!" Peggy shouted, very pleased with herself.

Maybe-Nancy's eyes grew so wide I thought they'd pop like over-inflated balloons. Willow and Roger looked stunned as well.

"Mika's fiancé is Rahul," Roger said. "That can't be a coincidence."

Peggy's face flushed. "Never mind, I did have it wrong. I'm so embarrassed. Her name isn't Nancy, it's Katherine. Katherine Tanney."

Things got quiet for a few seconds.

Roger broke the silence. "Mika talked a few times about her friend, Kat Tanney. Said Kat hated her for stealing Rahul."

Officer Daniels and the second policeman exchanged questioning glances. Daniels appeared ready to make some sort of move when Whatever-Her-Name-Was lunged at Peggy wrapping her big old hands around my friend's neck and screaming, "I'm going to kill you!"

Needless to say, we'd found our murderer.

And for once, it wasn't me that ended up almost dead.

* * *

Officer Daniels kept her promise. Squad cars carried all of us down to the Delray police department. My phone was confiscated on the scene since my video footage was evidence and we spent most of that day either waiting to be questioned or actually being questioned, despite the fact that the honeymooners were obviously key suspects. The police took pity upon our hungry tummies and fed us chips and soda from a vending machine.

In the police station hallway, just before giving us the all-clear to leave, the friendly, Viola Davis look-alike detective on the case updated Peggy, Roz, Roger, Willow, and me to the degree she was allowed. Apparently, Mr. and Mrs. Newlywed weren't newlyweds at all. Fake Mrs. was, in fact, Kat Tanney and Craig Bonner was her friend whom she'd enlisted to help her crash Mika's soft open, giving the resort a bad review as revenge for stealing Kat's fiancé, Rahul. Mika had no idea Kat was on the property, probably until the morning of the attack. That was it. All she could say.

"I guess we'll read the rest in the papers," I said. "But I think we're all guessing Mika went to the pool to put the finishing touches on the decor, Kat showed up wearing her ten gallons of perfume, and told Mika they'd give the QC a bad review if Mika didn't break up with Rahul. Mika said 'screw you,' and Kat lunged at her the way she did Peggy, smashing her skull on the concrete while strangling her. She fled, told Craig, who went to check to see if she was dead or alive, possibly get rid of any evidence, then I wandered up, ruining his plan to escape the scene undetected."

"And when she heard the sirens," Roz added, "she got spooked and decided to show up with a suspect in her back pocket. Joaquin probably told her and Craig the same story about the Cabana Bob feud so she decided to frame him."

Roger raised an eyebrow. "I wasn't guessing any of that."

"We've been around the crime scene block a few times," I said.

"Is it too early for a limoncello martini?" Peggy asked.

Roz and I moaned.

* * *

If you think our vacation was a total loss, you'd be wrong. Cabana Bob, it turned out, was quite a generous fellow. He learned of our plight and put us up, at his expense, in a five-star oceanfront hotel and gave us three whole days of free cabana time on the beach. Turns out, cabanas were the topic of his visit to the QC, the day I had seen him there. He was telling Mika his permit was back in effect and to warn her that her tactics wouldn't work with him. He'd been in Delray far longer than she and Roger, and he operated by the book. If she wanted to be successful in his town, she'd better learn to play by the rules too.

We accepted his offer gratefully.

As we lay on the beach our last day in Delray, soaking up the rays, relaxing to the sound of the waves crashing on the shore, I felt regret that I had to buy a cheap pair of sunglasses to shield my eyes from the sun. Since my designer pair had been in the pool area at the time of Mika's killing, they were being held as evidence along with my cell phone. Of course, I felt regret too, that Mika had died. She wasn't a nice person by most people's accounts, but she didn't deserve such a terrible ending.

Peggy opened her book, flipped a couple of pages, then closed it again. "I give up. I'm not in the mood to read. Tell me who did it, Barb."

"*Evil Under the Sun*?" I laughed. "It was the married couple. They plotted an entire murder just to steal the actress's diamond."

A newspaper landed on the sand at my feet followed by the sound of a familiar voice. "Speaking of murder, have you read the latest?"

The three of us looked up, shielding our eyes from the sun, to see Joaquin and his very handsome fiancé, Emmanuel, hand in hand. He introduced us then pointed to the paper. "The whole story is there. The man, Craig, has confessed that his friend Kat strangled Mika in a fit of rage when Mika would not agree to call off her engagement in exchange for a good review. This woman, it seems, has a history of violent attacks."

Peggy rubbed her throat. "Don't I know it."

I lifted the paper and read the short but succinct article. "Wow. It says here that we called it exactly: from Kat going to the pool to confront Mika down to Kat trying to frame Cabana Bob. Man, we're good."

"Yeah," Roz said, "but let's face it, we mostly stumbled into that revealing the guilty party. In fact, don't we usually stumble into those things? Think about it: if we ever tried to intentionally solve a crime with true, deductive reasoning, we'd probably fail miserably."

I laughed. She wasn't wrong. "Thank you for this, Joaquin. How about you, do you still have a job?"

He smiled. "Roger has been very kind to me and will keep me on. I will not call him a *culo* again."

After a bit more chit chat, Joaquin and Emmanuel said goodbye, wishing us safe travels home.

"Accidental or not, you know what this makes us, right?" I said, waving the paper in the air and humming the *Ghostbusters* theme song.

Roz and Peggy gave each other sideways glances.

I hummed more of the tune. "Come on, ladies. We came here to be wild and crazy; to throw caution to the wind. Get crazy with me now and shout the answer when I ask: who ya gonna call..."

"Coast Busters!" we cheered in unison.

I know, I know. Making fools of ourselves on the beach wasn't exactly wild or crazy, but we're middle-aged moms. Just how crazy did we *really* expect we'd get?

* * *

**Karen Cantwell** grew up on heavy doses of *I Love Lucy* and *The Carol Burnett Show*. She loves to laugh as much as she loves bringing laughter to the world. A USA Today bestselling author, Karen writes the Barbara Marr Murder Mystery series, the Sophie Rhodes Ghostly Romance books, and currently has a new humorous series under construction. When she isn't writing, Karen can be found wandering aimlessly, wondering why she isn't writing. If you enjoyed this Barbara Marr story, you may enjoy the novels, *Take the Monkeys and Run*, *Citizen Insane*, *Silenced by the Yams*, *Saturday Night Cleaver*, *Dead Man Stalking*, and *Dial Marr for Murder*. Book 7, *Risky Fitness* releases August 3, 2021. To learn more, visit KarenCantwell.com, AND, if you sign up for her newsletter there, you'll get a subscriber-exclusive Barbara Marr short story collection! If you are on Facebook, join her @KarenCantwellAuthor. Mostly, she hopes you find time every day to love well and to laugh a lot.

* * *

Recipe for Murder on the Beach, a killer cocktail:

*Ingredients:*

.5 oz coconut rum

.5 oz dry gin

.5 oz vodka

.5 oz blue Curacao

.5 oz fresh lemon juice

.25 oz simple syrup

.75 oz Sprite or 7-Up

drizzle of grenadine

ice

paper umbrella

Directions: combine coconut rum, gin, vodka, Curacao, lemon juice, simple syrup, and soda in a glass and stir; fill rest of glass with crushed ice; drizzle a bit of grenadine over ice; top with paper umbrella; enjoy. Also, when drinking, remember to make good choices, and try not to leave your sunglasses by the pool...

# Cabo San Loco
## by Eleanor Cawood Jones

MARTHA MCBAIN WAS NOT A GOOD FLIER, and she reached out to grip the drink cart as it rolled by her in the aisle.

"Ginger ale," she croaked.

"Oh, honey, this drink cart is as cold and empty as my heart." The flight attendant peered down at her through tiny tortoiseshell spectacles. "But let me grab you something from the front of the plane."

She pushed the cart on by and I was left with the impression of big blond hair, navy uniform, an ample frame, and a lumbering gait. I looked closer at her shoes. I hadn't seen a pair of brogues in years, but they did look comfortable.

"Ice," Martha called after her.

I reached across the aisle. "You'll be okay," I reassured my best friend.

Pathetic brown spaniel eyes looked at me from under a mop of dark bangs. I thought she looked so cute in her new bob haircut. It showed off her shiny brown hair. "You say that every time, Lorrie."

"And every time you're okay." I smiled at her. "Besides, we're on the way to Mexico for the first time ever! Think of the beaches, the sun, the surf, the drinks, the cheesy souvenirs you love to shop for, the Mexican dinners..."

She turned visibly green.

"Okay, maybe not the dinners. But likely we'll have some attractive, attentive waiters."

"Oh, there will be no shortage of those," Cidne DuPont said cheerfully. "You can make bet on that." She patted her immaculate red curls and straightened her paisley scarf unnecessarily. She was a glamorous forty-five, beautiful, an unwilling social media influencer, a philanthropist, and one of the nicest people I'd ever known.

A year ago, the first time I met her at her sprawling home in Great Falls, Virginia, she gripped both my hands in hers. "I'm Cidne, rhymes with kidney, like the bean," she'd told me. It turned out she unerringly introduced herself that way, so we all called her Bean, which, when you think about it, was thoroughly her own fault.

It was Bean's Gulfstream 550 in which we were currently winging our way to Baja, California, for a week-long stay at her friend Enrique's new resort on what she called "the good side of Cabo San Lucas." (Seriously, there was a bad side?) The trip was to mark the year anniversary of the day she, Martha, and our other companions were among the twelve jurors presenting a guilty verdict to a Fairfax County, Virginia, judge after a month-long sequester. The verdict had resulted in a life sentence for the young man accused of attempting to murder his girlfriend and was a tragedy for both his family and the victim's.

Martha hadn't talked much about it, which wasn't like her at all, but if any bright spot had come out of the whole thing, it was that the five women on the jury had bonded over the emotionally difficult ordeal and formed a fast friendship. They had been getting together for monthly dinners at each other's houses ever since. Martha had brought me along a few times, and when Cidne had decided to treat everyone to a jaunt to Baja, she'd included me to make it an even half-dozen travelers.

"I'm taking you somewhere warm and beautiful where we can enjoy two oceans, feel safe and secure in a nice resort one of my friends just opened, eat and relax, sit in the shade, and just enjoy each other's company. Somewhere where jury duty and murder will be the last thing on our minds."

Frankly, I thought she was including me to cheer Martha up, but I liked everyone in the group and I sure as beans (no reference to Cidne intended) liked the idea of going to Baja California Sur in a private jet on an all-expenses-paid vacation with these delightful women. I looked around and sank further into my comfy seat. The custom décor reminded me of my grandmother's living room, right down to the peach floral wallpaper.

"Petunia, why don't you bring ginger ale for all of us," Bean called toward the front of the plane to the flight attendant. Petunia made some sort of grunting noise in reply and clanked a tray on the kitchenette counter.

"I'm sorry about that extra turbulence when we made the fuel stop at Houston, Martha, dear," said Bean. "Texas weather, you know. Or maybe you don't know. Well, you never know with Texas."

Weirdly, I understood exactly what she meant. That had been a rocky landing and some ginger ale, preferred stomach soother of air travelers everywhere, would not go amiss.

"Petunia is a treasure," said Cidne. "She's been with the plane as long as the family has owned it. She's a dear."

I looked at Petunia lurching toward us, shoving the drink cart in front of her. She looked both determined and efficient. I wouldn't want to give her any sass. And I wished I could get my own straight blond locks to stand up that tall. I envisioned her moving through a cloud of Aqua Net.

"And Marvin and Val, the pilots. They've been with us forever, too. Well, Val not so long. We got her after the old co-pilot keeled over right up front during that one flight to Santiago, Chile. Flat out on the floor, he was, all of us looking at him and wondering who knew CPR the best."

Martha sat up and gripped the padded armrests in her chair (did I mention the chairs were like a favorite living room recliner?), swiveling it around to face Bean. "You're telling me you had a pilot die on the way to South America?" She grew even greener.

"Oh, no, dear. He didn't die. Petunia thumped on his chest and breathed the breath of life right back into him. She's a real pro at CPR and first aid."

I eyed Petunia again. I wouldn't stay dead with her working on me either. I'd be too scared of her to resist.

"But he never did pass his flight medical again. So we got a co-pilot who's, well, a little younger and fitter.

"And of course, we recently got Marguerite to help out Petunia," Bean continued chattily. I looked in the back of the plane at the slim brunette who was straightening towels on a rack. "Petunia finally admitted it would be nice to have a little cabin help on these long flights, right Pet?"

Petunia grunted and plunked a glass of ginger ale and a crystal ice bucket on a tray next to Bean.

Bean smiled. "But enough about our little crew family. We've all earned a break, ladies, and let's each share the bucket list items we want to accomplish in Mexico." She leaned over and fished in her navy-blue, Epi leather Louis Vuitton travel bag and emerged with a matching notepad and pen. She whipped the notepad open and looked around at all of us expectantly. She was superbly organized; I bet she ran a heck of a charity committee. "Maybe one big item each. Ashley?"

Ashley Johnson, the youngest of the group at twenty-three, lit up. "I read it's going to be sunny and warm all week. I just want to hang out in a hot tub and wear a different bathing suit every day, and have drinks and meet cute guys. There are hot tubs, right? In fact," and she looked at Petunia hopefully, "maybe Petunia has something a little stronger than ginger ale to get us in a festive mood."

"Ginger ale for now," said Bean firmly. "I promised your mother I'd keep an eye on you, as much as I can, anyway." Ashley still lived at home with her family and by all accounts had lived a sheltered life. I looked at her carry-on. It was her only piece of luggage and I wondered if she'd packed anything besides bathing suits. She weighed a hundred pounds soaking wet, so maybe she didn't need much room. With her striking dark skin, sparkling brown eyes, and sweet disposition, I didn't think she'd have any trouble with the 'meeting cute guys' portion of her bucket list. I made a mental note to help Bean keep an eye on her.

Bean wrote on her notepad. "Ashley, hot tub, bikinis, dates. Wear entire wardrobe of bathing suits."

She looked toward the back of the plane. "What about you, Book?" The other two jurors along for the trip were Karen Faulkner and Karin Garcia. To avoid confusion, one of them automatically acquired a nickname. Karen always had her nose stuck in a book and had the added benefit of sharing a famous author's last name, so we just called her Book. She was in her mid-thirties like Martha and me but, unlike us, was married with children—four of them to be exact.

"You mean in addition to bringing home souvenirs for the kids? I downloaded at least a dozen mystery and romance books on the e-reader, so I'm hoping to spend my week by the pool with Kinsey Milhone, Archy McNally, and some as-yet-unknown regency romance heroines." She paused. "But I'd really like to go on one of those sunset cruises with the food and the music to see the arch in the rocks at sunset. I heard there's even a rock out there that looks just like Scooby Doo!" Her enthusiasm was infectious, and we all laughed.

Bean added to her list. "Book *Los Arcos* sunset cruise for Book. Ruh-roh!" and grinned at her own cleverness.

No-nickname Karin, our senior member, piped up. "I saw photos of how you can walk down the beach near the resort and see the young folks surfing, and pose for pictures beside the rocks with the waves crashing on them. I'd dearly love to get that kind of photo of myself to send the grandkids. I have a reputation as an adventurous, fun-loving grandma to keep up, you know." She dropped her voice to a whisper. "I'd also like to have my hair done. Dark with red highlights, I think."

Karin was old enough to have opted out of jury service, but she had told us she felt it was her duty as a voting citizen to participate. A former college professor, she was widowed and lived for the chance to travel and visit her numerous grandchildren.

I thought Karin's new hairdo might make a nice change from her salt-and-pepper look. "I'd like to get highlights too," I said. wistfully. *And a good conditioning treatment*, I added to myself. A week of sea and sun was hard on fine hair.

Bean wrote furiously. "Karin, arrange highlights with Marcel and photo session at the surf rocks. Add Lorrie to salon session."

I hesitated. "And then there's the camels."

Everyone turned to look at me. Bean raised an eyebrow. "The camels?"

Martha put down the ginger ale she'd been slugging. "Lorrie saw this travel brochure where people are riding camels on the beach. She keeps talking about how fun it looks and how all ages are doing it and personally I think it looks a little scary and don't camels smell? But Lorrie lets on that she's watched some videos and everyone's having a good time and wearing desert gear and how great the photo ops will be, but it's really expensive and she didn't want to ask for one more thing that's not included in the resort fees."

I glared at her. "Well, I see you're feeling better, Miss Chatty Cathy."

"Oh, gracious, Lorrie. Don't hesitate to ask for add-ons. What good is it that I married money if I can't spend it on friends?" Bean wrote, "Lorrie, line up camels for beach ride." She paused, then added: "Find out how camels smell and what's to be done about it."

"Thank you, Bean," I said. "But everyone knows you married for love." We smiled warmly at each other.

"True," said Bean. "But the money doesn't hurt a bit, does it? And Martha, that leaves you."

"Hotel California," said Martha, promptly. "You can drive up the coast to Todos Santos and find the old Hotel California and have drinks and listen to music, and everyone says that's where the Eagles wrote the song, but the Eagles deny it and the hotel had to issue a disclaimer but really, who knows the truth about that kind of thing, anyway?" She paused for breath. "It's supposed to be a really cute town. Great surfing nearby."

"Hotel California it is!" Bean added Martha's item to her list, then the chief pilot was standing beside us.

"Just making sure you're all buckled up, ladies," he said. "We're about to start our descent into Cabo, and it's a beautiful day, 75 degrees and just a light breeze."

We dutifully checked our seat belts and gathered up our belongings.

Bean took a last look at her notepad. "Hot tubs for Ashley, sunset cruise for Book, salon and ocean photos for Karin, salon and camels for Lorrie, Hotel California for Martha," she read. "We'll make them all into group activities. Good thing we have a whole week!"

"What about you, Bean?" I asked. "What's your item?"

"Well, I've been to Cabo before, and I was thinking I've done it all, but there is this one thing. I always have to be so prim and proper, and I guess I'm kind of a natural goody-two-shoes, but I'd like to cut loose and sit up at the hotel bar and do that thing with the bottle of tequila." She hesitated. "You know, where they eat the worm?"

"Eeeeeew!" Ashley looked horrified, and Martha turned a pale green again. I burst out laughing.

"I'd love to see that, Bean, honestly," I said. "But let's not make that one a group activity."

"Amen," said Book, and Karin grinned.

"No photos, though. I can't have that trending on social media." Bean picked up her pen one last time and added a note. "Bean, eat the worm."

After a smooth landing on a sunny runway lined with palm trees, we waited for the four crew members to button up the aircraft, then piled onto the bus Enrique had sent for us. And by bus, I mean a 14-passenger Mercedes Sprinter luxury van. I peered out the windows at the tired tourists haggling for rental cars in the airport parking lot and was grateful to sit back in air-conditioned comfort. The charming resort hostess passed out pink fruit drinks with little umbrellas in them and gave a short welcome speech in Spanish, which Bean, Karin, and Book understood perfectly. I automatically handed Martha my umbrella, knowing she'd be collecting them, along with other random souvenirs, to paste into marvelously creative scrapbooks after we got back home.

The sun was setting when we reached Cabo San Lucas, and we pressed our noses to the windows as we rolled through the city. Throngs of gaily dressed tourists ducked in and out of little shops and bars, and ever so many restaurants.

"Oh, can't we open the windows?" Ashley asked. "I want to see it all!" So we did, to hear the noises and feel the breeze on our faces. Delicious cooking smells wafted in. We waved and honked at the big crowd outside Señor Frog's and Squid Roe. The mood was festive and relaxed, although Martha nudged me once to point out a passing flatbed truck sporting a machine gun on a platform, manned by a good-looking, bulky young man in a tight black sport shirt with *Policia* printed on the back across his shoulder blades.

"Reminds me of Fred," I whispered, referring to the event security chief she'd started dating recently at home. I was rewarded when Martha blushed.

"We'll eat at Edith's one night," Bean told us as we rolled down a slight incline and drove along the beautiful beach for a little way. "It's like nothing else." I caught a glimpse through an open doorway of a colorful interior, tall ceilings, and bustling waiters, and then we were by the city. We climbed up a long, narrow road lined with boulders before arriving suddenly to a small sign for 'Enrique's Enclave - Resort and Fine Dining.' We turned into the drive and entered a small tunnel.

I saw Ashley fussing with her watch.

"What are you doing, Ash?" Book asked her.

"I'm trying to figure out what time it is here so I can set my alarm for 7 a.m. and get in some hot tub time before you ladies are even ready for breakfast," she said.

Karin laughed at her. "Honey, it's going to be chilly at 7 a.m. You might want to wait."

"No way! I'll be fine. Hot tubs are warm, right?"

"Can't argue with that," Bean agreed. "And here we are!"

It was a shame we were too tired to properly appreciate the gates with two double E's woven into the ironwork, the grand entrance, and the beautiful red and blue tile work in the foyer, plus the splashing fountains, but the bellhops put us on golf carts and whisked us up the sidewalks to our assigned building. Bean had put herself with Ashley in the fifteenth-floor penthouse, which made Ash squeal with excitement. Martha and I were in an oceanside two-bedroom suite on the floor below, and Book and Karin were our neighbors in an identical suite next door.

It was idyllic, and I headed for our private patio and plopped down on a cushy orange chaise lounge to listen to the surf for a bit before we met up in Bean's suite for a catered dinner.

Martha sat down next to me and handed me a can of Coca Light from the full-size refrigerator. "Who would have thought we'd end up here because of that dreadful time on the jury?" she said quietly. "That young man we locked up deserved it, but he'll never see the ocean again."

"I know that was hard on you to convict him, Martha." My heart ached for her and the other jurors, and the families involved.

"It's been hard to forget about him in jail, and how his girlfriend will be in a wheelchair the rest of her life from her injuries. And I know his family hates us for convicting him. Those things they said on social media last year were so hurtful. You're my best friend, Lorrie, and I know you know it's had me down, but I'm going to try and put it behind me once and for all. It's been a year, and this is a good place to forget about old things and focus on the future."

She stood up and spread her arms. "Look at the pools and restaurants down there, and those palm trees and the beach! Listen to the waves. Breathe that fresh air." She flapped her arms like a bird, and I grinned at her enthusiasm. "It'll be dark soon. We can leave the porch door open all night to hear the ocean. We each have a king size bed. And have you seen our *bathroom* and that soaker tub? Plus, the food is bound to be phenomenal."

"Which reminds me," I said. "We're supposed to meet Bean in the penthouse in thirty minutes for a catered supper, and then early to bed so we can get up with the sun and hit the beach for a walk, or whatever else strikes our fancy."

"That's so perfect, Lorrie. I can't wait to feel the sand under my toes." We watched the sun slip into the ocean and out of sight in a spectacular sunset display, then Martha stretched and yawned. "You know, this may in fact be the closest we've ever gotten to paradise. What could possibly go wrong here?"

And nothing did, until shouting from fourteen floors below woke us up some twelve hours later.

I bolted out of bed and ran to Martha's room. "Is that my imagination, or does that sound like Ashley?"

Martha hopped up and immediately tripped over her robe, which was lying on the tile floor beside her bed. Mumbling, she grabbed it, tossed it over her 'Beach Bum' nightshirt, and made a beeline for the balcony. I didn't stop for my slippers but followed her in my palm-tree-themed shortie pajamas.

Far below, we could see a tiny person that looked like the equally tiny Ashley over by the largest hot tub. She was running in circles and waving her arms around. She screamed again. People were gathered around a figure on the ground, and a sturdy someone was bending over that person.

I squinted in the bright sunlight. "Is that Petunia and Ashley?"

"Throw on some clothes. What do you think happened? Do you really think that's Ashley? Is she okay? Did someone slip and fall? Do you think Petunia's giving first aid? Do you think it's anyone we know?"

That was way too many questions for someone who had been out of bed all of forty-five seconds. "It totally could be. Hurry up!" We quickly got dressed in yesterday's clothes and dashed to the elevator. Then, since we hadn't explored properly, we had to find our way out to the pool area. We followed a series of stone paths past an open-air sushi restaurant, a sports bar, two enormous swimming pools, and a sign pointing to the spa before finally arriving outside. We hurried toward the commotion.

Ashley saw us and hurled herself into Martha's arms. "They just took him off in the ambulance! If I'd been on time, it would have been me, too!" Martha patted her back and looked at me for help.

On the other side of the hot tub, I saw tall hair and, under it, Petunia. Well, I heard her first. She was talking loudly to a management type in a resort-themed red and orange sport shirt.

"What type of resort puts an ungrounded electric space heater beside a hot tub? Don't you know it can fall in and shock someone to death if it touches them? Which is exactly what happened to that poor man unless he gets a miracle! He was in full cardiac arrest!"

The manager in the sport shirt protested. "Madam! I assure you we do no such thing! I know February has chilly mornings, but we don't have space heaters in the resort area except back in the administrative offices. And we have no reason to bring one out to the hot tub! I can assure you we will get to the bottom of this."

Petunia's face was so red I thought she might be next for the ambulance. I turned to Ashley, who was quietly sobbing. "What happened, sweetheart?"

She raised her head off Martha's shoulder. "I went exploring last night and this British guy, Rudy, took a shine to me and he was *so nice*. He's too old, really, but when I told him I was getting up early to hit the best hot tub, the one as big as a little swimming pool, before my girlfriends got up, even though it was going to be like, fifty degrees, he said he'd join me. To be honest, I didn't mind." She looked slightly guilty, and I wondered exactly how old this new friend was.

"And I put on my red striped bikini, you know, the one I bought at Macy's sale rack with the matching cover and the matching beach shoes and bag, and I came down on the elevator except I was late because the gourmet coffee shack over by the south pool opens at seven and a cup of coffee and a donut sounded so good and the lady who runs the shack is my age and she's from Minnesota and so we chatted a little and she loves living here, and then I was *extra* late."

At this point I wondered if she and Martha were going to be future best friends as apparently they both firmly believed in no detail left behind when telling a story.

Martha nodded. (Of course she did.) "And then what happened?"

"So I'm walking across to the hot tub and I see Rudy in it and Rudy sees me and I wave and he waves and then he waves so hard he hits that heater which I hadn't even noticed and it falls right into the pool on him! I think he caught his arm in the cord. And I didn't know what was happening except he went under and I started running to go check on him and then Petunia was there and she moved me aside and all I had time to do is wonder who in the world wears black polyester pants at the beach because that's what she was wearing."

"That *is* hard to believe," said Martha.

Ashley detached herself from Martha at last and sat down on a nearby stone bench. The morning sun reflected off her red-frame sunglasses. We sat on either side of her.

"I'd forgotten about electricity and water not mixing, I guess. Petunia stopped me from getting in the hot tub. She jerked the heater plug out of the extension cord and went in the tub after Rudy. She got him out and did the CPR thing." She shuddered. "Then the ambulance came and I think they got him breathing, and I guess the police are next because Petunia is mad."

I pictured the buff young policeman with the machine gun from town, and shuddered. But we were guests of the resort owner and Ashley had done nothing wrong, so I suspected they would go easy on her.

I looked at the space heater lying on its side on the ground. The cord was unplugged but lying near a long, orange extension cord that ran into the main building. I looked up and met Bean's eyes. Then I saw her outfit. How anyone makes a caftan look elegant I'll never know, but she was awash in glamorous swirls of blue, orange, and yellow. Beach colors. Her red hair was tucked back under a white scarf.

"I got a call," she said to us quietly. "Ashley, why don't you come with me? Enrique isn't in town, but his managers and a few of the *policia* are in his office and they want to hear from you and Petunia what happened. Don't worry. They aren't accusing you of anything, but the man is seriously injured, and his wife is extremely upset. She's at the hospital with him now."

"His *wife*?" Ashley, Martha, and I said in unison.

"He never said he was married," Ashley said indignantly. In spite of the situation, I hid a smile.

"His wife, Brittney, is an acquaintance of mine," Bean said mildly. "I've run into her a few times at events in London and thereabouts. She's a bit of the jealous type, with a husband who's the stereotypical tall, dark, and handsome, and uses that to full advantage."

"I'd bet," said Martha. "I wonder if she had anything to do with this? I wonder if she's done anything in the past when she thought he was cheating? Is he a serial cheater? Anyone is capable of a jealous rage. I hope the *policia* look at her closely."

I wondered, not for the first time, what serving on a jury with Martha would have been like. No doubt each suspect would have been thoroughly considered.

"Book and Karin are on the way to the breakfast buffet," said Bean. "While Ashley and I are tied up, why don't you girls go meet them and let them know there's been a slight delay." She pursed her lips with distaste. "We will meet you there in a bit."

And when we all met up at an oceanside table, over scrambled eggs, donuts, hot chocolate, coffee, bacon, sausage, fresh fruit, and breakfast burritos (I was tempted to ask if I could have antacid as a side dish), Bean and a recalcitrant Ashley told us the two policemen had indeed gone easy on them, and that Petunia's fast action was already being credited with "saving Rudy's cheating life," as Ashley put it.

"It's a good thing Petunia's an early riser and was in the right place, right time," said Bean, mildly. I looked across the beach breakfast bar at the flight crew gathered at their own table. The two pilots were listening to Petunia, who was gesturing dramatically. Marguerite appeared to be reading her phone. Her hair hung over her face.

Bean continued. "Now, I suggest we put this incident behind us, keep our distance from the jealous Brittney when she comes back from the hospital and, Ashley, dear, maybe we can vet your dates a bit before the next one."

Ashley hung her head. "I'm sorry, Bean."

"Nothing to be sorry about, Ashley," Karin said firmly. "You're young and single and want to have a harmless good time. You remind me of my oldest granddaughter, who's a real sweetheart. But this is a thousand-dollar-a-night resort and it's not the local hangouts you're used to. You don't know who you're meeting. Just let us help out a little. But we promise not to hover, right, Bean?"

"Of course," Bean said. "And after all this, maybe you ladies will be glad to know I've booked us at the salon this afternoon after lunch. Highlights for Book and whatever else we want for ourselves. Does that work for everyone?"

It worked for me. I planned to get up the nerve to try highlights—just as soon as I'd slept off breakfast.

Martha and I took a quick nap, then hit the infinity pool for a quick dip with Ashley, while Bean, Karin, and Book attended a Mexican cooking class in the resort kitchen taught by Enrique's master chef. We spent time poolside speculating on how a heater got near the hot tub that morning. Was it an accident by a careless employee? Someone who wanted to cause random mischief or target Rudy? Worse yet, target Ashley? But why? We couldn't come up with a reason. But we were almost certain the three stunning, blond, middle-aged ladies across the pool staring daggers at us were Brittney, wife of the injured Rudy, and her friends.

"Not much for comforting her husband at the bedside, eh?" Martha whispered. "That's one chilly group."

We talked all of it to death, of course.

As promised, cute waiters were in abundance at the pool, and I gathered up all the umbrellas from our drinks again to save for Martha's scrapbook collection. She snapped them into a plastic case when we went back to the room to change for our salon session. I looked in her case. She had a plastic toothpick in there shaped like a shark, a coffee stirrer, and a few yellow flower petals.

"Nice flower, huh?" Martha smiled at me. "The little girl who brought me a drink with a flower in it said I should try eating the blossom, and I took a little nibble, but the petals are so pretty I thought I'd dry them out for the scrapbook."

I smiled back. It was good to see Martha starting to relax. "When did a little girl bring you a drink?"

"Y'all were in the pool, and she brought it over. She said someone across the pool wanted to buy me a drink and sent her over with it. I never did figure out who it was."

When I got out of the shower, I found her lying down. "You go on to the salon. I'm going to lie down a bit. I think I got too much sun."

I left her forehead. "No fever. You sure you're okay with me going? I can go another day."

"I'd really like to sleep." She curled up on her side. "Go on. I'll see you in a few hours." She yawned. "Maybe I'll call Fred."

"Be sure to tell him some stranger tried to buy you a drink and sent flowers," I teased.

She threw a pillow at me.

At the salon, Karin and I had the seats of honor in Marcel's color studio while Bean, Ashley, and Book treated themselves to pedicures with matching orange nail polish. I saw Petunia and Marguerite getting mud slathered on for facials, and I thought it was nice that Bean treated her flight crew as well as her guests.

Karin and I enjoyed the attention—and more umbrella drinks—while he and his assistants fussed over us. They colored Karin's hair a rich, mocha brown and trimmed it into short layers.

"Now I look like young Mrs. Garcia again!" she said happily. "I can't wait for my grandkids to see the pictures. But I've changed my mind about the highlights."

"*La chica bella,*" said Marcel unhappily. "You would look even more beautiful with the highlights, no?" He stood beside her with a plastic cup and brush at the ready.

"I'll take the highlights since Karin doesn't want them," I said. "Bring them over. Red highlights in blond hair will really pep me up, don't you think?" I never tried anything new with my hair. Martha would be proud of me.

Marcel turned the procedure over to his assistant, who began brushing color into my hair from the roots down to the ends with the little paintbrush.

"Is it supposed to burn like that?" I asked her.

Marcel heard me and rushed over, and then practically dragged me to the sink. He began shampooing me furiously.

Bean rushed over too. "What is it?"

Marcel added conditioner and, with no trace of an accent, said, "The chemicals were perhaps too harsh for her sensitive scalp. It is turning red here. And here and here."

"I'll be okay," I told him. "The burning has almost stopped."

"It is not okay," he told me. "I will find out who mixed the chemicals and fire them."

If the issue was my sensitive scalp, I wasn't sure how mixing the chemicals would have made a difference, but I didn't say so. After they toweled me dry—Marcel didn't want the added irritation of a blow dry—I saw the red highlights had created a few soft pink strands in my fine blond hair. I liked it and told Marcel so, but he just shook his head.

"I have never had an accident in my salon," he told me. "That is not how I have achieved my reputation. I apologize and hope you will not seek damages."

"I'm not a seeking damages kind of gal," I told him. Bean nodded approvingly.

"I'll bring Martha back so we can get one of those neon orange polish pedicures," I told Bean. Karin was already in the chair getting her polish. "But I want to go check on her now."

I stopped at the resort shop to get Martha a ginger ale and some crackers, then found my way back up to the fourteenth floor. I saw the door to our room open and a gray-haired man came out into the hall.

"Hey!" I called. "Who are you?" Alarmed, I headed down the hallway toward him.

"The resort doctor," he told me. "And your friend is resting comfortably, so don't worry. I gave her something to settle her stomach. We went over what she had eaten this morning, and I told her not to nibble on any more poisonous flowers."

"Poisonous flowers?" I stared at him blankly and opened the door to the room. Martha was sitting up in bed reading her e-reader. She looked at me sheepishly.

"I got so sick after you left, I called the front desk and they sent Dr. Morales, who reminded me we are in a foreign country, no matter how nice things are here and how much they cater to tourists. He said not to eat or drink things I wasn't familiar with, here, on the beach, or anywhere else on this trip. He was pretty firm about it, actually."

"We all ate the same things last night and this morning, though, Marth."

"After the doctor gave me something for the nausea and I felt better, he and I went over everything. He was interested in the little girl bringing me a drink since that was the only thing I did differently than y'all. I showed him the yellow flowers, and he said they are Mexican oleander."

"That's dangerous?"

"It's poison, apparently. That stuff is lethal. Good thing I didn't eat more than a nibble. I'd have been in the hospital with Rudy the cheating Brit."

"Not funny."

Martha grinned tiredly. "Dr. Morales asked me why I ate a strange plant and I told him the little girl suggested it. He may have mentioned that little kids eat dirt and crayons and listen to stupid things adults tell them and maybe they aren't the best culinary advisors. He said he'd have a word with the kitchen staff about what they are putting in their drinks, but they know better and probably the little girl was just playing."

She squinted at me. "Hey, is your hair pink or am I having hallucinations now?"

I laid down beside her and closed my eyes. "It's pink, all right. And the scalp is red if you look closely."

I felt her fingers in my hair. "I do see some red spots. What gives?"

"I think they just call it a chemical burn. They got it out fast enough to avoid any real damage. Marcel said it's a fluke."

Silence.

"Lor?"

"Yes, Marth."

"Is it just me, or are we having a run of really bad luck? Electrocution at the hot tub, chemical burns, and poison flowers at the pool? Does that seem a little odd to you?"

"And it's only the first day," I said. "It's all explainable, and I think it's just an oddity, but, hey, things come in threes, right? Should be over now."

"Mmmm." Martha drifted off to sleep and I moved to my own bed. I'd hang out and read and keep an eye on her for now. And though I didn't think for a minute that anyone was out to get Bean's little tour group, I was left with an uneasy feeling somewhere in my gut. Paradise is as paradise does, I said to myself.

Then I remembered the highlights that burned me had been meant for Karin, and my concerns returned. I made a note to talk to Bean about it and drifted into an uneasy nap.

We both woke up with late afternoon sun steaming in through the porch door and pounding on the room door. I hopped up and opened it. Bean,

Karin, Book, and Ashley piled in. They looked adorable in long, blue and orange striped, sleeveless dresses and matching orange neon pedicures. Bean tossed a bag at me.

"We bought you dresses at the gift shop too. Hurry up and get dressed. Drinks by the pool and then it's taco night Tuesday by the ocean!"

Martha bounced out of bed. "I could go for some tacos!"

I was relieved she was feeling better. I hopped into the shower and got dressed while she updated everyone, and Martha followed suit. No one seemed overly concerned by our rash of bad luck, and I decided to put it behind me for the evening and just enjoy the company of my friends.

We dined oceanside, at picnic tables under tents, and the attentive staff cooked us custom tacos, beans, rice, and fried plantains. We enjoyed the shade, stuffed ourselves, and went through three bottles of delicious red wine from Los Cabos Winery. We watched the sun set over the Pacific Ocean and listened to the rough waves pounding the rocks. Far down the beach, in the waning light, we could see the young surfers dodging the no swimming signs and running into the ocean near the cliffs to take their turns at trying to ride the tube.

"You can climb over those cliff rocks and wind up on Lovers Beach," said Bean.

"No, *you* can." Book giggled tipsily. "We're on the Pacific side now, the Divorce Beach side. When we go to Lovers Beach on our sunset cruise, you'll be able to walk on the sand from the Gulf of California to the Pacific. Isn't that neat?"

"There's a heart-shaped rock at Lovers Beach too," said Karin happily. "We'll be able to get some great photos there."

"I guess it would be mean to tell Brittney and her friends they could use a little Lovers Beach attitude?" Book giggled again and looked pointedly down the row of tables.

"Oh, no, are they back again? I swear I had no idea he was married." Ashley ducked behind the dessert menu.

"I wonder if they are the ones who sent me that drink with poison flowers?" Martha said. We all turned and looked at them.

"No," Bean decided. "It was probably some innocent child decorating your drink with shrubs, like the doctor thinks. We have no evidence, and we can't just accuse someone of attempted murder willy-nilly, can we? Besides, Rudy hit on me years ago and Brittney has had ample opportunity to harm me since then, and nada."

"Maybe this was the one that finally pushed her over the edge," Martha said. "I mean, look at Ashley. She's adorable!" She slugged Ashley good naturedly in the shoulder and grinned. Ashley blushed.

"Hey," said Ashley. "Where are all the people? I heard Cabo was crowded, and we saw all those people in town."

"Oh, they are over on the Gulf of California side," said Bean. "Those beaches are mobbed with tourists and salesmen. I've never even been. Would you like to go over there, Ash? We can go." Bean opened her voluminous purse and took out her notepad. "And we're putting this bad luck behind us. Let's see what's still on the bucket list. We have Lorrie's camels, Martha's Hotel California, Book's dinner cruise, and Karin's photos by the big rocks." She gestured down the beach. "That's the spot, where the surfers are, right Karin?"

Karin nodded happily.

"We'll have a free day tomorrow and hit the Gulf of California side," Bean decided. "And I'll book the camels and hotel on Thursday since they are way up the coastline. And Friday would be a good day for the dinner cruise. We'll fit Karin's beach photos in somewhere, too."

We were happy to let Bean plan our activities. We all nodded, full of tacos and wine and happiness, and went for a stroll and a few beach photos before heading to live music and the bar, then bed.

We rose early the next day, ready for another day in paradise. Martha and I headed upstairs to get our pedicures and I did a quick search on my phone for Brittney because I just couldn't let it go. As well as being prominent on the social media sites, she had been arrested twice for being a public nuisance, which apparently involved her drinking too much and yelling at her husband, so her temper was on display for the world to see. I didn't mention it to Martha, who was chatting happily with her stylist, but I resolved to be extra vigilant.

Bean had been shopping again and sent us all neon orange bathing suits and cover-ups to match, in a variety of styles and sizes. We giggled over the string bikinis and went for the one-pieces. In our suits, cover-ups, and flip flops, we met up with everyone at the breakfast bar, then packed our beach towels to head over to the Gulf of California side. Tourists mobbed every inch of available beach space. The shore was lined with hotels and timeshares, and local residents dressed in white and carrying huge baskets of bracelets and necklaces roamed up and down the sand hawking their wares to the tourists.

We all bought bracelets for ourselves, and Martha and I picked out bandanas and necklaces for the men and women back home at work. Then, to gloat just a little, we texted pictures of us on the beach to our friends at the office.

"You can tell them we're sitting on the beach at the Gulf of California or the Sea of Cortez, either one," Ashley told us. Her eyes were glued to her phone.

"Oh, really, Miss Google Maps?" Martha teased her.

She nodded earnestly. "It's important to get it right when you're posting on social media so people don't make fun of you."

Martha and I traded a look that clearly expressed our mutual gratitude we weren't twenty-three years old anymore.

"This is fun," Book said. "But I'm not getting any reading done. All I can do is people watch." Two adorable little girls were building sand castles next to her, speaking French to their mom, who was sporting a thong two-piece and eating a bag of pretzels.

With the magic that an unlimited checking account brings, Bean had beach umbrellas brought out to keep things shady. She ordered salads and umbrella drinks delivered to us right on the beach, and we ate, drank, swam, and dozed the day away. Then we rushed back to the hotel and changed into nice clothes to eat at Edith's, the famed local institution renowned for great food and spectacular service. I imagined we were dining on a stage setting for Casablanca, with the colorful tableware, tapestry, bead-lined walls, and constant, bustling activity. Brightly dressed waiters dashed here and there and I lost track of how many people were serving us. It was impossible to take it all in. Sunburned and content, we enjoyed a multi-course seafood dinner and the house specialty of bananas flambe for dessert.

It was the perfect day with not a care in the world and, best of all, nothing of note happened. We all agreed our bad luck was behind us.

"Camels tomorrow," I said happily to my best friend as we fell asleep not long after sunset. "I set two alarms!"

I could hear her grinning, and that was the last thing I remembered before waking up at dawn the next day. Martha was still asleep, and I staggered downstairs to the coffee shack to get us a large, American-sized dose of caffeine. I ducked behind a pillar when I saw Brittney and her friends in line ahead of me. Unfortunately, they were talking about riding camels later that day. My heart sank.

"All aboard the camel express!" Bean had appeared behind me. "Will you be having one hump or two with that coffee?" She laughed at her own humor and so did I. "Ashley and I just had breakfast. I'll meet you all at the front of the resort in an hour. I went ahead and chartered a bus for today's expeditions. Won't we have fun?" She handed me a bag and swirled off in yet another caftan, and I took coffee upstairs for Martha to roust her out of bed. When we looked in the bag, we found long-sleeved, oxford shirts with "Hump Day" and a smiling camel embroidered on the front pocket. We cracked up.

"Only Bean," said Martha, buttoning hers up over her tank top. We put on jeans and tennis shoes. "Let's pack a change of clothes in a beach bag in case these outfits reek of camel afterward," she added, so we packed sundresses and flip flops in a beach bag as well.

The six of us and the entire flight crew found ourselves riding up the Baja coast on the Pacific side, through miles of desert plants and bright sunshine. We all took the opportunity to doze or play on our phones, and finally pulled over to stop at a row of open-air buildings along the gorgeous coastline. We could hear the waves and sat at a row of tables to sign away any liability for the tour organizers while our camels were brought to the saddling area.

"No cell phones," our guide told us cheerfully. "You'll need all your hands and feet to hold on to your camels. Don't worry; we'll have plenty of pictures for you and the first one is free!" (I rolled my eyes, but I knew I'd probably buy the entire photo package.) "Put your belongings in the bin, put on your desert gear, and follow me." I saw Brittney and company putting on their headgear. They looked like they'd eaten something distasteful, and I nudged Martha and Ashley to watch.

Martha and I were assigned to an enormous camel named Humphrey, with Brittney and one of her cohorts directly behind us and the flight crew on two camels in front of us. I ignored them all and petted my beast, who snorted and moaned in what the guide told me were typical camel noises. They spread a blanket on Humphrey, and we mounted from a platform, and then we were off, many feet up in the air, swaying down the beach. I clung to my roll bar and Martha clung to me. The beautiful beach was on the right as we strolled along in a line. It was surreal, and I couldn't quit grinning, until I felt Humphrey moving to the right and left more than usual. He gave an extra loud moan and a twitch. I gripped the bar tightly and turned around in time to see Brittney swatting at Humphrey's rump in front of her with a scarf.

"That's unsafe, lady." I told her. "Do it again and I'll have you banned from the resort. Remember, it's all on film." I nodded at a drone overhead.

"Do you not have any sense? These things are big! Someone could get hurt," Martha added.

Brittney didn't reply but put her scarf back in place, and Humphrey calmed down.

After a ride that stopped just in time to avoid permanently sore backs, we took turns posing for photos with our camels. Humphrey stood nicely and gave me a camel kiss, then jumped and almost stepped on Martha. I looked down and saw tiny mice scurrying underfoot, and gave a shriek, which didn't help matters any. I saw a few pebbles bouncing off poor Humphrey's hindquarters and dropped his reins, running into the brush to see who had thrown them. I could see a figure in the distance but couldn't tell if it was male or female.

"What in the world, Lorrie?" Book had followed me. "You let your camel go. He was trying to stomp those poor mice and knocked Martha down. And the tour guide says they don't have mice out here and is demanding to know who brought them."

I turned and stomped back toward the photo area. "Someone was throwing rocks at Humphrey!"

"Oh, wow. That's bad," Book said. "That's what probably scared him instead of those mice. Mice scare elephants more than camels."

I didn't ask how she knew that. She was an avid reader. She probably knew lots of things. Book and I walked back, and I petted Humphrey apologetically while I reported the incident to the tour guide. He looked at me blankly.

"I have no idea who would do such a thing," he said. "All our employees have been here a long time and know how to treat animals. Maybe someone in your party was playing a joke? Unfortunately, we put away all the cameras after the ride, so we can't check that way."

I was starting to wonder if there was a single security camera in all of Baja.

"Look over there at the tequila-making demonstration going on for the group," said the guide. "Maybe we'll all have a drink."

That was a bit of a non sequitur. I opened my mouth to protest he wasn't taking the situation seriously.

"I noticed your camels don't really smell that bad," said Book. "Do you work hard at keeping them extra clean? But I was reading that there's this one village that had rogue elephants and they brought in camels because the camels smelled so bad the elephants wouldn't come around anymore, and it saved the day."

We all looked at her.

"Someone tried to make sure our camel was upset, smelly or not," said Martha. "We could have gotten stepped on or badly hurt. I hope our bad luck hasn't started up again."

The tequila-making demonstration ended, and a waiter plunked a shot in front of Martha. She picked it up and downed it, and choked.

"I believe I'll have one of those myself," I said. I saw Brittney and her friends snickering at us across the room. Martha was dirty and sandy where she'd fallen, and I was probably beet red from my short run through the desert vegetation. Not to mention the camel-sway backache that was setting in.

Worst of all, Martha, Book, and I were late getting to the delicious smelling lunch that had been spread out for us, and we found our plates splattered with what looked like red goo. The others had taken a short nature walk to learn the local plants and had eaten already.

"It looks like blood," Book said doubtfully.

"That red stuff isn't supposed to be there," said Bean. She stopped a waiter. "Did you add red sauce to my friends' plates?"

The waiter peered closer. "*Repugnante*! Absolutely not." He stuck his finger in it and tasted it. (Gross.) "If I had to guess, I'd say that was red gum sap. Those trees bleed red, and it gets sticky just like this. Regardless, we're out of food and I'm truly sorry. Someone is pulling a mean prank."

"The Hotel California is supposed to have great hamburgers," Martha said. "I'm sorry to miss this food, but we'll eat later."

They tried to refund our money, but Bean wouldn't hear of it. "Not the camels' fault, nor yours," she told them. "Best ride of my life. The meal was superb. And I'll take photo packages for my entire group. Here's their emails. You can send them along."

Good old Bean. Now we'd all have evidence that we had ridden camels at the beach, and that we were *not* professional camel riders.

Our chartered bus next took us toward the charming town of Todos Santos, pulling over along the way so we could see the professional surfers trying to outsmart the Pacific on one of the prettiest strips of beach any of us had ever seen. When we reached town, we wasted no time in joining the other tourists to get our photo ops at the charming old Hotel California on the main road.

"It's worth seeing, even if it's not the inspiration for the song," Ashley said. She took yet another selfie and then wandered off with Bean and Karin to roam the town and buy souvenirs. I wondered if there was anything else in the town besides souvenirs, but somehow it worked and wasn't tacky at all, and the merchants were smiling and friendly.

Book, Martha, and I walked through the dark, cool hotel, oohing and aahing, and found a shady picnic table on the outside patio. We ordered hamburgers with all the fixings, and they were as delicious as promised by the guidebook. Along with the other diners, we sang "Hotel California" and other Eagles hits to the accompaniment of an excellent cover band.

"Are we better at riding camels or singing, do you think?" Book burst into giggles and we laughed at her. "The kids would die of embarrassment if they could see me. And there's something so satisfying about embarrassing preteens." We used our phones to take a short film of her singing and dancing so she could horrify them.

"Oh, no. There they are *again*." Martha nudged me and I looked up to see Brittney and her two friends at a table near the four members of our flight crew. Fortunately, they weren't looking at us and we all voted to ignore them. The waitress put a fresh round of drinks on the table. I finished my burger and gathered up the little pink drink umbrellas for Martha's collection. I stuck them in my sundress pocket, stood up to go to the bathroom, and caught my purse strap on the chair. It slammed forward and ended up knocking over the entire table.

*Crash!*

The plates were a total loss, and plastic drink cups went flying.

Book and Martha jumped up, dripping drinks and sporting spots of ketchup and mustard. The waitress came running, and we all bent down to help pick up the pieces, but she waved us off. Martha bent down and looked closer.

"Not again!" She pointed to little yellow bits of flowers floating around in the pink punch. "I mean, I can't be sure, but those look like same thing that made me sick at the pool!"

I was sure they hadn't been in the first round of drinks. Maybe they were just decorative. I put some in a napkin, stuck it in my pocket, and asked for the manager. As I suspected, he told me they didn't use those flowers in their drinks and assured me they were most likely harmless. "Those flowers may have already been on the ground when the drinks fell," he pointed out. That was a valid point. We'd never know; naturally, there were no cameras.

No one seemed overly worried, but I resolved to show the flowers to the resort doctor and find out what they were. I looked over at Brittney. She and her friends were laughing uproariously at us. The flight crew was trying hard to hide their amusement, but even Petunia couldn't help grinning.

"What in the world?" Bean, Ashley, and Karin were suddenly standing beside us, big grins on their faces. "We bought Karin a dress for her photo session and, what the heck, I got one for everyone. Looks like you can use it about now."

She opened a bag and handed navy-blue, polka dot sundresses to Book and Martha, ignoring the mess all around us. "Try to keep these clean. Aren't they cute? They're sleeveless to show off your tans."

In the end, we all put on the polka dot dresses and the matching beach hats Bean had purchased and posed for photos outside Hotel California, to the amusement of the other tourists. And when we finally made it back to our own resort, we trudged down the beach to meet a photo crew for sunset pictures at Karin's rocks. (I had to hand it to Bean. She spared no expense on our Mexican bucket list items). Karin actually edged so close to the giant waves that she got knocked over, but stood right up, laughing and drenched. Those made the best photos of all.

"Your grandkids will treasure these!" Bean gloated.

And when we made it back to our rooms without further trouble, I went knocking on Bean's door to go over the incidents at the camel ride and the hotel patio.

"It's too much," I told her. "Some harmless pranks, but some really dangerous ones as well. I'm starting to think this run of bad luck is someone targeting our group."

Bean sat quietly for a moment. "I don't know anyone here but our group and Brittney's," she said. "I can't imagine any of them targeting us with real intent of harm, although I can see Brittney ruining the food or picking on a camel. She has a mean streak. But I didn't advertise we were coming here, and it isn't on social media yet, so it doesn't really make sense. I suppose someone could know we were all on a jury together and disagree with the verdict, but it's been a year, so that seems farfetched."

She sighed. "I've attracted my share of weirdos in my life, but most of them seemed harmless. Maybe it's someone who doesn't like people with money, and maybe we're not the only ones at the resort having this kind of luck. I'll call Enrique and talk to him about it. Maybe he has some disgruntled employees. We could consider going home early, or perhaps I can hire some security to watch out for us. Do you think that's overkill?"

I thought about oleander, portable heaters, and camels potentially stepping on one of us with big camel feet. "I don't know about leaving early, but I think the security is a good idea, although maybe we can keep it low key and if there is someone targeting us, they can catch whoever it is."

When we boarded the party boat the next afternoon for Book's requested arch sunset cruise, I noticed two muscular young men hanging out with our flight crew and looking around at everyone. I assumed this was Bean's security team and I wondered if there were others I hadn't noticed. I also saw Brittney and her ever-present friends, but at this point I was so used to them glaring at us I was practically immune.

"I wonder why I'm not tired of Mexican food yet?" Ashley giggled. We were serving ourselves from the buffet. She had met a young man at her hot tub that morning and spent the day with him by the pool, and she was in high spirits. "Oh, there's the arch with the sun shining behind it, and the Scooby Doo rock!" She dashed off to the deck railing and the rest of us followed.

"*Los Arcos* has to be the most photographed sight in Cabo San Lucas, and that rock actually does look like a profile of Scooby Doo!" I was delighted to see normally quiet Book so excited and happy.

We finished eating and danced to the on-deck band as the sun set and the lights of Cabo twinkled on the shore. The boat swung back around and passed the arch again. All of us but Book were relaxing on deck with yet another round of umbrella drinks, when the call came.

"Man overboard!"

All of us rushed unhelpfully to the side of the boat.

*Splash!*

The two buff men I'd pegged for Bean's security detail dived overboard. I could only hope they didn't land headfirst on a rock.

"Book! Book?" Ashley was calling.

"Oh, no! Where's Book?" Bean dashed about frantically on deck.

"Look! They are pulling someone up onto the dive platform." I squinted in the fading light. "I think it might be Book." I peered harder. "Whoever it is, is moving around. They're okay."

Ashley burst into tears.

Book was soaking wet but fine. "Those two men got me back on the boat so fast I hardly had time to worry that I can't swim."

Ashley cried harder.

"What happened?" Martha asked. Karin hugged Book, hard, water and all.

"Beats me. I'm standing at the railing and someone shoved me. I went over and in, and the next thing you know I'm in a rescue situation."

She was shivering, even though it wasn't cold, and the crew brought her a blanket. The captain listened to her story but had no explanation. No witnesses had come forward, and, as I'd finally accepted was the norm around here, there were no cameras.

"This has gone far enough," Bean growled. She turned and marched across the deck and the next thing I knew, was up in Brittney's face.

If it was possible to yell quietly, Bean did it effectively. Brittney and her two friends backed away from her and sat down. Bean joined them. After a heated discussion, she joined us at the other end of the deck.

"She admits to the ruined food at the camel ride and even to setting some mice loose around the camels, but that's all she admits to. Can you imagine hiding mice in your purse? She says she didn't throw rocks at any animals, though, or send any tainted drinks, or anything else. She fully denies the space heater incident at the hot tub, even though she and Rudy have been talking divorce." She sighed. "Apparently he's still in the hospital and not doing well at all.

"I threatened to make her look beyond—and I mean *beyond*—bad on social media if anything else at all happens to us, and, since that's all she seems to care about, I'd say we're safe from that end. But at this point I'm ready to call it a day, girls, and head back home a few days early. I'll talk to Enrique and to the *policia*, but I'd prefer to have my own connections at home look into all this. I'll hire a private investigator."

"Yes," said Karin, still holding on to Book. "Let's go ahead home."

"I'm starting to wonder if we'll be safe at home, either," said Martha. "The one thing we have in common, other than traveling around with Bean, is the jury duty and our verdict. If someone's out to get us for that reason, they can get to us at home, too."

Ashley sniffed. "I'll text Justin and tell him I won't be meeting him at the hot tub in the morning. He was going to take me to walk around the marina, but he'll understand."

Despite everything, I smiled to myself. Ah, the priorities of young love.

Bean smiled at Ashley, too. "I'll make sure we plan another trip later and maybe we can plan something near your young man."

"I'm game," said Book, her teeth chattering, "and I'm starting to warm up. I'm fine, girls. I'm ready to head home when you are." The captain had just brought her the cell phone she thought she'd lost in the water. The crew had found it on deck, and she was delighted not to have lost her pictures.

So, within two hours after the dinner cruise got back to shore, we were packed up and back aboard the Gulfstream. The two-man security team joined us for the flight back to Virginia.

We had packed quickly. Ashley had misplaced her polka dotted hat, I'd lost my favorite sunglasses, and Martha was bummed because her plastic case of souvenirs had gone missing from the room, and we puzzled over how it got lost or who would want it.

"Are you sure you want to make a scrapbook of this trip anyway?" Karin teased her.

"Oh, yes," Martha said absently. She was texting Fred to tell him she'd be home early. "It's been *exciting!* We got to hang out at the Hotel California, ride camels, swim in the ocean, and all those cute outfits Bean bought us. And the food!"

"What's weird is that every time we tried to do something on the bucket list, it went terribly wrong," said Bean. "I just can't quit worrying about it. At first I thought it was all just bad luck."

"Who knew about the bucket list?" I asked her.

"Well, we put it together on the plane, then talked about it on the bus ride to the resort," Karin said.

"And we talked about it at breakfast every day," Book added. "And in the bar. Remember, Bean, you had your notebook out and we checked off items as we did them."

"So, basically, the entire resort could have known about our list and planned to sabotage us," I said.

"I talked to Enrique while we were packing," said Bean. "He is, of course, horrified. He'd like us to come back at his expense, but that's beside the point. He said he doesn't know of any disgruntled employees. He also told me—surprise, surprise—that there weren't any security cameras in the hot tub area, so they don't know how the space heater wound up where it was. So I'm left wondering who dislikes me enough to try and hurt me and my friends, because when you have a lot of money, as I mentioned, you do attract your share of weirdos, and some of them are jealous and vengeful. But I think the most likely thing is our connection to the jury duty, and our security detail agrees."

Thing Number One and Number Two nodded. (Perhaps that's a bit irreverent, but we hadn't been formally introduced.)

"Some of these incidents could have resulted in one or more of us dying," said Book slowly. "It's possible we may not figure out why this has happened for a long time, or at all. To quote Kinsey Milhone, 'people murder for absurd reasons.' "

I had my tablet out and was researching old articles about the verdict the year before. "Anyone really threatening on social media or in person after the trial? I mean other than just hurtful stuff."

Ashley shrugged. "I'm on all the sites. The chatter died down a few weeks after the trial, and I know the police looked at the one or two really bad threats. Nothing stands out, and I think I read them all."

"Would you come back to Enrique's and Cabo San Lucas again?" Martha asked the group.

"Oh, sure," Karin answered. "We still didn't make it to Lovers Beach or spend any time at all downtown to speak of. And we rode camels, but you can also ride horses on the beach. I've not ridden a horse in many years."

"We could make a whole new bucket list!" said Ashley.

Bean's phone pinged with an incoming text and I heard her cry out softly in distress.

"It's from Brittney. Rudy didn't make it. She says he had a pre-existing heart condition, and the shock was too much for him." She looked at Ashley. "She said she's sad about their marriage and how it ended. She wants us to know she doesn't hold Ashley or any of us responsible and is sorry about how she acted."

We sat silently for a moment, thinking of Rudy and feeling bad for Brittney, whom we'd been so mad at the night before.

"That means whoever is doing this is now guilty of murder," I said. "That's not good at all."

Suddenly Marguerite was beside us. She had a bottle of tequila and six glasses on a tray. "This was delivered to the plane before takeoff, compliments of the resort," she said quietly. Her long hair hid her face as she set the tray beside Bean.

"Maybe they knew you hadn't completed your bucket list item," Ashley said. "I've never had tequila, and I'm certainly never going to have a worm. Look at that. Gross. It's all yours, Bean."

"That *is* gross," seconded Martha.

"We'll all have some," decided Bean. "I think we could use it. We'll toast Rudy. He was a scoundrel, but a likeable one."

She opened the bottle and began to pour tequila into the glasses. The pungent smell of alcohol filled the cabin. I continued to scroll through articles about the trial while waiting for my portion. I wasn't much of a drinker, but a strong belt of something right now sounded good.

I idly glanced at some photos from the trial, then stopped suddenly. I zoomed in on the accused's family after the verdict was read. They were an attractive, slim, dark-haired group. I zoomed in even further. I could guess who the mother was, as she was crying. Three young women surrounded her, comforting her. I zoomed in on the one closest to the camera, looked across the cabin, then jumped up and swiped the bottle of tequila and all the glasses onto the floor.

"*Lorrie*!" Bean was aghast.

"What is it with you and drinks lately?" Martha asked.

Everyone else in the cabin just stared.

"When did you hire Marguerite?" I asked Bean.

"Well, right before this trip. Remember, I told you she was new. We hired her to help Petunia."

"This picture is from the trial." I turned the tablet around and showed it to Bean, who studied it and then stood up.

"Marguerite, come here."

Marguerite, who was bringing a broom and a dustpan over to clean up the mess, stopped and stared at Bean, then at me. Petunia, who was behind her with a mop, ran smack into her and she stumbled, dropping the dustpan.

"I need you to explain this picture." Bean took the tablet from me. "Sit down here in my chair."

Marguerite slowly walked over and sat down, but she refused to look at the tablet. Bean put it in front of her face.

"There's nowhere to run, child. Tell me, is this your family in the courtroom? Is that you?"

Marguerite looked up and swiped the hair out of her face defiantly. The look she gave us was chilling.

"You had no right to do that to my brother! He's innocent. You've ruined his life and my family's. Just think. The biggest problem you had all week was how to angle your umbrellas to get the best shade, and he's holed up in jail. That's not right! You all deserve to be punished for what you did." She paused. "And you don't have any evidence at all that I did anything to you, even though I should have!"

"Is there anything in that bottle of tequila?" I asked her. "Because that's evidence right there. It will be easy enough to figure out where that bottle came from. Don't clean it up, Petunia. We'll leave it right there for examination."

I wondered if Marguerite had been in our room and removed Martha's plastic case of scrapbook items—we'd joked about that case more than once in public—and remembered the umbrellas and flower petals stuffed in my sundress pocket that I'd failed to throw out. I wondered if the wooden umbrella sticks had adsorbed some of the poisonous liquid, and if the yellow flowers were indeed oleander. Maybe there was a way to tie this back to Marguerite, and maybe there wasn't, but I hoped we could find a link. Perhaps someone had seen her tamper with drinks at the pool or Hotel California. Bean's investigator had his work cut out for him.

"We'll figure out what to do with you when we stop for fuel at Houston," Bean told Marguerite. "Meanwhile, you can sit with the security detail."

In no time at all she was buckled in a seat across the cabin, well away from us, and watched closely by two security guards and Petunia. We moved seats too, away from the sticky tequila mess.

"It was clever of her to find a way to get close to Bean," I said. "It must have felt like a bonus to have a whole group of the jurors along where she could get at them. The whole time things were going wrong and we didn't know where to look, she was clearly right there in front of us, but it's like she was in the shadows and we couldn't see her at all."

"Well, now we can," said Karin. "It's like the song."

"What song?" asked Ashley.

"*I can see clearly now.*"

Ashley shook her head. "Never heard of it."

"Before your time," Karin told her, grinning.

"Pull it up on your tablet, Ash," I suggested. "We could use an uplifting song."

"Think of how many ways to harm us Marguerite thought up in such a short time. If only she'd turned that creative brain of hers to something worthwhile." Bean sighed.

I was thinking ahead; thinking about how nice it would be not to have to worry about the safety of my friends once we got back home.

"That was quite a vacation," said Martha. "I think I'm ready to go back to work for a while. Might be restful. What about you, Lorrie?"

I smiled at her. "Never thought I'd say it, but yes. Yes, I am!"

And we all settled in for the long ride home.

* * *

Inspired by reading *Ellery Queen Mystery Magazine* at a young age, **Eleanor Cawood Jones** began writing in elementary school, using #2 pencils to craft crime stories starring her stuffed animals. Her more recent stories appear in several mystery anthologies, including "Keep Calm and Love Moai" (Malice Domestic 13: *Mystery Most Geographical*), "All Accounted For at the Hooray for Hollywood Motel" (Bouchercon's *Florida Happens*), and the 2021 Derringer Award-winning "The Great Bedbug Incident and the Invitation of Doom" (*Chesapeake Crimes: Invitation to Murder*).

A former newspaper reporter and reformed marketing director, Eleanor is a Tennessee native who lives in Virginia. She's an avid reader, people watcher, world traveler, and remodeling show addict who spends her spare time telling people how to pronounce Cawood (Kay'-wood) and making up long and elaborate story titles. You'll find her rearranging furniture or lurking at airports.

http://www.facebook.com/author.eleanor.cawood.jones

Girlsgonechillin.com

@eleanorauthor

This book is a work of fiction. Names, characters, businesses, organizations, places, events, and incidents either are the product of the authors' imaginations or are used fictitiously. Any resemblance to actual persons, living or dead, events, business establishments, or locales is entirely coincidental.

www.ingramcontent.com/pod-product-compliance
Ingram Content Group UK Ltd.
Pitfield, Milton Keynes, MK11 3LW, UK
UKHW041637190726
13854UKWH00006B/2535